Forever Lucky

*For Katie it seemed like the end,
but, in fact, it was just the beginning...*

By Gill Buchanan

Forever Lucky Copyright © 2017 by Gill Buchanan. All Rights Reserved.

All rights reserved. No part of this book may be reproduced in any form or by any electronic or mechanical means including information storage and retrieval systems, without permission in writing from the author. The only exception is by a reviewer, who may quote short excerpts in a review.

Cover designed by Gill Buchanan

This book is a work of fiction. Names, characters, places, and incidents either are products of the author's imagination or are used fictitiously. Any resemblance to actual persons, living or dead, events, or locales is entirely coincidental.

Gill Buchanan
Visit my website at www.gillbuchanan.co.uk

Printed in the United Kingdom

Second Edition Published in Great Britain 2019

ISBN: 9781079241754

Praise for Forever Lucky

Dollyrocker says: I have just finished reading Forever Lucky and feel sad to be leaving these characters behind. Gill Buchanan has managed that most tricky of tasks here: she's created a world in which a reader can fully immerse.
Right away I was gripped by our heroine Katie's plight. Newly bereft and plunged into debt, Katie bravely faces up to her nightmarish situation. Her daughters Alice (and especially the tempestuous Bethan) react pretty badly to their mother's straitened circumstances. I should imagine many mothers reading this book will feel a wave of recognition at the teenage fury and unreasonableness that the author conveys so well here.
Great book. Great story. Great fun.

Jane B. says: A great relaxing read - easy to get into, fun and poignant at the same time, with a feel-good ending. I liked the little personality quirks of each character.
Having really enjoyed her first book, Unlikely Neighbours, I was optimistic and this was just as good. Highly recommend it. The writing skips along, mixing a real sense of fun with deeper - sometimes even darker - interludes. Great first book.

Barbara says: the story flowed beautifully and I just had to keep reading to find ...
Gill's observations on people and their lives was most engaging, the story flowed beautifully and I just had to keep reading to find out what happened next. A most enjoyable read. I look forward to her next book.

Jane L. says: A thoroughly enjoyable read from start to finish. It was great seeing the characters develop and I didn't want it to end. Having enjoyed Gill's first novel this didn't disappoint. Can't wait for the next one.

To Tony

Chapter 1

Katie woke up from a cruelly short and restless sleep. The traumatic events of the night flooded her mind and her body was tense with pain. Could this really be happening to her? She felt very alone as she reached out only to feel a large expanse of cold bed. The sun defiantly shone through the Juliet balcony window and bathed her bedroom in brilliant white; a scene that would normally make her smile.

Her husband had looked so peaceful, lying there, when all the tubes and paraphernalia had been removed. The nurses had left him covered in a single sheet in a side room so that Katie could be alone with him. Finally, it was a moment of calm after the frantic attempts to save his life. His complexion was sallow but the beauty she had seen in him throughout their twenty and more years of marriage was still there; his defined cheek bones and roman nose; his dark hair, thickset even now at fifty-six years of age. Fifty-six. No time at all. Not enough, at least.

Snatches of conversation, during the family dinner they had shared to celebrate her fiftieth birthday, meandered through her mind.

'Champagne!' David had exclaimed, rather too loudly for such a refined London restaurant. 'Nothing but the best for my wife on her birthday!' His working-class background chipped away at him. She was the Cambridge graduate, him the grammar school boy, but it was his career that had always taken precedence. His old-fashioned pride demanded that he must be the one to provide a good living for his family, while she was a housewife and mother and sat on charity committees as if to prove her worth.

There had been a lively debate over which university Alice would go to. Bethan hadn't helped by suggesting that Portsmouth would be a difficult drive from Highgate; Nottingham would be a lot easier. Alice's face had looked anxious when she explained she needed to get an A grade for Nottingham.

''You'll get an A! No daughter of mine gets less than an A for French!' David, who had definitely drunk too much by that point, had almost bellowed. 'You know your mother went to the crème de la crème!'

Katie had felt her cheeks flush and shut the conversation down seeing Alice was close to tears.

How could they argue, on this, the last evening of David's life?

He had been quite agitated; checking his mobile phone a lot. Alice had told him to put it away but he didn't.

'Oh, leave him alone,' Bethan had said to her sister. She worshipped her father. Alice was always more measured with her feelings.

But now they could only be bereft.

Bethan appeared at Katie's door. She was wearing a khaki T-shirt that belonged to her father. Her long blonde hair was matted and messy and yesterday's make-up was smudged round her eyes. She looked younger than her sixteen years and burst into tears, falling onto the bed and into her mother's arms.

'Tell me it's not true.'

Katie hugged her hard. Tears came easily, over and over. Would they ever stop? Finally, Bethan was still and Katie held her head and kissed her.

'Where's Alice?'

'I think she went downstairs.'

'Let's go down; make some coffee.'

'Mum?'

'Yes, darling.'

'How? What? I mean…'

'I don't know.'

Bethan looked frightened.

'You said last night it was a heart attack; but he wasn't ill, was he?'

Katie brimmed with empathy for her daughter. 'I love you,' she said simply as she held Bethan's head and looked straight into her eyes.

Alice was staring out of the kitchen window on to the garden beyond. The white and blue asters looked pretty in the early morning summer light. Katie hugged her back.

'What are we going to do?' Alice asked vaguely. Katie turned her round, stroked her cheek and kissed her forehead.

'I'm going to make some coffee,' Katie whispered and moved to put the kettle on. 'Apart from anything else, I've had hardly any sleep; I need the caffeine.'

Both daughters stared at her, looking shocked.

'Would you like some?' Katie asked, despite their expressions, and neither answered her. She made a large cafetière of coffee with four heaped dessertspoons of fresh coffee and steaming hot water.

Alice and Bethan slumped into kitchen chairs at the table. Bethan held her head in her hands in despair; Alice looked vulnerable as she stared into nothing. Katie placed the cafetière on the table between them and added three mugs and a jug of milk. She too sat down and the full reality of what was happening smothered her yet again and she burst into tears. Alice put an arm round her while Bethan found a box of tissues and added it to the table. Eventually Katie blew her nose, blinked her eyes a few times and plunged the coffee.

'Can we see him?' Bethan asked. 'I mean, is he still at the hospital?'

Katie gulped in some air. 'They said something about the chapel of rest last night. Would I like him to be there? I think I said yes.'

'You think?' Alice asked her face demanding a more reassuring response.

Katie looked hurt but then composed herself. 'Yes, I mean yes, I think I said yes. It's all a bit of a blur.'

Alice covered her mother's hand with hers now. 'Sorry, I just need to know where he is.'

'I'll ring the hospital and check. And then we can all go in, if you like.'

'Yes,' Bethan said, a serious expression now, 'yes, let's do that,' she added and then lifted the cafetière to pour herself some coffee. Her hand was unsteady and she spilt some. 'Bugger.'

'It doesn't matter.' Katie got up to get some kitchen roll. The spillage dealt with she pushed the milk jug towards her daughter.

'No, I'll drink it black,' she said as if there was suddenly something wrong with milk.

Alice looked like she was deep in thought. Then she said, 'How are we going to cope, I mean, without Dad?' How on earth are we going to...?'

Katie reached out to her. 'I've no idea, my darling, but somehow we will.'

Chapter 2

As the three of them struggled through the days that followed, Katie hugged her daughters over and over. Bethan looked as if she was terrified of the future. Her father was her hero who could do no wrong, who bought her extravagant gifts, who could always lift her mood even on a wet Sunday in February. Alice ate nothing all day and then scoffed a whole tub of Ben and Jerry's banoffee pie ice cream. 'I feel sick,' she said disgusted with herself and discarded the empty pot.

Bethan insisted that Charlie, the cat, who rather unfortunately died two days after David, should be buried in the garden with a full ceremony. He had hardly left Bethan's bedroom for the last year, sleeping mainly, and he had peacefully slipped away at night.

'But darling, surely a quiet prayer would do?' Katie wondered as she said it, who they would be praying to and did she believe in God?

'No Mum, Charlie has been part of the family for eighteen years; we can't just throw him away!' Katie noticed Bethan was wearing another one of her dad's T-shirts, this time the grey one he had particularly favoured. It swamped her slim frame and she hugged it to her body. Katie said nothing.

Then there were the strange calls on David's mobile phone. Names flashing up that Katie did not know. She had told close relatives and his boss at work and that was hard enough; she could not face any more.

The first time they rang she answered, 'hello,' and they simply hung up. The second time they might say, 'can I speak to David, please?'

'Who is this?' Katie would ask.

That morning it had been Barry. 'I'm a friend of David's.'
'Really? He never mentioned you.'
The past tense had him worried. 'Has something happened?'
'Yes, he's dead.' Katie spoke the words but they did not resonate with her.
'Oh, I'm sorry to hear that,' they would say not sounding sorry at all, but more alarmed. 'You must be Katie, his wife.'
'Indeed.' The phone went dead. What on earth did all that mean?

Jane called round from next door holding a clear plastic sack of clothes. She was dressed far too smartly for a woman who was just 'at home' and had carefully applied some candy pink lipstick as she never left her house without it. Bethan answered the door.
'Oh, it's you...'
Jane looked affronted. 'Hello Bethan. You look dreadful, are you okay?'
'Well, you know, if not having a Dad any more is okay?' she said as if it was Jane's fault.
Jane looked confused.
'Dad's dead. I suppose you don't know,' she said almost angrily.
Katie arrived at the door.
'You poor darlings!' Jane's eyes looked like they might pop out of her head as she threw her arms around Katie. Bethan burst into tears and ran upstairs.
'Sorry Jane, it is a difficult time,' Katie explained as she moved away from their awkward embrace.
'Yes, yes of course! How did it happen?'
The question felt impertinent to Katie and it took an enormous effort for her to answer. 'It was all very sudden, heart attack, on my birthday.'
'That's dreadful. On your birthday?'
Katie wished she hadn't shared that detail. As if it mattered. They both stared at the sack of clothes Jane was still holding.

'These are for Save the Children, but don't worry I can come back another time.'

'Oh, I see. Yes, thank you. Just leave them there.' She pointed at the hallway which was already untidy so what did it matter.

'Are you sure?'

'Yes, of course. The children still need to be saved. Mind you, I think I need saving myself.'

'Oh, Katie, if there's *anything* I can do?'

'Well, unless you're a miracle worker.'

'When's the funeral?'

Katie looked aghast. Her mind went blank. It was all she could do to get through the day without facing up to the inevitable. She knew she had to take her head out of the sand and contact the funeral directors but the very thought of it made it all too real. She stuttered out, 'I haven't sorted that out yet.'

'No, no well in time,' Jane said and added, 'maybe that's something I could help with?'

Katie imagined Jane trotting up to the cemetery in one of her designer suits and full make-up, wielding a large spade and digging a big hole. 'Jane, you're very kind. I'll let you know.'

'Do you promise?'

Why wouldn't this woman go away? 'I'm not sure I should make any promises right now.'

'No, no. Silly me. Katie, I'm only next door,' she said as she squeezed Katie's hand.

Katie contemplated whether that was a good or a bad thing.

'Thank you, Jane,' she felt relief as she pressed the door shut on this intrusion.

For four days now they hadn't sat down to a proper meal and as it was Sunday, Katie decided to cook a roast for lunch. She considered that it would give her something to do even if no one felt like eating it.

'But Mum, I'm not hungry. Dad is dead. How can we eat?' Alice said as she popped a piece of raw carrot in her mouth.

'Well, it will be there if you want it, darling.'

Later that day Katie persuaded the girls to sit at the kitchen table and attempt the roast lamb she had cooked. It was not her best attempt but it looked reasonably edible. They always ate in the kitchen when it was just the three of them. They never bothered with the formal dining room unless they had guests or David wanted to eat in there. Bethan stared at her plate glancing up only momentarily with a horrified look on her face.

Alice began to eat cautiously. 'Actually, I'm quite hungry for decent food. I've eaten nothing but crap for days.'

Katie looked disapprovingly at her daughter.

'Sorry Mum, shouldn't have said crap at the table.'

They all managed to eat at least half a plate. Conversation was scarce.

Bethan asked, 'Did you get rid of Jane?'

Katie broke away from her thoughts, 'Jane? Oh Jane. She offered to help and I said I'd let her know and thanked her.'

'Very polite Mum,' Alice said. She waited until they'd finished eating before she asked, 'Mum, I know it's horrible to even have to think about it, but shouldn't we be sorting out the funeral?'

Katie sighed. Of course she had thought about it. When the man from the coroner's office rang to say the body was being released and the hospital mortuary awaited instructions, she thought how easy it was for him to say these words. After all, it was something he probably did every day. For her it meant that she was going to have to be really strong and cope with all the things you have to do in this situation and she was going to have to do it alone. The one person she always turned to when things were difficult, her rock, had been taken away from her.

Katie's mind went back to when she'd been alone with him in the chapel of rest. She decided that this was the last time she would see his face; there would be no open coffin at the funeral. And so she had stood watching him, stroking his face, his hands and through her tears she said, 'why David? Why did you have to leave me? Why didn't you tell me you were ill? We might have been able to do something. I know you hated the doctors, you always said you felt great even when your face said something different. You could laugh your way through any situation, and *I love that about you.* Maybe I should have done something, but you were so strong; somehow I thought you'd always be there for me and nothing else mattered.'

'Mum, are you all right?' Alice had her arms around her mother as she cried. 'I'm sorry. We don't have to talk about the funeral now.'

'Yeah, it's too soon. Don't worry,' Bethan added handing her mother a tissue.

Katie blotted the tears away and blew her nose. 'Don't be silly girls, of course we've got to face up to it. Tomorrow. Tomorrow, I promise we'll contact the funeral directors in the village.'

Just then the doorbell rang. They all looked at each other. Bethan got up.

'I'll go. If it's Jane again I'll tell her to keep her bloody Gucci blouses that no one who goes to the charity shop would want to buy any way.'

Alice let out a snigger and Katie smiled.

Bethan opened the front door cautiously until she saw who it was. 'Julia! You look brown.'

'Yes darling, Tenerife. Your mother knew I was away. Is she in?'

Bethan looked worried. 'Oh Julia, you don't know do you?'

'What? What don't I know?' Julia demanded, 'She's all right, isn't she?'

'It's Dad. He had a heart attack. He didn't make it. Mum's in bits. She needs her best friend right now but I warn you, as soon as she sees you...'

Julia rushed through to the kitchen and Katie got up from the table, her eyes red from crying, and they hugged each other hard.

'Oh Katie! My poor darling.' They both burst into tears.

Chapter 3

Julia turned up again on Monday morning as promised.

'Shall we walk? It's a sunny day.'

'Yes, let's. I've been cooped up in this house for too long.' Katie stepped out onto the street and took in a lung full of fresh air. She looked around her; somehow the world felt different.

'If we meet anyone you know, I'll deal with it,' Julia said with authority.

'Thank you.'

They proceeded arm in arm, Julia pulling Katie close to her, as they made their way down the hill into the village.

Sitting in the funeral directors felt surreal. Katie found herself struck dumb by the barrage of questions. Which type of coffin? Buried or cremated? Questions David had never answered. She wanted to please him and work out what he might have wanted. Then there were the "other people" being all those who are likely to turn up to the funeral; what would they expect?

'What was David like?' The funeral director, John Redgrove, was a statuesque individual and had a gentle way about him but still each question seemed impossible to answer.

'Big personality, great guy,' Julia said. 'Always the life and soul of the party, loved his family.'

Katie smiled at the accuracy of her friend's description.

'So what sort of ceremony do you think *he'd* have wanted?'

'One in about thirty years' time, I'd say.' Katie found herself staring at John. Julia was looking slightly alarmed and came to her rescue again.

'What do *you* want Katie? Let's just concentrate on that.'

Katie wanted to say a humanist ceremony but she wasn't sure if Redgrove and Crockett would offer such a thing. Were they allowed to keep God out of it? She took a deep breath, '*I would want a humanist burial, if it was me.*'

John leaned towards her and Katie became aware of the citrus notes in his aftershave. 'Lovely idea. I'm sure it would please David to know his wife has chosen for him.'

Once she decided to go with everything that felt right to her it all fell into place; bamboo for the coffin and it would be at Highgate Cemetery. John recommended someone he knew to conduct the ceremony, a man called Rupert Chandler. Katie felt some strange comfort knowing David's body would be lying there, just a few minutes' walk from her home.

As they stepped out onto the street again the slightest breeze caused Katie to shiver and hug herself.

'How about some lunch at The Flask?' Julia suggested.

Katie was about to say no and then thought about the rest of a long day at home on her own. 'Why not?'

Alice stood outside Chez Pierre unable to decide if she should go in or not. She couldn't explain it, but she felt she might get some comfort from seeing Jacob again. He had smiled across the room at her that night, put his arm round her even, when her Dad was on the floor struggling for his life. She liked him even though she didn't really know him. The last few days had been so gruelling for her. She took a deep breath to try and quell her nerves before opening the door. Immediately she wished she hadn't. She could not see Jacob anywhere. Maybe she should turn and run but it was too late; one of the waiters was asking her if she wanted a table.

'Oh, no. No, I'm just here...'

'Alice, isn't it?' How did he know her name? Was she somehow recognisable as the daughter of a dead man?

'Yes, yes.' Her eyes were everywhere but on him.

'I was here, the other evening,' he explained looking sheepish.

'Oh, I see.' Alice couldn't re-live that scene at this precise moment. She found the courage to ask, 'Is Jacob around?'

'He's on at twelve; should be here any minute. Would you like to wait?'

'Erm...'

She was about to say no when Jacob strolled in. Now she felt awkward.

'Ah, there he is.' The other waiter walked away leaving her standing there alone.

'Jacob,' she said hesitantly but just loud enough for him to hear. He came straight over to her.

'Are you okay?'

'Er, yes, yes, well you know, not really.'

'Of course. What brings you here?'

'I well, I...'

'This is where your Dad died, I know, must be awful.' He put a hand on her shoulder.

She couldn't stop the tears and now he was holding her; it felt good being in his arms.

She sniffed and he found her a tissue. 'Here, listen, would you like a coffee?'

'Yes.' Alice managed a smile now. 'Yes please, if that's okay?'

Julia had ordered a bottle of Pinot Noir and a couple of steak sandwiches. 'You look like you haven't eaten properly for days.'

'No,' Katie said vaguely, taking herself away from her thoughts yet again. 'Apart from yesterday when I attempted a Sunday lunch; I took some comfort from it actually, doing something normal.'

'I hope the girls are looking after you.'

Katie let out a nervous laugh. 'I don't think they can quite believe it. They both adored him... especially Bethan.' She was reminded of a moment so frequent in their lives, Bethan with her head on her Dad's shoulder, looking up to him. He would be offering advice to quell her latest crisis; she would hang on his every word.

'It's going to take time,' Julia said as she leant over to her friend.

'Oh, and Charlie's dead,' Katie said but wasn't quite sure why.

'The cat's dead? He was very old.'

'Yes, two days after David. Buried by Bethan in the garden with some sort of ceremony she found on the internet. Alice and I stood there as ordered and we were all weeping… for David I suppose.'

Julia was studying Katie's face. 'Well, if it helped her in some way.'

'Who knows? My mind is so full of David. I can't cope with anything else.'

'I'm not surprised.' Julia held a look of concern now. 'Listen, I don't want to even mention this, it's so unimportant in the scheme of things, but you know the Save the Children committee sits this week?'

'Oh gosh, does it? I'd completely forgotten.'

'Of course you have and I only wanted to say that I'll contact Malcolm and tell him what's happened and that you won't be coming for the foreseeable.'

'Would you?'

'Consider it done. And I'll tell him not to bother you with emails for a while, too.'

Jacob poured two coffees from the cafetière and handed one to Alice. He had an air of being in charge which she liked. They were sitting at one of the restaurant tables at the back.

'Are you sure this is okay?' she asked quietly, not wanting to be overheard.

He gave her an understanding smile and she looked at him, admiring his long dark eyelashes and clear olive skin.

'Yes, yes, you can see for yourself, Monday lunchtimes are always slow. What have we got, three tables in? Danny can manage that for half an hour.'

Alice sipped her coffee and didn't know what to say next. After all coming here was just a vague notion. She hadn't considered the implications of getting this far. Jacob broke the silence.

'When's the funeral? Do you know that yet?' he asked gently.

'No, Mum's sorting that out today. Julia, her friend, is taking her down to the funeral directors. I don't think she'd go otherwise.'

'Denial, the first stage of grief.'

'Yeah, you just can't take it in. One minute you're worried about you're A-level results and the next your life's fallen apart.'

'Can I come? To the funeral, I mean?'

'Oh yes, yeah.' Alice thought about it. 'I'd like that.'

'Will you let me know when it is? I'll need to change my day off.'

Alice smiled and felt warm for a moment as they exchanged mobile phone numbers.

Katie leaned back in her chair. 'Thanks Julia, I needed that.' The red wine had somehow numbed the pain.

'Don't be silly.'

'We haven't even talked about your holiday.'

'Nothing interesting there. Usual sun, sea and a couple of good paperbacks, oh and the occasional excursion to keep Andrew happy. He can't settle with a book.'

'No, David can't either. I mean...'

'It's okay.' Julia frowned and watched her carefully. 'By the way, Andrew is happy to help in any way if you need another bearer, that sort of thing. He was shocked when I told him.'

'Thanks Julia. I really should be thinking about these things but it's so hard. I keep noticing his car parked on the road, his beloved Mercedes, and wondering what on earth I'm going to do with it. The tax reminder came even before he died so it's well overdue but I still haven't done anything about it.'

'Maybe just tax it and keep it for now?'

'Yes, you're right. It will buy me some time anyway.'

'It will get easier. Somehow.' Julia put her hand over her friends. 'Now, let's get the bill.'

'I'm getting this,' Katie insisted. The waiter brought the card machine over to the table. She struggled to remember her PIN. The waiter took the card reader back from her and looked puzzled and said quickly, 'the card's not been accepted. Do you want to try again?'

Katie checked her diary where she had a prompt to remember the number. She *had* got it right, or had she? She punched the numbers in again this time feeling sure and passed the reader back to the waiter.

'Refer to bank?' He raised his eyebrows.

'Oh this is silly.' Julia took some notes from her wallet and handed them over. 'That should cover it.' She waved him away. 'Keep the change.'

'But Julia..' Katie was staring at her bank card. 'Why didn't it work? Is there no money in the account? I don't understand.'

'Now now, you don't want to be worrying about money at a time like this. I'm sure there's a simple explanation. Let's go back to yours and ring your bank.'

'My God, I've not even considered that money might be a problem.' Panic entered her voice. 'But of course we don't have David's salary now!'

Julia hugged her friend in an attempt to calm her. 'Come on, it's all going to be all right, I know it is.'

Chapter 4

'So there isn't any money in the account at all?' Katie's voice was shaking and her knees buckled under her. Julia caught her and gently lowered her into the chair at the desk of what had been David's study. She took the phone from Katie and said, 'thank you, goodbye,' before putting it back in its cradle. Katie's mind was whirring with all sorts of terrible thoughts.

'There must be some money somewhere?' Julia was the voice of reason. 'I mean what have you been living on up until now?'

'The thing is,' Katie's voice was hoarse and she had to clear her throat before she could go on, 'I know David was the only one working but there's the rent from his parents' place.'

'Up in York, you mean?'

'Yes, we get about twelve hundred a month for it.'

'Yes, I remember you saying at the time that you weren't going to sell it but to rent it out. I think the market was down a bit then.'

Katie remembered the conversation she and David had had. At first he was keen to sell but she had talked him round.

'Yes, yes, you are right as always,' he had said. 'I'll sort it out. You've got enough on your plate with all those charity committees you sit on.' Katie had thought at the time that that didn't make sense when he worked such long hours. But she was reconciled to it, as it was *his* parents' place.

Julia looked brighter. 'So does that money go into your joint account?'

'Well I assumed it did. But now I'm not so sure. I mean I don't look too carefully, there's no need normally.'

'So, how about ringing the letting agent?' Julia handed her the phone from the desk.

'Yes good idea; they should at least know which account they pay into.'

Katie found a card index file and looked through it. 'Here we are, Thomas Brompton, under y for York.' She picked up the phone and dialled the number on the card.

'Hello, it's Katie Green here. You rent out a property for us in my husband's name, David Green.' She read the address from the card, 'It's 4 Cheyne Gardens in York.' The man on the other end of the phone muttered something and then went quiet.

'They're looking it up.' Katie felt like she was on a cliff edge.

'Mrs Green?'

'Yes, yes I'm here.'

'We don't have a rental property at that address.'

'What do you mean? Well who does then?' Katie almost yelled at the man.

'Well, madam, we simply don't manage the rental of number four.' He stopped abruptly and she could hear a colleague interrupt him. 'Hang on a minute madam.' There was a pause before he said, 'ah, I'm just going to put you on hold for a moment until Kevin Klosters becomes available. He may be able to help you.'

Katie swallowed hard.

Julia disappeared and returned with a bottle of brandy and two glasses. Without asking she poured and handed a glass to Katie. Katie immediately took a large glug.

'Mrs Green?' Another man's voice said.

'Yes.' Katie held her breath.

'I'm Kevin Klosters and I can inform you that we were instructed to sell that property about four years ago. I think we got about...' his fingers drummed on the desk a few times, 'yes, two hundred and seventy thousand for the property if my memory serves me correctly.'

'Sold for two hundred and seventy thousand pounds!' Katie struggled to get the words out. Julia's eyes widened.

'Yes Madam. Perhaps you could ask Mr Green for the details.'

'Mr Green is dead!' The words burst from her as the horror of the situation dawned on her.

'Ah, I'm very sorry to hear that.' His tone remained professional. 'I'm very sorry.'

Katie was shaking as she put the phone down. 'He's bloody sold it for two hundred and seventy thousand!' she shouted. Had he really betrayed her in this way?

'So, what happened to that money?'

'More to the point, why didn't he tell me?'

'Yes, it's distressing, I agree.'

'Maddening more like! I just can't think what he would need that kind of money for!'

The doorbell rang. They looked at each other and Julia leapt up. 'I'll get it.'

Katie dared to think that it might be David and this had all been a nightmare. She buried her head in her hands. Alice walked in. 'Sorry Mum, I forgot my keys.'

Katie looked up and tried to compose herself; she must be strong for her daughters.

'Is it okay if Jacob comes to the funeral?' Alice was asking.

'Who's Jacob?' Julia and Katie asked in unison.

'He works at Chez Pierre; he's one of the waiters there.'

'Really?' Katie couldn't think straight. 'Why does he want to come?'

'*I* want him to come.' Alice blushed.

'Yes, of course.' It was too inconsequential to worry about.

'Good. Right. When is it?'

'Erm.... Tuesday, next Tuesday.'

'20th of July,' Julia added. 'Twelve noon at Highgate cemetery.'

'Right,' she said turning away but then came back. 'Well done Mum; can't have been easy.'

'Thank you, Alice.' Katie was looking back on her visit to the funeral directors as a cinch compared to what she was now dealing with.

Alice turned to go again but then she asked, 'Why are you drinking brandy in the afternoon?'

'Good question,' Katie said, pushing her glass away from her.

'We need a bit of Dutch courage,' Julia explained. 'We're just sorting out some of your Dad's affairs.'

'Oh God, awful!' This time she disappeared.

The two women looked at each other.

'Nothing's easy, is it?' Julia sympathised and then sat back in her seat a thoughtful expression on her face. 'There must be something,' and then asked, 'what about life insurance? I remember you saying he took out a policy years ago.'

'Yes, yes! You are quite right. Now where would that be?' Katie opened a filing cabinet and started taking files out, looking at them and discarding them to the floor. Finally she found something marked life insurance.

'Here it is!' She opened it up and scan read the first sheet. 'Oh, bloody hell, the last correspondence was March last year.'

'Is there a phone number?' Julia asked.

'Yes, here it is.' Katie tapped the number in to her phone. A recorded voice told her she had four options, including selecting two for existing customers with a life insurance policy. She selected two.

'Oh God, I've got to put in the policy number.' It seemed to take her an age to find it. 'Here it is.' She carefully tapped the number in.

'Sorry your policy number has not been recognised. Please type in the eight-digit number,' the machine threw back at her.

'I'm sure I got it right.' She put it in again.

Sorry your...

'Bloody hell!'

'Please choose from the following options.'

Katie didn't select anything this time and finally got through to a person in real time. The woman was terribly helpful and explained in sympathetic tones that the policy had been terminated in March two thousand and eleven on the instruction of the policy holder, David Green. The blood drained from Katie's face and the all too familiar feeling of nausea returned. She barely managed, 'thank you, you've been helpful,' and to put down the handset.

Julia didn't need to be told it was bad news. 'Oh Katie, I am so sorry. But the house sale, surely that money must be sitting in an account somewhere?'

Katie sank back into her chair in despair. Julia took up the mantle of riffling through more files. 'There must be something in here. Some clue as to where that house sale money went.'

'You'd think so,' Katie was defeated, any energy to continue with this search sapped from her. 'But God knows what we're looking for.'

Bethan held her hair up to the sunlight coming through her bedroom window. 'What do you think?'

Miranda was reading a magazine and didn't look up.

'What do you think, Miranda, about my hair?' She raised her voice this time.

Miranda glanced up. 'It looks good. Sort of... strawberry blonde.'

'It's not *meant* to be strawberry blonde.'

'Jessie J had purple hair the other day, well, half purple and half black.'

'I don't even like her.'

'Well anyway... what are you wearing to the funeral?' Miranda changed the subject.

'I don't know. That black dress I wore last summer I suppose.'

'Yeah, you look good in that.'

'It's a funeral, stupid.'

'There's a brilliant black jumpsuit in New Look.'

'Is there? I don't know. I haven't got any money. Dad used to give us money; I don't even know if Mum realised... anyway I'm supposed to be saving up.'

'Oh, for that NVQ course in Graphic Design?'

'Yeah, Dad said I could do it and well, now I've decided I really want to do it and it's nearly two thousand pounds. I've only managed to save up a hundred since Christmas.'

'Surely your mum will pay for it?'

'Yeah, I think she will when I make her see it's what I really want to do. I mean what's the point of staying in school? I know Alice has but she's naturally clever and she's going to uni.'

'Do you think she'll still go?'

'Oh, yeah. She'd better. I want her bedroom. It's much bigger than mine.'

Katie sat quite still now on a park bench and stared out across Waterlow Park as far as where the pale blue of the sky merged into the grey of the City buildings, the Shard standing tall amongst them. Julia had watched her with alarm as Katie chose flight over fight when the final piece of the awful truth was uncovered.

The plaque on the bench they were sitting on read:

> *In loving memory of Nicola Murray who enjoyed coming here for sun,*
> *walks and squirrel therapy.*

Julia wondered if this would be therapy enough for Katie after what they had discovered today. Instead of a house in York there was just fifteen thousand pounds in an account, thankfully in their joint names, even though Katie had no recollection of it. It had been one shock after another and eventually Katie could not take any more and ran out of the house as if she might otherwise explode.

A woman jogged with heavy limbs across their path. Purple and yellow irises adorned the grass below a copse. Further round the path several dog walkers sat with their pets, passing the time as if this was like any other day. A child squealed with delight on being freed from his buggy and ran bare foot across the grass, his mother's face fixed in a delighted smile.

Julia thought of a hundred things to say, all of them seeming grossly inadequate, and didn't say any of them. She turned to look at her friend. The anger had subsided and been replaced with a solid disillusionment, her breath still shaky. Julia took her hand and held it firmly in hers.

Finally, Katie looked at her and said, 'Do you know what the worst thing is?' She was close to tears. 'I'm wondering who on earth I've been married to for the last twenty odd years.'

Chapter 5

Katie was vacuuming the lounge carpet with an unnecessary vigour. Sleepless nights, grappling with the secrets David had apparently kept and the financial doom ahead of her, left her weary and depressed. Her back was sore with the strong repetitive movement to and fro, and she stopped to arch backwards, her hand in the small of her back for support, and cringed. She resented having to do this, the job of the cleaner, now sacked. The doorbell rang and she wondered which daughter had forgotten her key today. A small framed man with a friendly round face and a sympathetic smile stood on the doorstep.

'Hello?' Katie was half fearing he would be someone else who knew David but whom she had never laid eyes on.

The man simply held out a hand. 'Rupert Chandler, I will be conducting the service for your husband's funeral.'

'Oh yes!' She looked at her watch and remembered agreeing to a visit at eleven o'clock this morning. 'I'm so sorry, please do come in.'

He smiled broadly and stepped lightly on to the door mat.

'You'll have to forgive me,' Katie explained, 'I have a lot on my mind.'

'Of course you do. I do hope I can help alleviate some of the pressure you must undoubtedly be under.'

Katie wondered if he had a magic wand with him but simply invited him into the lounge. As she went in ahead of him she gathered up the sweeper and hid it behind a sofa, smiling apologetically.

'Do sit down.' She ran her fingers through her hair wishing she'd bothered to put some make-up on; she looked so pale without it.

He sat down and his diminutive figure was swamped by the cushions in the armchair he chose.

'Now...' His voice was soothing and Katie could see that he would be good at his job. 'The purpose of my visit is to get to know you and, of course, David a little and for you to tell me what you want from the service. Is that okay?'

Katie braced herself and tried to block out the events of the last few days as she gave Rupert a potted history of her marriage to David. What was easier was conveying how much he adored Alice and Bethan.

'They must be a great comfort to you at this time,' he responded.

Katie smiled through a sigh. 'Yes, they certainly are.' But in her own mind she knew that right now she felt a weighty responsibility for them; one which she had no idea how she was going to meet.

'Do you think either of them will want to say anything at the service?'

She knew the answer to this would be no. 'I think they're too upset.'

'I understand.' He placed his mug on the coffee table and tried to sit back in his chair but his feet left the floor so he shuffled forward back to his perched position.

'May I make a suggestion?'

'Yes, of course,'

'On these occasions it can be quite nice to ask if any from those gathered would like to say a few words.'

'Right.' Katie was struggling to think clearly but could not see any reason why this should not happen. Perhaps Julia would say something. 'Yes, that's fine by me. If you think that's best.'

'It can be very comforting to share our thoughts during the ceremony.'

*

On the day of the funeral Katie opened her eyes and immediately felt sick. She heaved her reluctant limbs out of bed and headed straight for the shower on some sort of autopilot to achieve what was expected of her.

As she dried herself she looked up at her outfit hanging on the outside of her wardrobe; the girls had been very helpful in sorting it out. A black shift dress and jacket, black tights, black shoes and a patent leather black handbag which Bethan had lent her. 'You can't possibly take your brown one Mum; it will look ridiculous.' Katie had smiled on receiving the rather fashionable alternative, more likely to be found on a teenager's shoulder entering a night club.

They had even laid out her underwear; a rather sexy black lace bra and matching knickers which David had bought for her last Christmas. It was as if she could not be relied on to think of anything herself. If only she could stop thinking about him and the awful predicament he had left her with. If only she could block all that out and simply grieve for her enormous loss; the man that was everything to her, gone forever.

One last look in the mirror and she decided she was as ready as she'd ever be to face her public. As she walked through the hallway she could hear her sister's voice. Patricia was telling Bethan that her dress was too short and totally unsuitable for a funeral. Bethan scowled back at her like a child on the brink of a tantrum.

'Patricia, you're early,' Katie said. Would she spend the whole day speaking her truth, no energy to lie? 'I mean, thank you for coming.'

Patricia hugged her sister but Katie remained rigid.

'Katie, I'm so sorry but Mark hasn't made it. Some meeting in Frankfurt he simply couldn't get out of. I said you'd understand.'

Katie did understand; Mark and David had never hit it off. David was always open to the possibility of a friendly pint but Mark's default position was that he always had somewhere more important to be. There was three years between Katie and her sister and it had made quite a difference when they were children and had always been an excuse, it seemed, for the older sister to look down on Katie. Their father had always been quick to feed Patricia's ego and praise her at every step, while Katie was almost forgotten and was merely good enough. After his death their mother had swept the past under the carpet and tried to redress the balance. But Patricia's patronising ways were fuelled by the fact that she had married so well, a banker, Mark Frobisher, who was earning a fortune in bonuses, while she considered David to be lacking ambition and too full of himself for his own good.

When their mother fell terminally ill with cancer, it was Katie who invited her into her home. Patricia had merely agreed this was the best option since she was too busy entertaining her husband's clients and maintaining their five-bedroomed house in Kensington. The fact that Patricia had chosen not to have children, while Katie was juggling a ten and a twelve-year-old alongside her charity work at the time, wasn't even mentioned.

'You're okay with this dress aren't you, Mum?' Bethan asked.

'Of course, darling, you look lovely. Your father would have been proud of you.' She knew that for sure.

'Any coffee?' Patricia asked. 'Yes, of course.' Katie heard herself say but wondered why the silly woman didn't just help herself.

'I'll get it.' Bethan seemed eager to go.

'What time are we going?' Patricia asked and the doorbell rang and Katie left her sister hanging and went to answer it. Julia stood there, her husband, Andrew, a few steps behind. This time she succumbed to a hug.

'All right?' Julia whispered.

'Ask me at the end of the day,' Katie managed and then, with her brave face fixed, 'now come on in and don't be nice to me or I'll cry and then my mascara will run and that wouldn't do would it?'

There seemed to be people everywhere by the time Alice appeared. She looked as glamorous as her sister, and Katie smiled at her and said in a lowered tone, 'be careful to avoid direct contact with your aunt; she seems to have an opinion on Bethan's choice of outfit.' Alice laughed and said, 'thanks Mum; you're the best.' Katie took a sharp intake of breath. 'Don't say anything like that to me until this is all over and I can break down and cry.'

'Oh Mum.' Alice's eyes watered. 'Come on darling,' she took her daughter's hand, 'let's be courageous together.'

'Is Uncle Mark here?'

'No. Patricia said something about him being abroad at a conference. Let's face it there was no love lost between him and your Dad.'

Katie was painfully aware that she hadn't said a word to either of her daughters about their financial ruin. It was important to her that they grieved today for the father they knew and loved. Tomorrow they would all have to face up to some impossible home truths.

John Lamont and Claire Davis from David's work arrived. Both were very pleasant and made their own coffee. Jane from next door donned a Prada suit, steely grey and clean cut to flatter her petite figure. She did her usual two cheek kiss, mwa, mwa and said, 'now is there anything I can do to help?' Katie had an answer. 'Oh Jane, it would be wonderful if you helped make coffee for everyone.' Jane looked taken aback as if she had staff at home for such menial duties. 'Of course, I would love to.' She carefully took off her designer jacket and placed it over a chair and with a concerned look she asked, 'right, do you have an apron?' Bethan handed her the one they all used even though officially it was David's. Katie thought about all the food that was smeared down the front, from messy hands, and the reaction that might bring and simply walked away.

Conversations in lowered tones seemed to fill the house. Katie happened to be looking out from the bay window at the front of the house when the hearse drew up and stopped in the middle of the road; there was no space for it to pull in. She felt drawn to it and went straight out of the front door. Was that really her husband in the coffin? John Redgrove appeared and went straight over to her. 'Katie,' he said simply taking her hand and rested his other hand on her arm. 'All right?'

Katie gazed at the coffin. It was smothered in beautiful white lilies just as she'd requested.

'Now remember we're here to make the day run smoothly so that it makes it just a little easier for you.' John was saying.

'There's no rush,' he added. 'We'll move off in about ten minutes.'

'But aren't you blocking the road?' Katie could see with cars parked down both sides of Bisham Avenue there was no room to pass.

'People are understanding. Now is everyone here or are we waiting for a few?'

'I haven't a clue really. We'll go when you say.'

'Of course.'

The funeral car pulled up outside Highgate cemetery and Katie and her daughters got out. She thought of all the times she had walked this way as it was so close to home and she had always considered it a peaceful spot. Today it took on a whole new meaning despite the warmth of the sun shining on the gravestones behind the black wrought iron fence creating a pretty picture.

As Katie entered the chapel, a man wearing a shabby pale suit came up to her.

'I'm sorry, Mrs Green, I know you don't know me but I was a friend of David's.' He seemed nervous.

'Oh?' Katie looked him up and down and wondered if he was lying as he didn't seem to be the type that would befriend David. He must have been fifteen years younger at least.

'Ross, my name's Ross.'

'He never mentioned you.'

'I don't suppose he did but we were very close.'

Katie's eyes widened now. Was today not traumatic enough without this strange intrusion?

'David worked for Hiscox Insurance,' the man said to prove his claim. 'He drove a black Mercedes; he'd had leather seats put in the front.'

All this was true but didn't make Katie feel any easier. 'Did you work with him?'

'No, no. I don't suppose he will have told you how we met. Mrs Green, I don't mean any harm; I just want to offer my condolences, show my respect. It was such a shock when I found out.'

'Right.' Katie turned and grabbed Bethan's arm desperate for a distraction. 'Where are we sitting?'

Jacob had turned up and was at Alice's side. 'Hello.'

'Oh hi!' She looked relieved.

'Did you think I wouldn't come?'

'No, no. Anyway, it's good to see you.'

Rupert Chandler talked about the man Katie had married; the man who had delighted her with his humour and generosity; the man who had always made sure they didn't want for anything. He took them gently and carefully through the chosen ceremony, in charge and in control. But then he asked those gathered there if anyone would like to say a few words.

The man she had met at the entrance who called himself Ross raised his hand and made his way to the front. Who on earth was he? Katie could not believe he was going to say something.

'I'd...' he cleared his throat. 'I'd just like to say a few words... about David as he was a good friend to me. You could say I was a friend in need as David helped me on the first stage to putting my life back together.' He looked out to his audience and rested his eyes softly on Katie before he continued. 'The main thing I want to say is that David was a good man. He had good intentions and only wanted the best for his family. He was so proud of his daughters...'

Katie flinched but he continued. 'And I will never forget what he did for me.'

She willed him to sit down, but no.

'I'd just like to read a couple of verses of a poem by Rudyard Kipling if that's okay?' He looked over to her. She took a deep breath and lowered her sight to the ground.

> *'If you can keep your head when all about you*
> *Are losing theirs and blaming it on you,*
> *If you can trust yourself when all men doubt you,*
> *But make allowance for their doubting too,'*

Katie covered her ears. Who is this man? How dare he! Why did he have to make her angry on the very day she just wanted to grieve? She grasped the hands of her daughters who sat close on either side. They both looked at her wide-eyed and innocent. 'What's he going on about?' Alice whispered. 'Who the bloody hell is he?' Bethan asked. Katie closed her eyes and gulped.

'If you can make one heap of all your winnings
And risk it on one turn of pitch-and-toss,
And lose, and start again at your beginnings
And never breathe a word about your loss;

Katie wanted to shout stop! But she would not create a scene; not today. Instead she stared at him angrily willing him to step down. Ross looked up from the poem and said, 'well, perhaps that's enough. I'm sorry if I've spoken out of turn.'

The poem was over. Ross shuffled back to his seat.

Rupert looked over to Katie and smiled. 'Our thoughts are with Katie, Alice and Bethan today. I'm sure we all want to reach out to them and for them to know that we are all deeply sorry for their loss and hold them dear in our hearts and are here for them.'

Alice's hand was red from being squeezed by her mother's and she had to release it. She put an arm around her to stop her keeling over.

Caterers had let themselves into the house for their return. People started to eat and to drink, the mood was lightened; laughter crept into the conversations; future plans were talked about. Katie maintained a polite smile throughout and said 'thank you' a lot in response to kind words of sympathy. She took some comfort from the hugs of her daughters and Julia.

'Don't worry,' her friend whispered in her ear, 'don't think about it today.'

Eventually people started to leave saying their goodbyes and making poignant comments to Katie as they squeezed her hand to mark their sincerity. 'We'll call soon,' some said but Katie did nothing to encourage them.

With the last one gone, she dropped to the sofa and wriggled her feet out of her high heeled shoes which were starting to pinch.

'Have you eaten anything Mum?' Alice sat next to her.

'No, I've not had a thing all day.'

'Let's have a drink, a toast to Dad,' Bethan suggested and got three glasses and found an opened bottle of Chablis.

'To Dad, we miss you Dad.' Alice said as they raised their glasses and they all choked back a tear.

'We'll be alright though, won't we Mum?' Bethan sought reassurance.

Katie didn't know the answer to that question. 'Of course, we will.'

Chapter 6

Katie opened her eyes on to a sun-drenched bedroom. She squinted at first, but then her gaze rested on her dressing table, an antique piece David had surprised her with just after they bought the house. Now her necklaces hung from the ornate detail of the mirror and her hairbrush was next to several bottles of perfume. The dark clothes of yesterday were strewn over the chair in the corner. She remembered how her limbs had ached and her neck had felt stiff as she had climbed into bed last night feeling a sense of relief but knowing that tomorrow would have its own ordeals.

And here it was. Her bedroom was a beautiful haven; her bed was wonderfully soft; each piece of furniture held a delightful reminder, a moment of happiness, now spoilt by the dreadful fear that it was all going to be taken away from her. How could she even contemplate selling this house?

As she walked into the kitchen she was surprised to see both her daughters at the table having breakfast almost as though they were keen to get back to some semblance of normality.

'Good morning my darlings,' she said with a heavy heart.

'Mum, you look dreadful.' Bethan got up and went to hug her.

'Thank you darling.'

'Mum,' Alice guided her mother into a chair, 'I'll make you a fresh coffee.'

'That would be nice.'

'Do you want toast Mum?' This felt like reverse roles.

'I'll try,' Katie said and Bethan put a slice of bread in the toaster.

They sat in silence for some minutes. This was the first day of the rest of their lives. Katie wondered how and when she was going to tell them that, owing to the fact that their father seemed to have lost most of their money, they were going to have to sell their beloved home. She noticed yet again the pile of unopened post at the end of the table. Anything that looked like a bill or a bank statement had stayed sealed from her eyes. Each time one of the ominous looking envelopes dropped on the doormat she promised herself she would open it the day after the funeral. That day had arrived.

The toast was hard to swallow; the coffee was gulped down as if it would give her strength to go on.

'Mum,' Alice said looking earnest, 'you know we don't have to rush into anything. I mean, I know things are going to be different now.'

'Do you?'

'Well, yes, we don't have Dad's salary.'

'No, no we don't.' It was obvious but Katie was still pleased that Alice had gone some way to realising that they weren't going to be as well off.

'But there is the rent from Grandpa's place, isn't there?'

Suddenly now was the perfect moment and before Katie had had chance to think it through, she said, 'actually, we don't.'

Both girls sat up and looked at her. 'What?' Bethan asked convinced she'd misunderstood.

Katie hated doing this to them but they had to know. 'What I mean is we don't have the rent from Cheyne Gardens. You see your Dad sold the house and, as far as I can tell, there is only fifteen thousand pounds of the proceeds left.'

'What do you mean, he sold it? Didn't you know?' Bethan's eyes were wide with fear.

'No, no I didn't know,' Katie said keeping her voice steady.

'But that's ridiculous!' Alice picked up a napkin and threw it across the room in some sort of pathetic defiant act. 'How could you *not know*? What did he do with the money?'

Katie took a deep breath and reached out to both her daughters. 'You know I love you both very much, don't you?'

Bethan's eyes watered. 'Of course, we do Mum, we love you too. But what the hell's going on?'

'I think your Dad might have lost the money somehow,' she said, her voice shaking. She was painfully aware that she wasn't making much sense.

'Lost it?' Alice shouted angrily now. 'What lost *all* the money from the house! Bloody hell! You've got to be joking!'

Katie flinched. She swallowed hard before saying, 'Yes, it's a lot of money.'

'A lot of money!' Bethan stood up. 'How can you be so calm about it?'

Katie stared down into her empty coffee cup. 'I've had my moment of rage, I'm left with a feeling of deep sadness now and..' She stopped herself. 'I think I'll make some more coffee.'

'Mum? Sad and what?' Alice demanded and the red of her neck flooded her cheeks. Katie stopped in her tracks and took a deep breath. 'Just sad; just sad that your father didn't share his problem with me.' Betrayed, was what she had meant and she was so pleased she had kept that back. She used every ounce of strength to stay calm but her hand was trembling as she put the kettle on. She made the coffee in silence and took it over to the table. Her daughters both stared at her and she felt an enormous sense of responsibility for these two innocent lives. She sat down.

'Listen my darlings, I don't know how, I don't have any answers yet but I know we'll get through this somehow. I'm going to look for a job and we've got a bit to get by on for a few months and well, we could always sell this house and get somewhere smaller.'

'Sell our home!' Bethan erupted. 'Sell our home full of Dad's memories! Never! Never! Don't even think about it!'

Alice looked shocked. 'Mum, you're not serious?'

The doorbell rang and they all ignored it but it rang again. Katie looked at the clock and saw it was nearly ten. Bethan got up. 'I suppose I'll go.' She stomped across the room and through to the front door. Jane was stood there looking slightly nervous.

'Hello Bethan,' she said timidly. 'Is your mother in?'

'Jane, she is, but you know this isn't a good time,' she said, her tone aggressive.

'I see. I just wanted to see if your mother wanted any help clearing up after yesterday. I suspect you've done it all now.' Jane looked offended.

'We've not even started! But who cares about the bloody tidying up? Dad's dead and everything is crap!' she shouted so that even her mother heard. She slammed the door and tears burst from her eyes. Katie appeared in the hallway. 'Who was that?'

'Jane! Bloody busy body Jane from next door! Who bloody cares?'

'That's enough swearing! It's not Jane's fault!'

'No, it's *your* bloody fault for saying you're going to sell this house!' She ran upstairs and Katie heard hysterical cries from her bedroom. Katie thought about going after Jane but decided against it. She walked back in to the kitchen. Alice got up to hug her and uttered through tears, 'Mum, we've got to find another way. Please tell me you'll think of something. I can't bear it.'

Katie knew that enough was enough and they could not take any more in today. 'I'll do my best, I promise.' And as she comforted her daughter, she desperately wanted someone to console her.

Chapter 7

Katie stared at the words on the screen:

> *If you can make one heap of all your winnings*
> *And risk it on one turn of pitch-and-toss,*
> *And lose, and start again at your beginnings*
> *And never breathe a word about your loss;*

At the funeral she had shut Ross's words out; she could not bring herself to even try to make sense of it. Now, a few days later, her denial was weakening. However upsetting, she had to discover the meaning behind those terrifying words.

She had typed: *If by Rud...*

That was enough. Google swept her to the poem in full and she easily found the offending verse. Now it was there in front of her; no room for misinterpretation.

And never breathe a word about your loss.

She walked as if on auto pilot to David's wardrobe; her need to know the truth was both desperate and urgent now. His suits hung silently; his smell gently filling the air. She gulped and started to check the pockets of his jackets. Then she remembered the suit he had worn the day he died and found it still wrapped in plastic as it was when it was returned by the hospital. She burst the bag open and went straight to the pockets. She soon found a betting slip that read:

Joe Coral, 2.35pm Goodwood: Forever Lucky: Stake: £3,000 3 to 2 on.

Three thousand pounds. Three thousand pounds on one horse, called Forever Lucky. Tears started to stream down her face as the ugly truth began to unfold. Her husband was a serious gambler.

Back online Katie searched for Joe Coral branches. There were none in Highgate but there was one near Leadenhall Street where David worked. She knew immediately she had to go there. She had never stepped foot inside a betting shop before but she had to experience this place for herself.

Warm summer rain fell as Katie emerged from the tube station. Office workers suited with shiny shoes went hurriedly about their business. All seemed to have a purpose; somewhere to go; someone to meet. Katie suddenly felt very lonely. She put up her umbrella; one spoke had broken so that it looked scruffy against all the rest. She searched awkwardly with one hand through her handbag for the street map she had printed off earlier to see which way she should go. It was difficult to find the street names high up on the city buildings and the first road she tried was the wrong one. She felt tearful as she turned back but told herself she must keep going and eventually she worked it out.

She could see Joe Coral a few doors up on the other side of the road. She happened to be outside a coffee shop and decided she would arm herself with a strong espresso before carrying out her mission. The queue was long but the staff worked quickly, no time for niceties.

'Your usual Sir?' The man didn't answer but nodded and handed over the right change, his mobile phone held to his ear with his shoulder. It was Katie's turn; she had her purse at the ready.

'Espresso please,' she said as she picked out the right money from the coins in her purse and was pleased she had it.

'Single shot or double?'

'Double.' Katie surprised herself but then this was no ordinary day. She looked around for somewhere to sit. Most were sat at tables on their own but glued to mobile phones or staring at laptop screens; in their own little world and not letting anyone in. Wet macs in the warmth made the air smell damp.

Katie approached a table; a man sat opposite and looked up long enough to notice her. He gestured to the empty chair and she sat down. The coffee tasted good. She had a newspaper in her bag but could not be bothered to get it out. After all she had hardly read a word, when she had it open in front of her on the tube, past an occasional headline. It all seemed so unimportant. Instead she watched as the people around her came and went oblivious of their surroundings.

The coffee was drunk; the moment of truth had arrived. She walked slowly up the road and stood outside the window for a moment. The display was shiny and inviting; no indication of the lives ruined by this evil domain.

Inside there were bright screens and a luminous green carpet but all the punters wore dark grey and the floor was littered with screwed up betting slips, discarded with disappointment. Katie was about to leave when she remembered the betting slip in her handbag. She approached the counter.

'Yes Mrs?' The man wore a wide tie loosened at the neck; his hands were podgy. She tentatively handed over the slip wondering if he would laugh at her because the horse had lost.

'Ah, Forever Lucky you are too Mrs. Would you prefer cash or a transfer to your account?'

Katie could not believe her ears. 'Cash,' she said feebly leaning on the counter for support.

'I'll just be a moment.' It was just a normal day for him. Katie had hardly had time to work out the significance of this when he returned and started to count out the money.

She stared at the fifty-pound notes; not something she was familiar with.

'And that's your 5k.' He put the money in an envelope and noticed her expression. 'Are you all right there?'

'Yes, yes. Yes, I'm fine.' She paused for a moment. 'So, the horse won?'

'Of course!' He was puzzled now.

'Right.' She took the money, put it into her handbag, zipped it up and wandered out on to the street in a daze. She felt like a robber having collected her stash of the stolen cash, part of some undercover world. And then she realised that this must be a world that David was very familiar with. 'Oh, David,' she muttered under her breath, 'your bloody horse won!'

Back in Highgate village Katie felt an enormous sense of relief; the City had unnerved her. She suddenly had an overwhelming sense of how lucky she was to live in such a lovely place. She had taken it for granted in the past. Now that it represented a luxury she could ill afford she was desperate to hold on to it.

Finding herself at home alone she took the money from the envelope and counted it out on to the kitchen table. She stacked it into five piles of one thousand pounds. What would she do with it? Put it in the bank and use it to survive on when her savings ran out? That would be the sensible thing to do. Put it on another horse? That was what David would have done. It was too big a decision for her to make right now. She bundled it up and hid it in her wardrobe.

Chapter 8

'Do you have this in a size eighteen?' A large woman asked.

'This is a charity shop, darling, we don't do sizes. It's just what people donate, I'm sorry,' Julia explained.

'Well, all I can say is that there are a lot of skinny rich people around here!'

Katie stifled a laugh and Julia noticed her pretending to be interested in a second-hand book entitled *Rich Dad Poor Dad*. The annoyed woman thrust the size ten garment into Julia's hands and walked out. Katie stole a laugh and Julia joined in.

'What are you doing in *here* darling? You normally only pop in to drag me out for a browse around that lovely vintage shop.'

'Ah well, I'm poor now, shopping in charity shops; it's come to this.'

'That is not funny,' Julia said.

'No, it's certainly not funny.' Katie was struggling to stay focused on the here and now.

'You need a plan,' Julia said in an upbeat way.

'A plan, ah yes, do you stock those?'

'No, but the cafe down the road does.'

'Really?'

'Yes, let's go to Fegos. I've had many an inspirational thought in there. I'll even buy you a cappuccino.'

'That would be good but what about the shop?'

'Rachel's due any minute; she'll cope on her own for an extra hour.'

Alice knocked on the bathroom door. 'Bethan, you in there?'
There was no reply.

'Bethan, how long are you going to be?' Alice knocked louder.

She finally opened the door and appeared with a towel clutched around her. 'For God's sake; can't I have a bath in peace!'

'You've been ages! I need to go out.'

'Where're you off to?' Bethan asked. She seemed genuinely interested which seemed odd to Alice.

'I'm going to... look for a job.' Alice avoided her sister's gaze.

'What? I thought you were going to uni.' Bethan hoisted her towel up and tucked it round her chest to leave her hands free to run her fingers through her wet tangled hair.

'Uni or not, I'm broke! Aren't you?'

'Well yes, of course. I was going to ask Mum for some money the other day but when she said she might sell the house I thought bloody hell.'

Alice was thoughtful. 'Do you think she knows that Dad used to give us two hundred pounds a month each?'

'Mmmm... somehow I don't think so.'

'This is really crap isn't it? Anyway, I'm going to try and get a waitressing job.'

'How much will you get for that?'

'I don't know. Jacob earns quite good money but he's a Maître d' and has experience.'

'They might start you in the kitchen washing up, can you imagine?' Bethan looked horrified.

'Well I'm not stooping that low.'

'Too right.' Bethan agreed and then she said, 'sorry about taking so long; I was just having a wallow, you know, thinking about Dad and how rubbish life is without him.'

'That's okay; I understand.'

'Actually Mum's out so you could use her bathroom.'

'I know, I just needed my shampoo and stuff.'

'Oh right, well come in and help yourself.'

'Thanks sis'.'

Katie stared down at her coffee. Julia had said, 'yes', to chocolate sprinkled on to the milky foam and it was shaped like a leaf. She looked up at Julia, 'I need to sell the house and the girls *hate me* for it. *I* hate me for it!'

'You do know that teenage girls are a nightmare, don't you? As you will recall, when Daisy got to eighteen, I decided I couldn't take any more and persuaded Andrew to buy her a flat just to get rid of her!'

Katie smiled.

'Sorry, I know that's not an option for you.' Julia bit her lip.

'No, I'll be buying a flat for all three of us at this rate.'

'Now stop that. We're here to devise a plan.'

'I'm all for a plan darling but let's face it, selling the house is the obvious thing to do, isn't it?'

'Well, it's certainly *an* option and probably the sensible one.'

'I can hear a but, even in your voice.'

'Well let's just think about this...' Julia gazed into the distance as if she was looking for inspiration.

'David's car needs taxing, remember? And the girls don't want me to sell it. The fridge freezer has been playing up and that's something we can't manage without. And if Bethan wants to go back to school to do A-levels there will be school fees which are astronomical!'

'Oh God yes, it's all pretty grim isn't it? Can't she go to a sixth form college to do her A-levels? Then you won't have the fees.'

'Yes, if she can be persuaded. She's always turned her nose up at going to college; it might all be too much for her.'

Julia rested her hand on her friends. 'Poor you. And the girls; how are they coping with all this? How much have you told them?'

'I've certainly been economical with the truth so far. But I've stopped their allowance which they are beginning to get upset about.'

'Can't they get some casual work during the school holidays?'

'Good idea; but how do I suggest that when they are still traumatised by their father's death.'

Julia sighed. 'Hey, we're supposed to having a planning session to lift your spirits.'

'Sorry, just telling it like it is.'

Julia leaned in. 'So, what's the bottom line? Have you managed to access that money in your joint account?'

'Yes, I've got just about enough money for a few lean months and then that is it. If I don't sell the house it will be repossessed by the building society and that would be even worse!'

Julia squeezed Katie's hand. 'Okay, so you need to downsize. Your house is too big anyway what with Alice going off to uni...'

'If she goes!'

'If she goes, what do you mean?'

'I have a feeling she's thinking about taking a year off,' Katie said with an air of resignation.

'To do what? Be unemployed and drive her mother mad?'

'She hasn't said as much yet but her enthusiasm for uni has definitely waned.'

A man dressed smartly in a suit came and sat on the next table. He placed his coffee down and opened up the Financial Times newspaper. They both stared into the bottom of their empty cups.

'Same again?' Julia asked.

'My turn,' Katie said standing up.

'Don't be silly.'

'It's all right, I won five thousand pounds on a horse,' Katie said matter of factly.

'What?'

'Well, David did to be more precise. He placed the bet on the day he died.'

'What kind of bet was that?' Julia looked amazed.

'It's beyond me.' Katie picked up the empty cups and went up for two more cappuccinos. The man with the pink paper looked up.

With Katie back in her seat Julia leant forward. 'What about taking in a lodger?' Her face was hopeful.

'I have thought about it, but I just can't imagine sharing my home with a stranger.'

'I know what you mean, but if it was a woman it would be safe, wouldn't it? You could give her your guest bedroom with the en-suite and then you wouldn't have to share a bathroom.'

'Well, I suppose so; as long as she wasn't a sex-crazed lesbian,' Katie said flippantly.

The man opposite made an indistinguishable noise behind his paper which metamorphosed into a cough. The paper was lowered. Katie glared at him accusingly. He smiled, 'sorry,' he felt the need to say and disappeared back behind his paper. Julia sniggered.

'So,' Katie summarised, 'is that it? The plan?'

'No, no. I was thinking you could get a job as a PA like you did before the girls were born. I mean at the moment you spend a lot of time working for charities for free.'

'Well, I'm certainly willing to get a job but PAs are few and far between these days. It's all computers now doing everything for you. And let's face it things have changed a bit in the last eighteen years.'

'Yes, you've got a point. But there must be something you can do?'

'Julia, let's face it, at fifty in the current job market I might as well save my breath. I mean even to be a receptionist you need to be beautiful, wrinkle free and wearing a vacuous smile and a miniskirt.'

The FT man's paper hit the table. He leant across. 'I'm sorry, I hope you don't think it impertinent of me, but may I make a small suggestion?' Katie and Julia looked at each other in astonishment and then back to the man as he continued, 'It's just that nowadays there is a great demand for virtual assistants.'

'Virtual what?' they said in unison.

'Virtual assistants; it's basically being a PA to one or more clients but working from your own home,' he explained.

'That sounds interesting.' Julia was warming to him. 'So what sort of things do virtual assistants do?'

'Anything from booking appointments, making travel arrangements, writing reports to answering the phone.'

'Well that sounds easy.' Julia's wide eyes looked straight at her friend.

'Yes, it sounds interesting,' Katie was willing to concede but was not at all sure about this. 'But how do you get your clients?'

'Business networking, social media, you could advertise locally, but you can be a VA to anyone, anywhere in the world.'

That sounded daunting to Katie. She smiled and thanked the man for the suggestion. Julia wasn't going to let it go though. 'Do you have a virtual assistant?' she asked.

'As a matter of fact I do; Nancy in New York; works well for me.'

'What's wrong with London?' Julia asked.

'Nothing at all, but you see distance doesn't matter. Admittedly the time delay can be a bit of a problem,' his head tilted from side to side as if it was a minor inconvenience. 'Anyway, I must go. It's been lovely meeting you.' He put his business card on their table before a quick goodbye and he was gone.

'Harry Liversage, CEO of Greenfield Investments,' Katie read from the card.

'Are you going to call him?' Julia asked.

'Whatever for?'

'Well, keep the card, you never know.'

'Oh, if it pleases you.' She dropped it into her handbag so that it was in no particular place. They sat quietly for a moment and then Katie said simply, 'what I really wanted to talk to you about was a viewing I've arranged for a flat.'

Julia did not look pleased. 'Oh, where's this flat then?'

'Archway.'

'Archway!' Julia repeated sounding alarmed.

'Yes, exactly and it looks really small compared to my house despite having three bedrooms. *But* I can just about afford it with the capital in the house with some left over to live on for a year or so.'

'Right, okay, so when are we viewing this flat?' Julia had her bravest face on.

'Oh thank God you said "we". I don't think I could do it on my own.'

'Of course I'll come with you and I promise to be positive.'

'It looks pretty grim online but I persuaded myself it might have potential.'

'Okay, so what time is the viewing?'

'Three o'clock so we need to leave now,' Katie said looking apologetic.

'Oh, look at the time!'

'Yes, we'll leave now,' Katie said as if it was the last thing she wanted to do. They looked at each other as they stood up and Katie decided that it was best to not think about anything at all.

'Let's go in my car,' Julia said as she gave her friend a hug. 'Now, no tears until we get there.'

Katie allowed herself a smile.

Chapter 9

Julia pulled up outside the mansion block. 'I think it's here, somewhere.' She craned her neck to look up. Katie held her hand and they looked at each other in the same way as Thelma and Louise did just before they went over the cliff edge. Katie was about to say 'forget it, let's go,' when a young man in a navy-blue suit with a boyish face and poor skin tapped the driver's window. Julia put her window down.

'Mrs Green? Here to see number 15 High Mount,' he said cheerily.

'Er yes, this is Mrs Green,' Julia pointed to Katie. Now she had nowhere to hide.

'Ah right, brought a friend along, good idea,' he said uncertainly. 'So where are you currently living?'

They both got out of the car warily. 'Highgate village,' Julia replied as Katie didn't.

'Ah right. Yes, this block is very popular with divorcees,' he said as he smiled and winked at Katie.

Katie gave him a withering look but stayed silent. Julia thought that this man was not making it any easier. He led them into the communal hallway which was dusty and had a lot of unclaimed post and junk mail. The walls bore the scars of many years of comings and goings and were grey with dirt.

'Lift's unreliable, I'm afraid,' he said and started up the stairs. 'No need to join the gym,' Julia quipped. Katie did not laugh. They reached number fifteen, the gold numbers were doing their best on a battered blue painted door.

'Paint your front door blue if you want to sell your house,' the estate agent chanted gaily. He walked down a dark, narrow hallway and straight into the first room and announced 'so this is the living room, a good size, I'm sure you'll agree and double aspect; not all the flats in this block enjoy that.' He looked very pleased with himself as he delivered his patter.

A damp smell hit Julia straight away. The walls were beige and marked where pictures had once hung; there were two wonky shelves which had been put up badly and housed nothing but dust and a random electric cable. The white imitation-leather sofa was stained and the carpet was threadbare in places. Julia was squeezing Katie's hand. Katie looked like she was dumbstruck. The estate agent continued to dig himself into a hole.

'What do you think? First impressions?' he asked.

'Not sure it's *exactly* what we're looking for,' Julia offered by way of explanation for Katie's silence. 'I tell you what, we'll look round the rest on our own; I'm sure we won't get lost.'

'Oh, okay.' The estate agent was winded. 'Well I was going to...' Julia had led Katie out into the hallway. They took a cursory glance into the kitchen which hadn't been updated since the seventies and still had Formica units in dirty white with a brown trim. There was a very small table squeezed in with two orange plastic chairs. Julia imagined Alice and Bethan's reactions to this place and knew they would be horrified by the very thought of living here. Katie was looking ill, nauseous even.

The curtains in the main bedroom were drawn making the room dark but they could just make out a lurid green patterned carpet.

'Do you think the current owner is blind?' Julia asked. Katie spluttered a laugh but it was quickly replaced with tears. Julia hugged her. 'You know, I don't think this is really you.'

Finally she articulated what she was feeling. 'I think if I moved in here I would kill myself.'

'Probably time to leave then.' They met the estate agent in the hallway as they tried to escape. He looked like a kid who'd just been told he couldn't play his favourite computer game.

'It's not right,' Julia cried out before he could say anything. She steered Katie out and down the stairs.

'Oh, wouldn't you like to look at anything else?' He was shouting down the stairwell now. 'I believe number four is vacant.'

'No, no thanks.' Julia shouted back up to him as they both picked up speed and started racing down the steps.

'Oh, oh well I'll just lock up then…'

They jumped into the car and Julia hit the accelerator as they headed down the road and back to Highgate. Katie wept as the full realisation of what was happening to her hit her hard. Julia said nothing until they pulled up outside her house. 'You're coming in for a glass of wine,' she commanded. Katie looked at her. 'Am I?'

'Yes, it's not optional, it's entirely necessary.'

With half a bottle of Pouilly Fume drunk, Katie allowed her shoulders to drop. 'Thank you,' she said. 'I couldn't have done that on my own; not without biffing that estate agent.' She took a deep breath and sighed.

'Hey you,' Julia reacted, 'you're not going home until you're incapable of even a sigh.'

Katie smiled. 'Being with you certainly helps but the elephant's still in the room.'

'No, it's not. I don't allow elephants in my living room.'

They looked at each other. Katie could not have been more serious. 'I have to find another way, don't I?'

'Yes, it's the lesbian lodger after all.' Julia clunked her friend's glass and Katie let out a giggle.

'That's better,' Julia said. 'I might let you go home eventually.'

Chapter 10

Katie opened her eyes and realised it was past eight o'clock. She hadn't slept in so late since the fateful night. Her head felt sore and her mouth dry. She remembered the wine she had drunk at Julia's. Just as she reached for her glass of water there was a knock at her bedroom door. 'Come in,' she said surprised as Alice appeared with a tray.

'Morning Mum, thought you might like breakfast in bed.'

'Oh darling, how thoughtful,' she said relieved to see it was just a piece of toast and some coffee. She sat herself up in bed. Alice placed the tray on her lap. They looked at each other and Alice sat on the side of the bed sheepishly. Katie sipped the coffee and there was an uncomfortable pause before Alice said carefully, 'Mum?'

'Yes darling.'

'I've got my A-level results; well actually I had them a few days ago.'

'Oh darling, I'm so sorry; I completely forgot. Silly me; what did you get?'

'Don't worry Mum; I know you've had a lot on your mind.'

'Yes, but this is important.' She took her daughter's hand. 'So?'

'So, I got an A and two Bs.'

'That's great. Well done!' Katie moved the tray to one side and hugged her.

'Thanks Mum, but actually,' she looked down at the bed cover, 'the thing is the B is in French.'

'Oh. Does that matter?'

'Well it means that Nottingham won't take me. But Exeter probably would.'

'What do you mean probably?'

'Well I mean they would. That was my offer; a B in French.' She started stroking the bedspread looking thoughtful and Katie gave her time. 'The thing is, I've been thinking.'

Her mother braced herself.

'I just can't leave you and go off to uni now,' Alice continued, 'I can always take a year off and go next year.'

Katie was about to take a bite from the toast but put it back on the plate.

'I'm going to get a job,' Alice announced, now confidently.

'Really darling?' Suddenly Katie felt relieved. She realised that she didn't want her daughter to leave her at this moment in time.

'Yes, there's a waitressing job going at Chez Pierre where Jacob works.' It was as if Jacob working there justified it somehow even though it was where her father had died. 'I'm not sure if I want to work *there* but there are other restaurants.'

Katie was pleased for this last token. 'Maybe not a good idea to work in the same place as your boyfriend.' Katie winced as soon as she said it. She was making an assumption. 'Jacob is your boyfriend now, I assume?' She prayed that she was right about this and hadn't put her foot in it.

Alice blushed. 'Yes Mum. Anyway, The Lemon Tree are looking for people so I'll try them.'

'Good idea.'

'And then I'll be able to help out with the food shopping and stuff and well that will help won't it? Make things a bit better?'

'Yes, of course it will.' Katie thought that David would have wanted Alice to go to university. It felt selfish wanting her to stay and help her face this nightmare but, as Julia had pointed out last night, maybe it was time to put her own feelings first. A waitress's wage was hardly the answer to her problems but it felt like a small step in the right direction. What was more heartening was the fact that her eighteen-year-old daughter had some small understanding of their situation.

Both Bethan and Alice were out when the doorbell rang later that morning. Katie smiled at the thought that it might be Julia coming to share hangover snippets after the wine they had drunk yesterday. So when she opened the door to see the man who read the poem at the funeral, this time in jeans and a t-shirt she gasped for breath.

'Please don't shut the door,' he said quickly and desperately. 'It's me; it's Ross; I only want to help.'

'How on earth can you help me?' Katie suddenly felt angry and upset.

'I know you don't know me; I know I am asking for a huge leap of faith. I understand,' he said. 'I knew David; I knew him well. We shared a problem, an illness if you like.'

Katie wanted to scream at him to make him go away but something was stopping her. There was an awkward pause before the man said, 'I'll be in the coffee shop in the village. Fegos. I'll wait for you there. It's up to you Mrs Green.' He turned and walked away.

Katie shut her front door pressing hard against it long after it was closed. She was trembling and hated everything about the situation but knew deep down that she had to go. Somehow she calmed herself and went upstairs to put on a jacket and sandals. She applied some lipstick, took a deep breath and walked down to the village.

Fegos was quite busy for a Wednesday morning but she spotted Ross straight away. He looked pale but relieved to see her. He smiled and waved hesitantly and Katie felt very strange as she approached his table and sat opposite him.

'Thank you for coming,' he said meekly, 'may I get you a coffee?'

Katie, in her heightened state, wanted to say *what on earth is in this for you* but instead took another deep breath to calm herself. 'Yes, yes please, a cappuccino.'

Ross attracted the waitress's attention and ordered the coffee.

'So,' Katie said as ready to listen as she ever would be, 'where did you meet my husband?'

'At GA. At Gamblers Anonymous, the Camden branch,' he said with a stark honesty and Katie felt like she had been kicked in the stomach.

'Is that a shock to you Mrs Green?'

'Of course it is!' She realised reluctantly that this man was worth listening to; he may well be able to help her understand what was going on in her husband's life before he died. 'Call me Katie, please.'

'Thank you Katie. We met two years ago,' he went on. 'My wife had left me; she was so sick of the gambling and I'd lost my job. I knew I had to do something. Anyway, I was stood outside the hall where the GA meeting is and wasn't going to go in when David appeared. We looked at each other and he said, "are you coming in?" "I don't know" I said, I couldn't face it. But then David said in a really gentle kind of way, "Well you're here now," and made way for me to walk in first. Thank goodness he did.'

'So you're cured now?' Katie was looking at a man whose hair had greyed prematurely and who was thin with worry. What was there to thank goodness for?

'I've not gambled for a year now. I have a mentor who helps me. I can ring him in an emergency. Now I've seen what's happened to David I'm even more determined to keep it up.' He quickly added, 'Sorry, I didn't mean that to come out like that.'

Katie could not hold back a tear. 'So, David didn't manage to give up?' Of course she knew this; he had placed a bet on his last day.

'He tried Katie, really he did. He really tried but he kept saying he had to win back some money he'd lost before you found out. He always believed he'd do it. He had to. He couldn't bear the thought of failing his own family.' Katie wanted to hug and punch her dead husband at the same time.

'How could he be so stupid?' She hadn't meant to say that out loud.

'It's an addiction; it's like an illness. He did try. You see the trouble was David had some big winnings. He could get it right and win tens of thousands on accumulators but he didn't know when to stop.'

Katie thought back over the years. Sometimes David had seemed unusually high; there had been fleeting moments of absurd generosity. At the time she had thought it was just the way he was. And then there were other times when he seemed subdued and she had sensed he was making an effort to appear his usual self. 'Bad day at work?' she would ask in ignorance. 'Yes, difficult day darling,' he would explain and that was that. If ever she probed for details he brushed her off with, 'I don't want to talk about work now. Let's forget it. I'm with my family; that's the important thing.' And that would be enough for Katie to be reminded once more how much she loved him. Tears were rolling down her cheeks now. Reaching for a tissue from her handbag she said to Ross, 'I'm sorry'.

'Don't be silly; of course you're upset.'

Katie blew her nose and composed herself. 'Thank you,' she said, 'I mean thank you for telling me. I needed to know even though it hurts so badly.'

'David was very kind to me; it's the least I can do.'

Katie wondered what had gone on in this secret friendship.

'I know it sounds silly,' he said, 'but I'd like to help in any way I can.'

'Why?' The word slipped from Katie's mouth.

'Because David helped me, that's all.' He looked uncomfortable for a moment.

'I can't imagine what you could do unless you happen to have about half a million pounds spare that you don't need right now.'

Ross smiled. 'Sorry, not quite. Let me give you my card.'

He handed over a small blue business card. Katie picked it up and read: *My Mag, Highgate and Hampstead, keeping locals informed.*

'What's that then?'

'It's a business I bought a few months ago. My Mag is like a local directory of businesses. I sell the advertising space, get it printed and put it through all the doors in the area.' He had come alive now as he talked about his new venture.

'Oh yes, I've got a copy at home, I remember now,' Katie said. 'Do you make much money?'

'Yes, it's not bad at all. Keeps me very busy but of course that's a good thing.'

Katie was beginning to realise that there was something to admire about this man. At first she had hated him for what he stood for, but actually he was just the messenger and she really should stop shooting him down.

'Anyway,' he said, 'I have to go now but I really meant what I said. If there's *anything* I can do, just give me a call.'

Katie looked straight into his eyes for the first time. 'Thank you,' she said and popped the card into her handbag, 'I will.'

Chapter 11

Bethan's GCSE results were in cyberspace somewhere or perhaps on an internet site, which only Bethan could log in to. Katie and Alice drank coffee and wondered what her grades might be as they sat at the kitchen table.

'Shall I go and wake her?' Alice asked her mum. It was ten o'clock.

'Probably not a good idea.'

Alice got up scraping the legs of her chair against the floor loudly. 'Well I can't wait around here all day.' She went over to the kettle and refilled it. 'More coffee?'

'I think I might burst.'

'Well I'll make some anyway. Bethan might want some when she eventually comes down.'

Katie smiled. She felt strangely calm about the results. After all, life had thrown some pretty big hurdles at her recently. Alice sat down again and ran her fingers through her hair. 'What if she's failed? She didn't do very well in her mocks.'

'She'll have passed.' Katie looked wistful. 'She'll have passed for her Dad. She would do anything to please him.'

'But that's the trouble, isn't it? She doesn't want to go to college and do A-levels because Dad's not here, so she thinks there's no point.'

Her words hung in the air as Bethan walked down the stairs, through the hallway and straight out of the front door. Slam. Alice looked as if she had been personally affronted and her mother smiled again.

Katie was wandering around Highgate village yet again; anything to distract her from the massive predicament she found herself in. She found comfort in going up to the cemetery and thinking her thoughts out loud to David. She told him about how his horse, Forever Lucky, had won that day, about the frightful flat in Archway and the latest update on his daughters, which she knew he would appreciate. Today she would have told him about Bethan's exam results, but of course she didn't know what they were. It surprised her how calm her reaction to this fate was. What little anger it had invoked had dissipated. She didn't feel the need to reprimand him; just a deep sadness and an enormous reluctance to face up to the naked truth of the matter.

Back in the village she bought the local paper, the Ham and High and scanned the appointments section over a coffee. She wasn't sure if she was disappointed or pleased that there was nothing suitable. Waiting in the queue for the till to pay for a few groceries in the local shop, a postcard on a noticeboard caught her eye. It read:

Writer requires room in house to escape the distraction of his own. Clean shaven, well-mannered and can make a mean cappuccino. Call Birch on 07700 900987.

Katie smiled. She liked the sound of Birch and found herself saving his number in her mobile. Of course she would not phone him. She remembered the two business cards in her handbag, one from Harry Liversage and one from Ross. She seemed to be collecting new contacts. What a strange turn life had taken.

Back home she looked at the aubergine she had bought and remembered how David had occasionally cooked the Italian dish, Melanzane, and how much the girls loved it. It did occur to her that it was likely to be more to do with the fact that their father had prepared a meal for them and the precious attention they were getting from him, than the food itself. Her own attempts to cook something new were usually unrewarding, but she was at such a low ebb that she felt she had nothing to lose. She found a recipe in a Delia Smith cookbook, but realised it wasn't the one David had used as the page was pristine and not splattered with grease marks. Nevertheless she had heard good things about Delia. This sentiment quickly disappeared after reading the first instruction under method:

First prepare the aubergines: cut into smallish pieces, pile them in a colander, sprinkle with salt (2 heaped teaspoons), then place a plate on top of them. Weigh it down with a scale-weight and leave to drain for one hour.

'What a palaver!' she exclaimed out loud but Delia wasn't listening and persisted in her instruction. Just then her mobile rang and she could see it was Malcolm, the chair of the Save the Children committee.

'Hello Malcolm,' she answered, her voice struggling to sound upbeat.

'Katie, I'm sorry to have to call; Julia told me to leave you alone and I will, of course, but first my deepest condolences for your loss.'

'Thank you. Actually I'm glad you've called because I've been thinking and..'

'About your position on the committee?' he interrupted.

'Yes.' Katie wished he would let her finish.

'It's just that there's quite a lot of work building up for the Autumn Fete,' he continued, 'and I totally understand if you don't feel up to it..'

'I don't actually.' Katie was blunt. It was the only way of getting his attention.

'You don't?' Malcolm was somewhat taken aback even though he had suggested as much himself.

'Yes, you see I have a lot to worry about right now and I'm going to have to start working again. For money, I mean. So you see, regrettably,' she wiped away a silent tear, 'I'm going to have to stand down.' She sniffed and hoped he hadn't heard. 'I just won't have the time anymore.'

'Oh well I'm sorry to hear that.' His tone indicated that he was most put out now. 'You will be sorely missed of course and we will need to find a replacement as a matter of urgency.'

Katie thought back at the long hours she had devoted to this charity. It was a shame that Malcolm's thoughts were more about the gap she was leaving rather than an immediate desire to thank her for all the work she had put in over many years.

'I'm sure you'll find someone,' she said feeling quite sad about it now.

'Yes, well if you know anyone?' he had the cheek to ask.

Katie was tempted to suggest her neighbour, Jane, but decided against it. She was the sort of woman who meant well even if she had no idea what actual affect she was having on people around her. She decided not to answer his question. 'Goodbye Malcolm and best of luck,' she managed to say before ending the call and allowing herself to cry out loud. Why was this affecting her so much?

By the time the assembled dish went into the oven Delia's book had been discarded and a large glass of white wine poured. She remembered last night's alcohol consumption being somewhat over a healthy limit, but noted the respectable time of six o'clock and raised her glass to the kitchen clock. She felt uncomfortable drinking alone at the table and started playing with her mobile. Then she remembered Birch and his amusing advert and, before she let herself consider whether or not it was a good idea, she found his number and pressed call. After a couple of rings she heard his voicemail:

'Hello, this is Birch. Please don't hang up. I'm in the middle of writing the next gripping chapter of my novel and I promise I'll get back to you if you just let me know who you are.'

Katie liked his voice and warmed to him as she heard his message but still she hung up. She took a large slug of wine and listened out for one of her daughters at the front door. But they didn't come. The house was still. She downed the rest of the wine in her glass and called him again. This time she left a message.

'Hello, er, Birch, erm, this is Katie. I saw your advert and well, as it happens, I have a spare room. You're probably fixed up by now. Anyway, just in case, my number is ....' and she left her mobile number.

Having ended the call, almost as a reflex action, she re-filled her wine glass in a heavy-handed way pouring far more than she normally would. The house was still quiet. Their road didn't get much traffic. Despite being part of a terrace she rarely heard the neighbours; the walls were thick. In the silence she wondered what an earth she was going to do with the rest of her life. Her girls would leave home; how would she fill this house with life again. Just then she heard a key carefully turn in the front door as Alice arrived home. She knew it was Alice because Bethan was far more careless and tended to lurch clumsily into the hallway invariably knocking something over as she went.

'Oh, you are in Mum,' Alice said as she reached the kitchen. 'I thought I could smell something cooking. What is it? You haven't cooked Dad's melanzane, have you?'

They waited for Bethan to appear and when there was no sign and no message by seven o'clock Katie said, 'she must be out celebrating her GCSE results with her friends.'

'Or drowning her sorrows and unable to face us,' Alice added unhelpfully.

Katie served up two portions of the melanzane and they ate without commenting on it. Alice talked about a job she had now secured at The Lemon Tree. 'I'm sure I will soon be up to five days a week and that should be a decent amount of money. Jacob says we'll have to try and get the same shift pattern. I'm not sure, I mean I don't want to push my luck in the first week.'

They heard the front door open and waited for Bethan to appear. 'Oh, you didn't wait for me then?'

'Sorry darling, we weren't sure what time you were coming home.' Katie wished she wasn't immediately on the defensive all the time.

'Did I say I'd be late?' This was definitely confrontational now.

'Would you like some dinner?' Katie asked ignoring her.

'S'pose. What is it?' Bethan sat down and Katie served up a small portion in case it was rejected. She didn't say what it was. After Alice's reaction she decided to keep quiet about it.

'Wine?' She wasn't in the habit of encouraging her daughters to drink, especially on a week day but she had an inkling that somehow desperate measures were called for.

'Yeah Mum, but what's the matter?'

'Nothing is the matter, I'm just offering you a glass of wine with your supper.'

'This is about my results, isn't it?'

'No! I don't even know what your results are.'

'Don't you?'

'No! I promise you. We don't, do we Alice?'

'No, we don't; you slinked off this morning without telling us.'

'I did not! I didn't know myself this morning!'

Katie sat down and decided not to have any more wine. She let the awkward silence remain in the hope that both her daughters would at least calm down. Eventually she said, 'Bethan, why don't you tell us what you got; we love you whatever it is.'

'Huh! I knew you'd think I'd done badly! Well! Four As and five Bs actually!' She took a large glug of wine.

'Well done darling,' Katie said in a measured tone.

'What were the As in?' Alice demanded.

'English lit, art, DT and media studies.'

'Mmm..' Alice sounded unimpressed.

'What do you mean, mmm?'

'Nothing.' Her sister was affecting innocence.

'So,' Katie changed the subject, 'which A-levels are you going to do?'

Bethan stared at her with disbelief in her eyes.

'I told you, I want to do an NVQ in Graphic Design! Don't you ever listen?'

Katie could not recall this but knew her mind had been all over the place. 'I'm sorry, darling, what does this NVQ involve?'

'It costs two thousand pounds,' Alice interrupted.

Katie now knew this was not something she had been told about. She would have remembered that.

'Yes!' Bethan glared at her sister. 'Yes, but I am trying to save. I mean I had a hundred pounds put by before Dad...' She started to sob.

'Look perhaps we should talk about this tomorrow.' Katie said desperately. 'It's been an emotional day, I mean let's just sleep on it and...'

'And by tomorrow,' Bethan yelled, getting to her feet. 'By tomorrow you'll have come up with some reason why I can't do what I really wanted to do!' She stormed off down the hall. 'What Dad said I could do!'

Katie closed her eyes and sighed.

Alice raised her eyebrows. 'I knew it!' After a quick look at her mobile she said, 'I'm off to see Jacob. See you later Mum,' and was gone.

'Oh?' Katie was left bemused.

Just you, me and the kitchen clock, Katie thought as she picked up her wine glass. She looked at the table; Bethan had hardly touched her food and Alice had left some. No one appreciated her culinary efforts; no one had offered to load the dishwasher. Yes, they were grieving, but so was she. All this left her feeling the need to reach out to someone for support but she would not lean on Julia again today even though she knew she could. She picked up her phone and saw she had a voicemail message from Birch and she felt quite excited.

Hi Katie, Thanks for your message. I'm not fixed up actually so would love to hear more about this spare room of yours. Do call me back; you've got my number.

He sounded warm and friendly and she immediately wanted to call him back. She needed cheering up; she needed to do something for herself. She would call him. Right now.

Chapter 12

Birch stood at Katie's door at ten minutes after the appointed time of eleven o'clock. Katie had been fidgeting and meddling for at least twenty minutes, nervous about his imminent arrival. One thing that had gone in her favour was that both her daughters had had reason to go out; she had not told either about him. She composed herself, smoothed her hair and opened the door.

'Katie?' he held out his hand.

'Yes, you must be Birch. Do come in.'

He smiled at her, an infectious smile. He was tall and slim with fine, fair hair swept back from his forehead. His bright blue eyes sat in a slightly freckly face and his lips were thin. He wore an open neck shirt and skinny jeans and carried a shabby looking briefcase.

'Funny business this, isn't it?' he said and Katie felt relieved.

'Yes, I must admit it's a whole new world to me.' Katie wondered whether she should have said that. They walked into the kitchen, which was beautifully tidy due to her earlier efforts. She had woken at six o'clock and her thoughts and worries had got her out of bed to start cleaning and tidying the house, which had been neglected for some time, especially as she had let her cleaner go. A vase of summer flowers, brought around by Julia earlier, prettied the kitchen table.

'You have a lovely home Katie,' he said sincerely.

'Thank you. We have had a bit of a tidy up,' she was willing to admit.

'Would you like some coffee?' Katie remembered his advert.

'Good idea.'

She looked at the makings of coffee that she had laid out earlier in readiness and wondered how on earth, one made a mean cappuccino. Birch picked up the packet of fresh coffee. 'Excellent choice!' he said, opening it up and weighing up his tools. Katie was more pleased than amazed.

'Now where's the fridge?' he asked instantly making himself at home.

She showed him. 'Milk?' she assumed.

'Yes, good good. A small pan?'

Katie found the same and placed it on the hob. And before her eyes he turned into a barista and set to work with a cool efficiency that Katie could only stand back and admire. Eventually he said, 'deux cappuccino, Madam.' He placed the cups on the table. 'May I sit down?'

They sat and Katie sipped the coffee; it was delicious.

'So,' he announced, 'this is the bit where we both ask careful questions to make sure we're not weirdos with some strange agenda.'

Katie was immediately concerned.

'Oh dear,' he backtracked, 'That was meant to make you laugh. I was joking. My silly way of trying to make this easier.'

'Don't worry,' Katie offered.

'Listen, I have references from law-abiding citizens who have known me for years,' he said and pulled out a scruffy piece of paper from his briefcase. He tried to flatten out the creases on the table as he looked up at her.

'Katie, you look like a lovely woman with a wonderful home, I do hope I haven't put you off. From what I've seen so far, this house looks like just the haven of tranquillity I am looking for...have I messed up?' His honesty was endearing.

Katie smiled. 'You should know I have two teenage daughters in this *haven of tranquillity*,' she said.

'Well done! And you're still sane. Marvellous!'

She was laughing now. 'So that doesn't put you off?'

He paused for a moment in consideration. 'Are they noisy?'

'They're pretty good, and both have iPods so they can always listen to their music through their headphones.'

'Sounds perfect. I tend to write from elevenish into the afternoon and sometimes into the evening. Not a morning person you see. I promise to be quiet if leaving late.'

Katie lent back in her chair and observed this unusual man. 'Do you mind if I ask you something?' She was tentative.

'Not at all, ask away.'

'Why don't you write at your home?'

'Ah well, you see, the wife teaches musical instruments, violin mainly to schoolchildren afternoons and evenings. It would be all right if one or two of the blighters could actually play a decent tune, but sadly not. It's enough to drive a man mad!'

'Oh dear,' Katie sympathised and wondered if his wife should perhaps be the one looking for premises.

'Celia, my wife, won't hear a word said against them. So when little Johnny came round a couple of weeks ago and made a noise which would make you seek out a pneumatic drill for relief, I decided enough is enough! I barged in and said, "this is ridiculous! Go home and practice until you can at least hang a tune together".'

'Oh dear.' Katie tried to hide her amusement.

'Mmm...' Birch drained his cup and gestured to offer Katie more from the pot.

'Yes please,' she said in reply and then, 'I don't suppose that went down too well.'

'You can say that again. I'm lucky if I get so much as a grimace out of my wife and little Johnny is apparently in therapy!'

They both laughed at the ridiculousness of it all. The doorbell rang and Katie remembered that Julia had offered to come round in case she needed rescuing from the potential lodger if he turned out to be a nutter. 'Excuse me,' she said.

At the door Julia whispered, 'how's it going?'

'Pretty good, I think.'

'You think? Can I come and have a look at him?'

'Yes, but what's your excuse?' She was still whispering.

Julia held up some clothes in a Save the Children charity bag. 'Come in Julia,' Katie said now in a normal voice. Julia swept into the kitchen and introduced herself. 'Hello, I'm Julia, Katie's friend.'

'Ah, come to check up on me, very wise.' He stood up and shook her hand.

'May I offer you a cappuccino? I shall have to make some more.'

'Oooh, lovely thanks.' Julia made a show of placing the charity bag in a corner of the kitchen. Birch looked puzzled.

'I sit on a charity committee,' Katie explained, 'or at least I did.'

'Oh right,' he said, and got on with making more coffee.

In all the commotion Katie hadn't heard the front door go and Bethan wandered into the kitchen looking very confused. 'What on earth is going on?'

'Oh, you haven't met Birch, have you?' Julia jumped in and Birch turned to introduce himself.

'Birch, meet Bethan, Katie's daughter.'

Meanwhile, Katie positioned herself behind her daughter and frantically waved her hands around, whilst shaking her head from side to side.

'Birch is thinking of joining the save the kiddies committee,' Julia said confusing everyone.

'Ah yes,' Birch was quick to catch on, and joined in. 'I feel particularly strongly that children all over the world need to be saved.'

His attempt at being earnest tickled Katie and Julia. Bethan could not have looked more serious.

'Whatever,' she said, and wandered out and up to her room.

'Oh no! Have I blown it?' Birch whispered.

'Don't worry,' Katie said, 'leave Bethan to me.'

'Have you seen the room yet, Birch?' Julia said, 'it's really lovely, gets the sun in the evening and has an en-suite.'

'Sounds very good. I didn't want to appear too pushy, but I'd love to see it.'

Julia looked at Katie, 'only if you're sure?' She stroked her arm. Katie had a smile of resignation. 'No time like the present,' and all three trotted up the stairs. Bethan's door swung open angrily as they passed her room. *What is going on?*

'We'll talk later.' A confrontation was the last thing Katie wanted right now. She spoke calmly but the look she gave her daughter left Bethan in no doubt that she had overstepped the mark.

'Right!' Bethan was indignant but closed the door slightly less aggressively than she had opened it. Julia turned to Birch. 'They've just lost their father; we have to make allowances.'

'Oh, how dreadful, I'm so sorry.'

Katie's eyes watered and she gulped before leading the way up more stairs to a second-floor. 'It's just here.' She opened the door. The bed had fresh linen on it and was sprinkled with cushions. There were more flowers in a vase on the dressing table, and an armchair was loaded with yet more cushions. Birch walked straight over to the window and looked out onto the park beyond the railings.

'Look at that! Green! Trees! I love it!'

Julia was beaming. 'It is rather nice, isn't it?'

He looked round the room. 'Thanks for putting the flowers in, lovely thought.'

Katie blushed. 'I suppose you'll need a desk?'

'Yes, yes, for my laptop.' He looked thoughtful, 'could I bring my own over?'

'Yes!' Julia said a bit too quickly. And then, 'sorry, I'm jumping the gun here. I don't even know if you two have talked money.'

Katie's heart skipped a beat. This is where it could all fall down. She had no idea how much to expect from this kind of arrangement. Birch came straight to the point.

'How does eight hundred pounds a month sound?'

Katie quickly worked out in her head that it would be enough to pay the mortgage, which would be a huge help. Let's face it, she thought, she was desperate and that kind of money every month sounded wonderful. She looked over to her friend who looked like a schoolgirl about to burst with excitement.

'Yes, eight hundred pounds is fine,' Katie said trying to hide the massive relief, she was feeling. Birch walked over to her and shook her hand. 'Thank you, Katie; you won't regret it.'

Chapter 13

Jacob placed a glass of white wine in front of Alice. He grinned as he said, 'I've not had a girlfriend who drinks Chardonnay before.'

Alice was pleased that he had called her his girlfriend as it was the first time. 'Am I too sophisticated for you then?' she teased.

'No, no, you're a bit posh but lovely with it.' He raised his pint glass to her. Alice blushed.

'How's work? Has that horrible girl, Jo, left yet?' he asked.

'No,' Alice twisted her auburn hair around her finger. 'The manager decided to give her another chance.'

'Oh no! That's not right. I mean being rude to a customer. At Chez Pierre they would throw you out there and then.'

'Yeah, I don't understand it either. She thinks she's so wonderful. Miss Perfect. She says she's only waitressing until she gets spotted as the next Kate Moss!'

'Right! Is she pretty then?'

'Oh, you're interested now?'

'I might be!' Jacob was playful. 'Nah, don't be silly. I'm sure she couldn't compete with a classy girl like you.'

'You've got a point there; she certainly didn't go to the same school as me.'

'Nor did I!'

'Well it was all *girls*!'

'Ah, well that would explain it!' Jacob looked wistful as he leant back into his chair. 'What does your mum think?'

'Think about what?'

'Well, you know, you dating the Maître d' at the local restaurant?'

'I don't know! She's not said anything.' Alice looked flustered.

'Have you told her about me?'

'Er.....Yes.... of course I have.'

'And what did she say?'

'Nothing. Nothing much. She's cool with it, I'm sure.'

'That's good.' Jacob leant over and kissed her. 'Another Chardonny?'

Birch was trying to manoeuvre his desk down the stairs. He had taken the legs off to make it easier and asked his wife to help him but she was still sulking over the little Johnny incident. He huffed and puffed and groaned his way down to the hallway where he placed it down leaning precariously against a console table.

Celia appeared from the living room door. 'You'll never get that in your car.'

Birch looked at her and decided to say nothing.

'Where is it you're going, anyway?' she asked.

'I told you; just down the road. Bisham Gardens.'

Celia stared at him. 'I can't believe you're doing this!'

He walked up to her and placed his hands on her waist. She tried to wriggle free and averted her eyes.

'Listen, I just need somewhere peaceful to write,' he said. 'I've got my publisher breathing down my neck for this next manuscript and I need to get it finished.'

'So you're leaving me,' she said and turned to walk away.

'Don't be ridiculous!' Birch was losing his patience with her. 'I'm just going there during the day to write!'

'And it's a woman who owns this place?' She turned back, her arms were tightly folded.

'It's a family actually. A woman recently widowed and her two teenage daughters.'

'And you think that's going to be more peaceful than here?'

'Yes!'

She said nothing more and went through into the living room slamming the door behind her. The legless desk top fell to the floor and one of Celia's treasured objet d'art broke in to several pieces. 'Bloody hell!' Birch picked up the desk and marched out.

'I never liked that stupid thing anyway,' he muttered under his breath.

Katie opened the door to see Birch standing there with what looked like half his desk.

'Hello Katie. Work in progress I'm afraid.'

'Oh?'

'Yes, would you believe I've actually walked round here with this thing!' He held the desk up.

'Right. Well do come in.'

'Thank you.'

'Cup of tea?'

'Ooh lovely, yes please.'

Birch carefully placed the piece of furniture where it was unlikely to fall and followed Katie into the kitchen.

'I haven't had chance to tell the girls about our arrangement yet but I'm hoping to this evening,' Katie explained.

'Oh right, no problem. I shall get the desk upstairs and hide it under the bed or something until I get the all clear from you. Meantime I'll return to domestic bliss chez moi!' He laughed mockingly.

'More violin lessons?' Katie assumed.

'No, no, well yes, but added to that my wife has turned into a disapproving Angela Merkel type.'

Katie poured boiling water into the tea pot and bought it over to the kitchen table where Birch had sat himself down. She was thoughtful. 'I hope I'm not the cause of any of this disapproval.'

'Oh no no, not at all; everything is my fault in Celia's eyes. Oh God, and that reminds me, I left a little blooper behind; what I mean is, one of her treasured ornaments fell and broke! Accidently, of course, in fact it was probably due to her slamming the door on me but there's no point in me even putting up a defence.'

Katie poured the tea into mugs. 'Oh dear,' she said and then, 'I seem to be saying that a lot around you.'

'Yes!' Birch became animated, 'I have a bit of an "oh dear" life at the moment! But don't worry, as soon as I get my next novel off to Henry, he's my publisher by the way, I will get what's owed to me, hand most of it over to Celia to spend on designer clothes, cushions and more objet d'art and she'll be as happy as Mary Berry with a perfect lemon meringue pie!'

They laughed together. 'You know I feel much better already,' Birch said and Katie decided she liked this character but didn't say so. 'I'm pleased it suits you here,' she allowed herself and they sat amiably sipping tea.

Bethan arrived home first. She found her mother in the garden.

'Hello darling.' Katie needed this evening to go well.

'Hi Mum. Alice not here yet?'

'No, but I had a text from her and she'll be here soon.'

'Right, I'll just go and shower.' She disappeared back into the house.

Katie took the opportunity to lay out some nibbles and drinks on the garden table. It was a lovely August evening and she thought being out in the sun would put everyone in a good mood. She had procrastinated about whether to open a bottle of wine or make some fresh lemonade and decided to offer both. Her daughters were young adults now and they could make up their own minds. Anyway, she had a distinct feeling she was going to need a bit of Dutch courage.

Alice appeared. 'What's all this?'

'I just thought as it's such a gorgeous evening we could sit out here for a bit.'

'You're going to tell us we have to move house aren't you?'

'No! No, I'm not.'

'Well what then?'

'Alice please, let's wait until we're all together and then I will tell you the good news.' She was pleased she had termed it like that.

'Good news?' Alice said with disbelief.

'Yes! Good news!' Katie suddenly felt daunted by the task ahead and reached for the wine. She stopped herself. 'Now, I just need to get something out of the oven.' She escaped to the kitchen.

Just a few minutes later, Bethan sank down in her chair and folded her arms. Alice busied herself pouring drinks.

'Wine, Mum?'

'Thanks. Lovely.'

'We are having wine? Again?' Bethan asked.

'If you like or there's a homemade lemonade.'

'What, you made it, Mum?'

'Yes, yes, I did.' She didn't add that Julia had relayed strict instructions over the phone to avoid failure at all costs.

'So what's all this about?' Alice was restless. 'You said it was a *good* thing.'

'What?' Bethan was agitated. 'What have you been saying behind my back?'

'Nothing!' Katie was adamant.

'How can it be nothing?' Bethan would not let go. Katie offered round some olives. They both took one without thanking her. She took a deep breath and a large glug of wine and leant back in her chair trying to remember what she had rehearsed earlier.

'Are we going to be sitting in silence all evening?' Alice glared at her mother. Katie decided that this was not a good moment, but she had set it all up: the warm bread rolls with oil and balsamic dip, the Greek olives, the nuts, the wine and the lemonade. It was all there in front of her saying that this evening was special and she had an announcement to make. It was supposed to be making this easier but was only serving to make her feel trapped. She had reached a point of no return.

'Well?' Bethan sat up in her chair now.

Katie reached for her wine. 'The thing is,' she began, 'I've found a solution to our problem, which means we won't have to move house.'

'Really?' Alice was astonished.

'Yes,' Katie braced herself. 'I'm renting out our spare bedroom – daytimes only I might add – to a writer.'

'Not that weirdo, that was here the other day?' Bethan looked worried.

'What weirdo?' Alice asked. 'Why don't I know about this?'

Katie sighed. 'His name is Birch.'

'*Birch?*' The two cried in mocking unison.

'Yes, I know it's an unusual name.'

'Unusual?! Sounds very dodgy to me!' Alice poured herself some wine in a clean glass and pushed her lemonade away.

'He writes novels,' Katie said trying to make him sound normal.

'So that makes it all right?' Bethan had a point.

'Yes, he was advertising in The Corner Shop for a room where he can write during the day. He will be going home to his wife in the evenings.'

'He's married?' Alice asked.

'Yes, he's married to Celia, and they live just a couple of roads away.'

'Why on earth,' Bethan started, 'does he not write at home?'

'Ah well,' Katie was pleased she had a good answer to this question, 'his wife is a violin teacher and he finds the noise very distracting.'

'What kind of an excuse is that?' Alice said in disbelief. 'Anyway Bethan, how do you know he's a weirdo?'

'He was in the kitchen the other day, when I got back from Miranda's, making coffee!'

'Making coffee? In our kitchen? Is this true?' Alice's eyes widened.

'So he's good at making coffee; why do you hold that against him?' Katie was trying to make light of it.

'But you don't just walk into a stranger's kitchen and start making coffee!'

'I agree it's a little eccentric,' Katie admitted, 'but actually I was rather pleased. It meant that I didn't have to make it.'

'So why did Julia say he was on the save the kiddies committee?' Bethan asked.

'Ah, so Julia's in on this as well!' Alice was getting louder. 'It seems everyone but me knows about this!'

'Julia came round.... just in case.' Katie tried to explain.

'Just in case, what? Just in case he's a weirdo?' Alice looked straight at her mother.

'For goodness sake! Can we stop calling him a weirdo and calm down!' Katie said realising she had raised her voice and was rather worked up. There was a pause for thought and Alice topped up all their wine glasses. Katie hoped upon hope that they were all mellowing in this short interlude. Eventually she said calmly, 'if,' she didn't mean *if* but she thought it might soften the next bit, 'if Birch rents our spare room at the top of the house, he will pay us eight hundred pounds a month which will cover the mortgage payments, which would be a *huge* relief to me. If I manage to get some work we will be able to get by, and more importantly, we can stay in this house, a home we all love.'

Her daughters remained silent. She looked to both of them for a sign; a sign of acceptance at least, better still approval. Finally Alice spoke.

'I want to meet this Birch; I want to see for myself why you think this arrangement is going to be okay.'

'No problem.' Katie prayed that he would meet her approval.

Bethan stood up. 'No one cares what I think!' She turned to go inside the house.

'Bethan,' Katie called after her, 'why don't you both meet him properly together?'

'S'pose.' Bethan didn't turn round and continued into the house and Katie considered that that was the best she was going to get from her today.

Alice was quiet for a while and then she said, 'eight hundred pounds a month?'

'Yes, that's right.'

'It's such a mess up there, you know.'

'Actually, it's not. Julia and I cleaned it up.' Katie remembered the desk under the bed and hoped it was well hidden.

'Sounds like you've thought of everything.' Alice relaxed back in her chair. Katie reached for her daughter's hand. 'You know I wouldn't be doing this if I didn't think it was the right thing. And well, he seems very nice.'

'Mmm, okay, I'll give him a chance.'

Chapter 14

Harry Liversage swung round in his big black leather chair away from his computer screen to take in the view from his penthouse flat over the heath and towards the City. He sighed and began to regret his decision to work from home. At four o'clock on most days he would be in a meeting discussing the investment portfolio of one client or another. His partner, Ben, was great for bouncing ideas off. They made a good team. Ben had also worked at Cazanoves in the City when they first met. They were both star performers and after a couple of years of competing for "best fund manager of the year" they decided to join forces and set up their own firm. Harry was happy to have a Hampstead address for their office, after all, they could be in the City in twenty minutes if a client preferred to meet there.

He dialled Nancy's number.

'Harry? Everything okay?' He loved her directness which Americans do so well.

'Yes, yes, everything is fine.'

'Okay.' She fell silent.

'I'm working from home.'

'Good.... getting lots done?'

'Mmm... well I was.'

'Blood sugar levels taken a dive maybe? Still, it must be four-ish UK time.'

'Yes, yes it is.' Harry swivelled back to his computer. 'Did you get that report from 3M?'

'Yes I DHL'd it to you. You'll have it tomorrow. Did you need it sooner? I scanned it just in case.'

'Oh right. No, tomorrow's fine.'

'Anything else? My nanny has to leave soon, so I have to get a whole lot done before then.'

'Oh yes, yes sorry. Thanks Nancy.' He put the phone down and decided to make some coffee; he doesn't drink tea. His apartment is modern, open plan and monochrome with track lighting and an impressive looking surround sound system. One of his girlfriends commented that it was the epitome of a bachelor pad but he could not remember which one. The kitchen was rarely used except for finding a plate to eat his takeaway off. He mainly enjoyed the eateries around Highgate village.

The espresso machine started to gurgle as his mobile phone rang. He rushed over to his desk. Not a number he knew but it was local.

'Hello?'

'Oh, hello, is that Harry Liversage?' The woman sounded nervous.

'Yes, that's me.'

'You won't remember me but I was in Fegos with my friend and you gave me your card.'

'I do remember. Delightful woman; very English; very Highgate village.'

Katie was not sure how to take that. 'I, I hope I'm not wasting your time.'

'No, no, not at all.' He was pleased for the distraction.

'The thing is I saw from your business card that you are an investment fund manager.'

'That's right.' He walked over to his coffee machine and grabbed his coffee.

'It's only a small amount I have, just five thousand pounds, but I was just wondering if you would be able to advise me on how to invest it?'

'Oh right. Well it's certainly a small amount but as you're local I'd be happy to help.'

'You live in the village, do you?'

'Certainly do. Listen we might as well meet up then we can discuss how you want me to manage the money, attitude to risk etc… Would that be okay?'

'Yes, that would be great.'

'Fegos seems like the obvious place. How are you fixed?' Harry clicked to the calendar on his screen and suggested, 'Thursday morning at eleven?'

'Yes, that's fine with me.'

'Great.'

Julia appeared right on cue at mid-day holding a big cool bag.

'Oh Julia, you're a life saver!' Katie took the bag from her friend. 'Are we having a picnic?'

'No no, it was just easier to bring the food over in this.'

Katie peered in. 'So what are we going to make?'

'It's a pasta salad with cold meats, mozzarella and tomatoes.'

'Sounds lovely. Thank you.' Katie hugged her friend.

'No trouble but do you want me to stay when they all arrive or disappear so you can pretend you made it?'

'Oh stay! Please! That would be even better. This is going to be bad enough without back up, I can tell you!'

'But Birch seems really personable; I don't see how the girls can object to him?'

'Yes, but they are so emotionally raw since David died, especially Bethan. Even if I say something nice she snaps my head off. I've come to realise that "s'pose" is the best I'm ever going to get.'

'Ah, I remember it well; Daisy's "s'pose" phase. Luckily she's grown out of it since she went to uni.' Julia started unloading the bag. 'Were you planning to serve wine?' she asked looking hopeful. 'It might help smooth the waters for us at least.'

'It's a strategy I have been adopting a lot recently.' Katie was thoughtful. 'Not sure if it helps or not but they don't drink much, well, not in front of me anyway.'

'I think we go for it then.' Julia pulled a bottle of Chablis out and put it in the fridge. She turned to Katie, 'now how long have we got?'

Birch wore a pale blue shirt hanging over chinos that were badly ironed. He knocked on the door of his wife's study. She didn't answer so he opened it a little and peered round only to be presented with her back.
'Darling?' he said mildly.
'What?' she seemed instantly annoyed.
'I'm just going out for a couple of hours,' he said as gently as he could hoping not to distract her too much.
She looked at her watch. 'So you're going out for lunch?'
'Yes, that's right.' Birch prayed that she would not ask for any details.
'Who with?' The question he dreaded.
'Henry,' he lied.
'Henry? What publisher Henry? You're going down to the West End then?'
Birch was suddenly in knots. 'No, he's coming this way,' he said, thinking he wouldn't be long enough to justify a central London trip including a long lunch with Henry. 'Anyway got to ...'
'Since when?' she said loudly and turned in her swivel chair to look him straight in the eye, 'since when has Henry come up to Highgate?' Her eyes were searching.
'Since today. Got to dash.' He threw her a kiss, not daring to get any closer and made a quick exit, grabbing a bottle from the console table in the hallway before reaching for the front door. Once on the pavement he moved quickly off breaking into a jog until he had turned a corner. There he slowed to a walk to get his breath back and smiled to himself. He saw the funny side but had it really come to this, running away from his wife?

'Hello erm Bethan?' he said as if he was answering a quiz question and held out a hand.

'I'm Alice.' She shook it, looking at him with a critical eye. Her mother noticed that Alice had made an effort to look presentable and was wearing a pretty blouse over jeans and had her long hair swept back in a high ponytail.

'Sorry; sorry about that.' Birch handed her a bottle of Prosecco. 'I thought this might go down well with luncheon.'

'Thanks, I like Prosecco.' She looked surprised and Katie hoped that was one point to team lodger.

'Excellent.' He looked at the kitchen table which was already set for lunch with some cheerful yellow roses in a vase in the centre. 'Shall I sit here?'

'Yes, sit where you like,' Katie said breezily not realising where he meant.

'That was Dad's seat,' Bethan said flatly as she suddenly entered the room. She wore a faded khaki T-shirt and a pair of ripped jeans and looked effortlessly beautiful despite her defensive stance.

'Birch, why don't you sit next to me?' Julia patted the chair to her left.

'Yes, yes good idea.' He moved swiftly.

'So you must be Bethan,' he held out his hand as if he had nothing to lose. Bethan looked uncomfortable as she shook it.

Katie placed a large bowl of pasta salad centre stage. She was pleased with how it looked with the bright colours of the salami and the red peppers against the creamy mozarella. 'Help yourselves.'

'This looks good,' Birch said cheerily, 'did you make it?'

Katie nodded towards Julia. 'Joint effort,' Julia explained.

'Is that meat?' Bethan asked prodding a piece of salami with her fork.

'Yes darling.' Katie was trying to keep her exasperation at her daughter's behaviour at bay.

'I'm not eating meat anymore,' she said as if everyone should have already second guessed this whimsical change of heart.

'What, so you're vegetarian now?' Alice asked her sister.

'Yes, I've decided I don't want to eat dead animals.'

'Wasn't that a vegetarian quiche I saw in your fridge?' Julia looked pointedly at her friend.

'Ah yes, that's lucky.' Katie reached it out. 'Would you like me to warm it in the oven for you?'

'Then I'll be eating after everyone else. I'll have it cold,' she said playing the martyr. Katie glared at her.

'I hear you're a writer,' Alice said turning to Birch.

'Yes, novels mainly and a column in The Times.'

'A column in The Times?' she sounded impressed. 'What's your column about?'

'I review restaurants. Great job when it's a good restaurant!' he added.

'Oh God, you're in trouble now Mum, a restaurant critic!' Alice pointed a smug look at her mother.

'Not at all! This lunch is delicious! Far better than most restaurants might serve up.'

'I suspect that's down to Julia; Mum's no great cook,' Bethan said coldly.

'Birch isn't going to be here to critique your mother's cooking; he's here to write.' Julia said and smiled supportively at Katie.

'Seems odd to me.' Bethan viewed her quiche suspiciously.

'Yes, I suppose it must seem a bit strange to you,' Birch said switching to a mellow tone. 'You must miss your father terribly and to have some man like me just turning up, but...' he paused momentarily as if to gather his thoughts, 'but I'll be tucked away on the top floor, you'll hardly know I'm there. Writing is a pretty quiet pass time after all.' His amiable manner met a half smile from Alice at least.

'What sort of novels do you write?' Katie filled a pause in the conversation feeling a little more confident.

'Thrillers. Contemporary, humorous....

'Oh wonderful; I'd love to read one of them.' Julia chimed in.

'Well Julia, I shall get you a signed copy!'

'Oh me too please,' Katie joined in.

'So are you still at school Bethan?' Katie admired Birch's bravery in tackling the most challenging person in his audience.

'I've done my GCSEs and I want to do an NVQ now in Graphic Design but Mum won't let me.'

Katie sighed. 'We haven't discussed it. I think this is a conversation for later, don't you?' Her eyes met Bethan's sullen face.

'Oh God I'm sorry. Sorry I didn't mean to interfere.'

Katie wondered where Birch's next paintball might be fired from.

'You didn't,' Alice said, 'Bethan just doesn't want to do her A-levels like I did.'

Bethan put her fork down, the quiche barely touched, and pushed her plate away from her.

'Have you got your A-level results yet?' Julia turned to Alice.

'Yes, but I'm not going to uni, this year at least; I'm having a gap year. I'm working at The Lemon Tree at the moment.'

'Ah yes, The Lemon Tree. I've been there a few times, it's not bad.' Birch said.

'Have you written a review?' Alice sounded interested.

'Yes, of course. Means I can put it on expenses!' He smiled at her and it looked like Alice might be warming to him.

'Shall we have coffee in the garden? I think it's stopped raining,' Katie was brighter now the food part was over.

'I don't want any coffee,' Bethan announced and stood up dragging her chair noisily. 'I've got stuff to do.' She was half way out of the room. Katie was astounded by her behaviour.

'But hang on a minute. Birch has come round especially to…'

'It's okay really.' He smiled at Katie. 'Really it is.'

'Bye then.' Bethan skulked out of the room.

Alice reached out to her mother and turned to Birch. 'I hear you're rather good at making coffee?'

Chapter 15

'What the hell do you think you're playing at?' Katie burst into her daughter's room to find her lying on her bed, small headphones in her ears.

Bethan reluctantly removed the music and met her mother's angry gaze. 'What?' She looked affronted.

'I said,' Katie tried to take some of the emotion out this time, 'what do you think you're playing at? Behaving like that in front of Birch. How do you think it makes me feel?'

Bethan looked stunned. 'How do you think *I* feel having some weirdo coming into my home, trying to take my Dad's place before we've even got a headstone up on his grave!'

'But that's ridiculous; can't you see! No one will ever replace your father.'

'He even tried to sit in Dad's chair!'

'How does he know that was Dad's chair? Anyway, he won't sit there again; certainly not after the look you gave him!'

'I don't like him! I don't want him here! I mean, is he going to have his own key? I don't think it's safe!'

Katie sighed and sat on the edge of her daughter's bed so that she was now at her level.

'Darling, I wouldn't be doing this if I thought it would put you at risk in any way. I've checked him out on Google; he does write for The Times and he has sold millions of books. He just wants somewhere quiet to write and we have a spare room at the top of the house we hardly use so it seems silly not to rent it out.'

'What if I want my friends round to stay?'

'You can still have a friend or two to stay; Miranda always sleeps in here with you anyway, doesn't she? Then there's the sofa in the study.'

'We're a bit old for sleeping on sofas, Mum!'

'Darling, we have to manage with what we've got.' Katie wished she didn't have to keep spelling out the predicament they found themselves in. As if it wasn't bad enough to live through it without having to bring your daughter to her senses every single day.

'I just think it would be better if you got a job instead; then we'd be all right wouldn't we?'

Katie sighed. 'I wish it was that easy,' she said calmly. 'You know what the job market is like. I'm fifty and PAs don't really exist anymore; it's all virtual assistants and technology which is pretty mind boggling for someone like me.'

Bethan looked thoughtful. She pulled herself up and sat next to her mother. 'But do you fancy Birch?' She was looking straight into Katie's eyes. 'I mean it's obvious you really like him.'

Katie raised her eyebrows in disbelief at this revelation. 'Don't be silly! Is that what you think this is about? I *like* the fact that he's going to be paying us eight hundred pounds a month in rent!' She thought carefully about the next bit. 'I do like him, yes, but then I wouldn't want someone in my home who I didn't *like*!'

'You see you admit it, and I think you fancy him.'

'No! That is not what this is about!'

Bethan swung her leg from the knee down to and fro like a sulky schoolgirl. 'So if we have all this money coming in can I do an NVQ?'

'Darling, the money is for the mortgage.'

'But if you get a job...'

'I'm sorry darling, I really am.' Katie was racked with guilt now knowing she was meeting Harry Liversage to hand him five thousand pounds in cash but somehow that money was special to her, it was the last bit of David she had. It felt like the right thing to do, to invest it.

'We just can't afford your NVQ. Why don't you go to Sixth Form College like your sister and do A-levels? Any subjects you like; you choose.'

'It's not fair! Dad would have let me go; I even told him about what I want to do and he said, if it was what I really wanted...'

'*After* A-levels I seem to remember,' Katie butted in.

'But what's the point!' Bethan was tearful now.

'The point is you've got to do something!'

'Why have I? What's the point in anything anymore! Dad's dead! I hate everything!'

Katie moved towards her daughter, fearful she might lash out at her, but as she got closer Bethan succumbed to a big hug and cried until her emotions were spent. Katie, for the first time since her husband's death felt strong enough to provide comfort without breaking down herself. She was on her own now and she had to make a life worth living for her and her daughters. She brushed the wet hair away from Bethan's face and wiped her tears lovingly with her hand.

'We haven't celebrated your GCSE results yet have we? You did so well; I'm really proud of you.'

Bethan sniffed. 'I did it for Dad.'

'I know.' Katie let that go. 'So how about you and I go shopping and get you something, maybe a new dress, whatever you want.'

'But Mum you keep saying we haven't got any money.'

'I'll find a hundred pounds from somewhere.'

'Okay. Can we go on Friday? I don't want Alice coming too.'

'Friday it is and we'll lunch in Thai Square on Oxford Street, your favourite restaurant. Still?' She looked into her daughter's eyes.

'Yes Mum, still.'

Chapter 16

Katie walked down into the village and arrived at Fegos just on time but Harry was already there looking very smart in a suit. She had decided against taking the cash with her, it just didn't seem right. She was nervous enough without carrying that kind of money. He stood up and smiled as she approached and shook hands heartily with her. She hadn't looked at him properly the other day but now she could see he was devilishly handsome with his blonde hair falling in a fringe over his high forehead, his stunning blue eyes and he could easily get away with designer stubble. She was thankful that he was far too young for her.

'Hello Harry, thanks for meeting me. Is it okay if I call you Harry?'

'Of course! So much more friendly to be on first name terms. Some of my clients insist on calling me Mr Liversage. Nancy, my VA thinks it's hilarious, her being American that is. Anyway Katie, what can I get you?'

They chatted about the village which Katie was pleased about; she was still wondering if she was doing the right thing. Harry then began to talk about his background.

'I started at Foreign & Colonial after graduating, worked my way up to a position where I was managing a European fund. Then I moved on to Cazanoves where I met Ben Goodshaw who is now my partner. We're both very good at what we do and took it in turns to win "best fund manager of the year" in our sectors. Those were good days, great fun, but in the end we decided to set up on our own. This way we get to meet our clients and can offer a more personal service.'

He passed a file over the table to her. 'In there is the investment performance figures of some of the funds and stocks we've chosen for our clients. They have all brought in exceptional returns over five years. Obviously it's no guarantee that we will do as well for you but hopefully it will provide some reassurance.'

Katie was very impressed by his spiel and was trying to think of a question she could ask him but didn't want to sound too ignorant about the whole thing. He rescued her with, 'let's talk about you now, Katie, and what you're trying to achieve. Tell me a bit about yourself.'

She felt more at ease now and decided to relay the story of David's horse, Forever Lucky. She found herself explaining to him that she wanted to do something worthwhile with the money as it was one of the last things David had done and she didn't want it to come to nothing. He listened attentively and when she had finished, he said, 'well I'm privileged Katie. You are entrusting me with this five-thousand pounds and I promise you I will do everything I can to meet your investment objectives. May I take it that you are looking to provide yourself with a nice little nest egg in the future?'

'To be honest that sounds great but I hadn't given it much thought. I mean I just live from day to day at the moment. My daughters are proving to be quite a handful even though they are sixteen and eighteen.'

'May I ask, I don't mean to pry, what sort of income you have for your day to day needs?'

Katie was relieved the answer was no longer nothing. 'I've just taken on a day lodger; the income from him will pay the mortgage.'

'That's a good idea. What's a *day* lodger?'

'Oh well, he's a writer you see and needs somewhere quiet to work during the day.'

'How wonderful! An established writer, I assume?'

'Oh yes, he writes for The Times.' Katie was pleased she could say that. 'And he's written many novels, bestsellers, his name is Birch. You may have heard of him?'

'Do you know I think I have; such an unusual name!'

'Yes, it is, isn't it? I read online…' Katie blushed realising she was revealing the snoop she had done on Google.

'Good for you; checking him out I mean, very wise.'

'Yes,' Katie said suddenly feeling much happier about the whole Birch scenario. 'Anyway, he only uses the name Birch, I don't know if it's his Christian name or surname. It's a bit like Lulu. Still, each to their own.'

'Yes, why not! Makes him more intriguing, I think. That sounds like a great way to create an income.'

'If only it was enough.' Katie looked thoughtful.

'Did you give any thought to my idea about becoming a virtual assistant?'

'I have. I like the idea of working for myself from home; that would be perfect. But I'm not sure I would know where to start to be honest.'

'Why don't you give Nancy a call; she'll be happy to help. Okay she's in the states, but she could advise you on how to get set up. With the internet it's not much different where you are these days.'

Katie was surprised by his generosity. 'Oh thanks, I'd like to do that.'

'Tell you what, why don't you come to my office in Hampstead and call her from there. We have a free phone service to the States set up so you can chat as long as you like.'

'That's very kind, thank you.'

'I'll let you know when Ben's not going to be around and you can use his desk.'

'Great.' Katie wondered why he was being so nice to her.

'Now, let's talk about the logistics of investing this money for you.'

By the time she left Fegos and was wandering back up the hill Katie felt excited about the idea of investing the money. Harry had talked in detail about where he proposed to place it and what he might achieve. She was also enthused at the prospect of talking to Nancy and perhaps launching herself into a new career. Whilst each new day was certainly a challenge, somehow she was beginning to feel more alive than she'd ever felt before.

Chapter 17

Birch came and went each day without a fuss. Sometimes he seemed to spend hours on end in his room without even venturing into the kitchen to make himself a drink. Katie sat alone at times wondering if he might appear. It was strange that he was in her home but they had so little contact.

He had paid her for the first month's rent upfront with a cheque. Katie was so pleased to finally have some money coming in and she thought about how easy it was to have a day lodger. For the first few days she made sure she was there to let him in in the mornings and each day he bid her good morning and made his way up the stairs to his room without a fuss. On Friday she was leaving before eleven which was his usual time for turning up, although Katie noticed it varied between ten forty-five and midday so he wasn't a creature of habit. So the day before she went up to his room and knocked gently on the door.

'Come in!' he said cheerfully.

'Sorry to bother you.' Katie said from the door.

'Not at all! Do come in.' He beckoned her with his hand. She noticed the room was tidy but the bed cover was ruffled as if someone had been lying on it. She went over to him and presented him with a set of house keys.

'I think you should have these. It's silly me having to be here to let you in each day and as it happens I'm likely to be out tomorrow morning.'

'Oh thank you. Yes, makes sense,' he said simply. 'Going anywhere nice?'

'I'm taking Bethan shopping. It's a kind of present to her as she did so well in her GCSEs.'

'Oh good.' He looked thoughtful, 'I hope it's not anything to do with *appeasing* her after *my* arrival.'

'Well funnily enough it's a bit of that too.' Katie surprised herself as she confided, 'I suppose it's a chance for us to bond; spend some quality time which has been missing lately.'

'Good idea. But is she okay with me being here?' Birch swung round in his chair and looked intent. 'I must admit I've only bumped into her briefly on my way out yesterday. She said hello at least.'

'I think so. It will take time. She was so close to her Dad; she's really struggling with life at the moment.'

'It's understandable.'

'But we see so little of you.' The words slipped out as Katie noticed a flask, mug and food container on the desk.

'Yes.' Birch followed Katie's eyes to the evidence of his self-contained existence. 'Well I thought I better keep myself to myself.'

'Really you are most welcome to use the kitchen; help yourself to drinks at least, use the microwave.'

'Okay I will. Thank you.' And as if to demonstrate he was happy with this new arrangement he said, 'would you like some coffee now? I'll make it.'

'Yes okay.' Katie was surprised but pleased. 'As long as I'm not interrupting you in full flow.'

'Believe me full flow is a rare and wonderful thing!'

Alice was waiting for Jacob to finish his shift. There was always one table of customers that seemed oblivious to the fact that they were the last ones there and Jacob wasn't prepared to hurry them. She watched him as he moved efficiently and discreetly around the restaurant; he looked handsome in his uniform. He had an excellent reputation as a maître d' and, no doubt, he wasn't going to lose it over a couple of lingering diners.

He approached Alice. 'Shouldn't be long now,' he said as he looked longingly into her eyes but would not touch her.

'Can't you give them their bill?' Alice whispered.

'No!' He laughed. 'Is that what you do at The Lemon Tree?'

'We don't seem to have this problem; our clientele always seem quite happy to leave after they've eaten. Maybe the ambiance isn't as good as here?'

'Yes, and the menu not so expensive.' Jacob smiled cheekily.

'Waiter!' The man in a suit and tie summoned him over.

'Yes sir.' Jacob was by his side in an instant.

'The bill, please.'

Katie was showing Birch where everything was kept in her kitchen and as she did he selected what he needed to make the coffee.

'Ah, now the milk pan is where?'

'This cupboard here.' Katie pointed and let him reach for it.

'This kitchen is exceptionally tidy; you should see mine!' Birch said as he went about his task.

They stepped carefully around each other. Katie realised that she had been tidying up a lot more since he started lodging; she could not help it. With the coffee made they sat at the table.

'I see you've bought the Times today.' Birch smiled and found his column.

'Yes, I've read your review of the new Turkish restaurant in Hampstead. Sounds good. I was wondering, do they know you're a critic when you book the table?'

'Well I don't actually tell them but I do book the table in my name so some of them twig. I get Celia to book if she's coming with me but she didn't come along to this one.'

'But you talk about your dining companion?' Katie was curious.

'Yes, I took Bob with me; a friend of mine. The thing is if you go alone, armed with notepad and pen or Dictaphone, it's so obvious.'

'Yes, I can see that.'

'Also it means you can order more dishes without looking like a sad glutton!'

Katie laughed. 'Nice job to have though.'

'Yes, I quite like it.'

'Why didn't Celia go with you?' Katie surprised herself with that question; he was easy company and the words just fell out.

'Oh, she had some excuse or other. Often she says she's on a diet; some silly restrictive thing where she can only eat cabbage soup for a week!'

'Oh I see.' Katie wondered about the state of their marriage and didn't know what to say.

'Where are you going shopping tomorrow?'

'Oh, Oxford Street. Can't stand the place myself but it's Bethan's choice. She loves Miss Selfridge and Top Shop which at least aren't too expensive.'

'Mmm, I don't envy you.' Birch looked at his mobile which was ringing. 'Henry, would you believe, my publisher, probably checking up on me. I swear he's telepathic.'

Alice put her arm inside Jacob's as they walked away from the restaurant and into the village. 'Fegos?' Jacob suggested as they approached the café.

'My mum's taken to having coffee in here.'

'Oh?' Jacob hesitated. 'Does that make it no go?'

Alice looked through the window. 'No, it's fine.' They walked in. 'She's not here anyway,' Alice said scanning the tables.

'Do you not want me to meet her?' Jacob looked serious for a moment.

'No, it's not that, silly.' She doubted herself as she said it. 'I just want you all to myself!'

They sat at a table for two and Jacob ordered. He sat back in his chair. 'So?' he asked with a mischievous smile now.

'What do you mean, so?'

'So you haven't waited for me to finish work and dragged me here for nothing. What is it?'

'I have not *dragged* you here!'

'Only joking.'

He was still laughing as she blurted out, 'I got a B in French. French A-level. Just a B.'

'Okay. A Grade B sounds okay. Any others?'

'Yes.' Alice was mildly irritated. 'An A in Art and a B in English lit.'

'Grade A in Art. I'm going out with an artist! Yay!'

'Oh stop it. The point is I need an A in French to go to Nottingham. I can go to Exeter with a B but I'm not sure I want to.'

'I see.' He leant forward towards her. 'So does this mean you're trying to tell me that you're moving to Exeter?'

'No! I mean, no I'm not planning to go this year but maybe next September.'

'Okay.' He looked puzzled.

'Right now I don't really want to go anywhere; I want to be here for my mum.'

'Of course,' he said and nothing more.

Alice eventually said, 'The thing is, if I did want to go to Nottingham I'd need to re-take my French A-level and get an A.' She looked down into her coffee cup. 'You see that's what my Dad wanted.'

'Right, so you want to do it for him.'

'Do you know, I don't know anymore.' She sipped her coffee deep in thought. 'All this stuff about him losing all our money; I'm just so confused. It's like, did I really know him?'

Jacob stroked her cheek and lifted her chin so that he could gaze into her eyes. 'I'm sure he was proud of you; you could see it in his expression when you walked into the restaurant that night. And he'd want the best for you.'

'Yeah... I just don't know what the best is any more.'

'May I ask a question?' He said carefully.

'Of course.'

'Why don't you do art at university?'

Alice looked confused. 'Art? Not academic enough, I suppose. It was just a filler at A-level.'

'Right,' he said looking even more muddled. 'So what do you want to do in the end? I mean career wise?'

'I haven't got a clue,' Alice said as if this question had never occurred to her before.

'Okay. Not a clue. Interesting. Maybe that would be a good starting point? I mean knowing what you *want* to do.'

Alice looked straight into his eyes. 'Let's not talk about this now; it's all too much.'

'I'm with you there!' he agreed and changed the subject. 'Did you know there's a band playing at The Flask on Saturday and it's my evening off?'

Chapter 18

'Oh Mum, I love it!' Bethan lifted a slate grey dress away from the rail and up to the light.

'Why don't you try it on.' Katie considered that it looked very short but at least it had a high neckline and if Bethan loved it her mission was complete. Her legs were already aching even though they were only on their third shop.

'Yes, yes I will. Oh and what about this faux fur shrug to go with it?'

Katie was tempted to check the price label but thought better of it. 'Perfect. Try them together.'

Bethan emerged smiling from the changing room to show her mother. 'Fabulous! Looks great on you,' Katie said hoping her daughter felt the same.

'Yeah, I really like it, especially with the shrug. So is it okay if I take both?'

'Of course it is.'

The Thai restaurant was buzzing and people were queuing so Katie was pleased she had booked. They were swept past those waiting and to a small table for two where they both collapsed into their chairs and dropped their bags.

'Starving!' Bethan announced and her eyes lit up as she scanned the menu.

'Mm, quite hungry myself,' Katie said as she took a quick look and decided on a dish she recognised. Her mobile started ringing and she decided it was safest to ignore it.

'Aren't you going to get that, Mum?'

'I suppose I could.' It was Harry.

'Hello,' Katie pretended it was a number she didn't recognise.
'Katie?'
'Yes, hello Harry, how are you?'
Bethan stared at her mother.
'Katie, sorry to disturb you, you're obviously out and about, I just wanted to let you know that Ben's out tomorrow so if you want to call Nancy?'
'Oh great, yes, I can do tomorrow.'
'Good, I'll email the address to you and see you there. Afternoon will be best as Nancy is five hours behind us.'
'Oh yes, of course. About two?'
'Perfect. See you then.'
Katie felt her cheeks redden as she put her phone away.
'Harry! Who's Harry?' Bethan's eyes pierced through her mother's conscience.
'Yes, Harry Liversage.' Was adding his surname making this any easier? 'I happened to meet him in Fegos when I was having coffee with Julia.'
'What? You've met a man and you're seeing him tomorrow?!'
'No, no, don't be silly. For goodness sake he's half my age. He told me about virtual assistants. He happens to have one himself, Nancy, she's in America.'
'What's a virtual assistant?'
'Well it's like a PA, which of course is what I used to do, but you work from your own home.'
'Oh, so are you going to be Harry's virtual assistant?'
'No no, he's already got Nancy.'
The waiter appeared and they ordered. Katie was pleased when he disappeared again and she could explain properly. Of course she left out the five thousand pounds investment bit, which did make it sound a bit implausible, but hopefully the chance of her getting some work and earning some money would overshadow that in Bethan's eyes.
'Harry is kindly letting me telephone Nancy from his office tomorrow, so she can tell me how I might set myself up as one of these assistants.'

'Why? I mean why is he helping you so much?'

'Well he's kind. He overheard Julia and I talking about what kind of work I might do to earn some money and he simply made the suggestion.' That part was true but somehow it seemed far-fetched now.

'Oh Mum,' Bethan was almost laughing, 'and you honestly don't think he fancies you? Inviting you to his office with the excuse that you can phone this Nancy in America! For goodness sake!'

'Bethan, darling, I can totally assure you he does not find me in the least bit attractive and he is just being kind!'

'Mum, you are *so* naïve!'

Katie sighed deeply. 'Bethan, what can I say to convince you?' She had an idea. She would do anything to make today a success. It was so important that this time was special and they bonded. 'Listen, why don't you come to Hampstead with me tomorrow and you can meet him for yourself and you will realise that he is just a nice guy.'

Bethan looked uncertain. Their food arrived and Katie lifted her glass, 'cheers darling, here's to you. Well done on your exam results.'

Reluctantly Bethan took a sip of her wine. 'Okay, I will come with you tomorrow to meet this Harry.'

Katie was pleased to get home; the Bethan summit had been exhausting both physically and emotionally. They both dropped their bags in the hallway and headed for the kitchen where Birch was sat at the table with a pot of tea and The Times newspaper.

'Oh hello,' Birch took one look at Bethan's face and hurriedly folded the paper and got to his feet. 'Sorry, sorry about this; I'll go back up to my room.'

'Don't be silly.' Katie looked for a sign from her daughter that this situation was acceptable to her but didn't find one. 'Any tea left in that pot?'

'Er no, but I can soon make some more.' He went to put the kettle on.

'Would you like a cup, Bethan?' her mother asked hopefully.

'Thanks, but no. I'm okay.' She smiled at Katie as if to prove it. 'I think I'll go up to my room to try my new clothes on.'

'Oh, successful shopping trip, was it?' Birch asked.

'Yes, it was. Mum's bought me a lovely dress and a couple of other bits.'

Katie was relieved.

'Oh good.'

Bethan turned to her mother. 'Thanks Mum. I love my new clothes and lunch was great. Can't wait to meet Harry tomorrow.' She winked as she grinned and stepped lightly out of the room leaving Katie bemused and slightly embarrassed.

They both waited as if they needed to hear the sound of Bethan's bedroom door closing before they could talk.

'Sorry, sorry about that.' Birch looked concerned. 'The last thing I wanted to do was to spoil your day.'

'What, by having a cup of tea in the kitchen? Don't be silly. She'll have to get used to it. Anyway, that's the best reaction I've had from her for a long time.'

'Oh, I do hope so; I do want this arrangement to work. I'm finding it perfect for writing up there; getting lots done.' Birch made another pot of tea and Katie sat down. They sipped in silence and then eventually Birch said, 'So you're both off to see Harry tomorrow? Not some kind of family shrink I hope?'

'No, not a shrink,' Katie said laughing. 'It's a long story,' she added wondering if it was one she wanted to share with Birch.

'Sorry, don't mean to pry.'

'Actually, it would be rather nice to tell someone. I haven't even told Julia yet.'

'Now I'm intrigued,' Birch said leaning in.

'But first I have to swear you to secrecy.'

'The plot thickens.' He had an amused glint in his eye.

Katie looked pointedly at him. 'So?'

'So my lips are sealed,' he said emphatically.

When she had finished her tale she felt better for sharing her secret. Birch had nodded in all the right places. He tried to pour more tea from the pot into Katie's cup but there was only a dribble.

'Shall I make some more?' Katie offered, 'or do you need to get back to your writing?'

'Oh, don't worry about that. But actually I'm full of tea at the moment.'

'Yes, me too.' Katie suddenly felt awkward but then Birch said, 'do you mind me asking about the Mercedes outside gathering dust? Is it yours by any chance?'

Katie looked down. 'David's Mercedes actually. To be honest I've got my head in the sand over this one. It's overdue a service and MOT and needs to be taxed and I really want to sell it but I just know the girls will go mad if I suggest that. They want to hang on to every last bit of their father.'

'Mmm difficult one, it's a fine looking car.'

'Yes, David's pride and joy.'

They both looked into their empty cups and then Birch said. 'What if I was to pay to make it legal for you and then have it on sort of loan, you know, use it when I need a car, which isn't very often to be honest. You see my wife and I only have one car and she pretty much monopolises it.'

Katie was so tempted to say yes. 'Oh, that's a very kind offer but I would be worried what the girls would think especially if they saw you driving it.'

'Yes, I can see that. Silly me.'

Katie started fretting again about the fact that it wasn't even legitimate to have it sat outside the house. 'Oh, blast those girls! This is ridiculous. It's a great idea!'

'Oh good! That's settled then.'

They both smiled and Katie was pleased.

'Well I suppose I better get back to my writing.' Birch stood up. 'I've enjoyed our chat.'

'Me too.' Katie stood up as well and then to her surprise she added, 'you must come down for afternoon tea more often.'

'Yes, yes I will.' He shuffled out of the room with an uneasy wave as he made his way into the hallway and up the stairs.

Chapter 19

'Okay Nancy, I'm handing you over to Katie now.' Harry gave the handset to Katie who was sat at Ben's desk feeling rather strange. Bethan was sat opposite her looking intrigued. Harry had been the perfect gentleman and made them both a fresh coffee from a rather flash-looking machine. The office was small but smart with a large brown leather sofa and cut flowers in an elegant vase.

'So Katie, lovely to talk to you.' Nancy's voice exuded warmth. 'Harry tells me you're going to become a VA.'

'Well, thinking about it. Yes, certainly thinking about it.' Katie was nervous.

'Do you mind me asking what your background is?'

Katie didn't mind; this woman sounded nice. 'Well I was a PA in the City, London that is, but that was a long time ago. I worked part time for a bit when my girls went to school but then my husband persuaded me I didn't need to work.'

'I see,' Nancy said politely.

'I was sitting on the Save the Children local committee up until recently,' she felt better for adding. 'I was the secretary for many years.'

'Great, well let me tell you what you need to do to set yourself up as a VA at home.'

Bethan watched Harry as he stared at his screen typing occasionally, rather well she noticed. He looked up and their eyes met. Bethan quickly looked away.

'Sorry if you're a bit bored,' he mouthed and smiled. Bethan smiled back. Harry went over to her. 'Why don't you come and sit over here?' He moved her chair over to his desk.

'So, are you still at school?' He spoke quietly.

'Not really. I've done my GCSEs and I want to do an NVQ now.'

'Oh right, straight into the world of work; I like that. An NVQ in what?'

'Graphic Design but it doesn't matter because my mother says she won't pay for it.'

'Difficult age, isn't it, sixteen? You just want to be independent.'

'I'm nearly seventeen actually.' Bethan then thought about what he had said. 'Yes, you're right. I do so want to be able to make my own decisions. My Dad would have let me do the NVQ, I just know it. He was the best Dad you could ever have.'

'Must be really tough for you.'

Katie was making notes now and pleased she hadn't forgotten her shorthand. 'So I need to decide what I'm going to call my business and get my email set up?'

'Yes. Are you okay with that?' Nancy asked. Katie wasn't at all okay with it.

'You know Harry has an IT guy who helps him out with all that techie stuff,' Nancy continued. 'Ask him for his card. I'm sure he doesn't charge much.'

'Great, is he local then?'

'Not sure but you know they work with you over the phone and can access your computer remotely these days.'

'Gosh that sounds good.'

'Yeah, don't worry we all need a bit of technical help from time to time.'

Katie imagined she would need more than most.

'So, is there anything else you would like me to cover off now?'

Katie didn't want to let her go. 'Actually, the main thing I'm worried about is how I'm going to get some clients.'

'Good question. Well I got my clients through networking mainly and then when you've got a few happy customers you'll get referrals.'

'Okay so how do I network?'

'Your charity committee might be a good starting point. There must be people on there that could use a VA or they might know someone.'

'Good point.' Katie wrote that down and put a big star next to it.

'Then there's a lot of business networking groups for the self-employed and small businesses, certainly here in the States, and I know Harry goes to one; they meet for breakfast.'

'I see.' Katie felt daunted at that prospect.

'Ask Harry about that one.'

'Have you ever actually met Harry?' The question slipped out before Katie could check herself.

'No!' Nancy laughed. 'Not in person anyway but we've skyped. Handsome devil, isn't he?!'

Katie blushed. 'Yes, I suppose so. So how did you become his VA?'

'Ah, yes of course. Well social media. I was particularly targeting investment companies, it's good to have a niche by the way, and we met on Twitter.'

Katie suddenly felt overwhelmed by the whole venture ahead of her. The world of social media was almost alien to her, although Save the Children did have a Facebook page and she had looked at it with Alice's help.

Nancy seemed to read her mind. 'Listen, the best way to go about this is one step at a time. Write yourself a plan and break it down into action points.'

'Yes, that's a good idea, I will.' Katie decided it would be best to bring the conversation to a close now. She looked over at her daughter who seemed to be getting on *too* well with Harry.

'Okay, well I think that's enough for now but hey call me any time Katie.'

'Oh thanks, you've been great. Thank you.'

'Not at all. Have a good day now.'
Katie sighed as she looked through her notes.
'How did it go?' Harry asked.
'Good thanks, I think.'
'Lots to take in?'
'Yes, certainly that.'
'Don't worry, you'll be fine.'
'Actually, I've got a couple of things I need to ask you.'

Alice noticed the space on Bisham Gardens where her father's car had sat for weeks. It had been gathering dust in the summer heat, was now occupied by another unfamiliar car. She reassured herself that her mother must be using it; after all she knew she was out. However, when she looked up and down the street for her mother's car she could not see it.

'What are you doing?' Jacob looked puzzled.
'Looking for my mum's car.'
'I thought you said your mum's out.'
'Yes, she is, but the thing is my Dad's car is missing too. She can't be out in both cars at the same time.'
'Maybe it's in the garage? Maybe it needs a service?'
'Yeah but it's strange, I mean with both cars out at the same time.'
'I see.'
'Do you?' Alice was agitated. 'What if it's been stolen?'
'Good point. Why don't you ring your mum?'
'Yeah, I could do.'
'But?' Jacob looked at her squarely.
'Well, she's with this Harry bloke over in Hampstead.'
'Really! Some sort of date? Seems a bit soon.'
'No silly, she's talking to his assistant in America or something.'
'Right.' Jacob had an air of resignation about him.
Alice decided to text her mother.
Hi Mum, Dad's car is missing, worried it's been stolen. Alice x

She put her phone back in her pocket. 'Mum takes ages to text, we might as well go in.'

Katie saw the text on her phone from Alice and wanted to reply straight away. 'Just got to send a text message.'

Harry leant towards Bethan. 'Have you thought about doing an apprenticeship? A lot of young people are opting for them nowadays.'

'Isn't that slave labour; minimum wage?'

Harry looked at her carefully. 'Well look at it this way, it won't cost you anything and at least you'll be earning something as you learn. I think most apprenticeships turn into proper jobs at the end.'

'Actually, now you put it that way it sounds quite good. But can you do an apprenticeship in Graphic Design?'

'I don't see why not.' Harry sat back in his chair looking pleased with himself.

Katie looked up from her phone. 'Are we ready to go now?'

'Just a minute, Mum.'

Harry sat up. 'A client of mine has a web design business; might be worth me asking him...' He looked over to Katie for approval. 'If you don't mind?'

'Okay, thanks.' Bethan said regardless. 'Shall I give you my mobile number?'

'What's all this?' Katie interrupted.

'Harry's going to ask a client of his if they do apprenticeships in graphic design.' Bethan looked brighter than she had for a long time.

'Well I can't promise anything but I'll let you know,' Harry added quickly.

'So this is where you live.' Jacob took a good look round the kitchen. 'Very nice. You must have views over the park at the back.'

'Yeah we have but you can only really see them from upstairs. Great view from the top bedroom,' Alice's eyes flitted upwards with mild disgust, 'occupied by our lodger, of course.'

'Oh yeah,' Jacob looked interested, 'is he here now?'

'Who knows; I suppose so. He's pretty quiet but he does come down to use the kitchen.'

'Ooh I hope he does. I'd love to meet this Birch character.'

'Jacob!'

'What's the matter?' He put his arms around her and kissed her. 'Want me all to yourself again, do you?'

'Jacob, not here.' She moved away from him. 'Mum will be back any minute.'

'Doesn't your mum approve then? Is she one of those "not under my roof" mums?'

'I don't actually know. I've never, well you know.'

'Mm, I could be the first.' His eyes lit up.

Alice ignored him and checked her phone; there was a reply from her mother.

Hi Darling, Dad's car is at the garage; needs a service MOT etc.. No need to worry. Home soon love Mum x

'You were right; in the garage.' She melted into his arms this time.

Birch appeared at the kitchen door and knocked even though it was open. 'Er sorry, am I interrupting?'

'No mate, not at all.' Alice watched on as Jacob immediately extended a warm handshake. 'You must be Birch?'

'Indeed. Yes, listen I can make myself scarce. Come back later.'

Jacob looked at Alice and she said, 'no, it's okay, I was going to make some tea anyway. Would you like some?'

'Thanks Alice, that would be great.' Birch sat at the kitchen table and Jacob joined him.

'Do I know you from somewhere?' Birch was looking quizzically at Jacob.

'Chez Pierre? I'm the maître d' there.'

'Ah yes! That's it. I reviewed your restaurant just a few weeks back, not for the first time either.'

'I see. I hope we were up to the mark.'

'You certainly were. Very much so.'

'Great. So how are you finding it lodging here with three beautiful women?'

'Very good, as you can imagine.' He laughed but then stopped abruptly. Alice looked troubled as she poured the tea.

'So, have you two known each other long?' Birch asked.

'Couple of months.' Jacob replied and then added, 'I'm a very lucky chap,' and beamed at Alice who blushed and sat down at the table.

They all looked at each other as they heard the front door open and Bethan and Katie appeared in the kitchen. 'Hi Mum.' Alice got quickly to her feet nearly stumbling. 'This is Jacob.'

'We've met, haven't we? At the restaurant,' Katie said with a half smile.

'Yeah, I suppose so. Anyway, how'd it go, Mum?' Alice was at her mother's side.

'Mum's being a bit of a technophobe and worried about Twitter and stuff,' Bethan answered for her mother.

'Well it's all very new to me,' Katie said with a defensive tone.

'I'm with you there,' Birch added.

'Why do you need to go on Twitter?' Alice asked.

'Well as far as I understand it's all about networking; that's the way Nancy got her clients and she met Harry through Twitter, whatever that means.' Katie waved a dismissive hand in the air and asked, 'any tea in that pot?'

'No, sorry.' Alice sighed. 'Shall I make some more?'

Birch was already on his feet. 'I'll put the kettle on; it's no trouble.'

'Oh thanks.' Katie sat down. 'Are you joining us?' she asked Bethan.

'Okay just a quick cup then I'm going on the internet to find out about graphic design apprenticeships.'

'What's this?' Alice perked up.

'Harry was telling me about apprenticeships.' Alice looked horrified. Bethan added, 'they sound quite good actually.'

'Yes, I was reading about them in The Standard. They are more popular than degrees these days,' Jacob added.

'You're much more likely to end up with a job.' Birch said.

'But hang on a minute!' Alice was quite alarmed by the level of support for the scheme. 'Isn't that where you work ridiculous hours for virtually no money?'

'Maybe you're thinking of internships?' Birch said but met a scowl from Alice.

'Yeah, I know you don't earn much as an apprentice,' Jacob said. He was squeezing Alice's hand under the table. 'But surely they have to pay you at least the minimum wage and you have to be learning a skill or something.'

'But can you do an apprenticeship in Graphic Design?' Katie asked Bethan.

'Harry seems to think so.'

Birch handed mugs of tea to Katie and Bethan.

'I hope that's all Harry is thinking.' Katie was staring at her daughter.

'Mum! What are you saying?'

'How old is this Harry anyway?' Alice needed to know.

'Too old for you, Bethan.'

'Oh for goodness sake Mum; he's not that old.'

'He's too old for *you*.' Katie said resolutely.

'How old is he then?' Jacob asked now.

'In his thirties, I would guess, given his experience,' Katie said.

'Far too old!' Alice pronounced judgement on her sister.

'I'm going upstairs.' Bethan picked up her mug and backed out of the room. 'See you later,' she said smiling.

'That's right, skulk off again,' Alice said after her.

There was an awkward pause. Jacob broke the silence. 'So you're setting yourself up as a virtual assistant, Mrs Green?'

Alice looked embarrassed. Her mother looked exhausted.

'Possibly. It's been quite a day so far.'

'Jacob, let's go and watch a film.' Alice started to manoeuvre him out of the room. 'I need to chill; I'm working this evening.'

Jacob looked surprised but followed her anyway.

Katie looked relieved. 'That's better,' she said looking straight at Birch. 'Just you and me.'

Birch smiled broadly.

Chapter 20

'Why do you keep looking at your phone?' Miranda looked annoyed.

'Oh, nothing.' Bethan quickly checked the screen of her mobile again which told her there were no new messages. She put the handset down on the café table and finished her cappuccino. 'Shall we have another one?'

'Don't know.' Miranda smirked. 'Not sure what we're doing in Fegos anyway? I mean it's hardly the trendy place to go round here.'

'It's all right.' Bethan was defensive.

'I thought you said your mum comes here?'

'She did... once.... maybe twice.'

'Judging by the clientele she'd be a regular here; we must be the youngest in here by miles.'

'I'm nearly seventeen.'

'What's that got to do with anything?'

Bethan squirmed in her chair and then said, 'look I've met this guy, right. Harry, his name is. He's absolutely gorgeous and he's got my mobile number. Mum reckons he's too old for me but he's not.'

'How old is he?'

'About.... thirty.'

'Golly that's quite old, Bethan. Anyway, how did you meet him and how on earth does your mum know about it?'

Alice had only been in Mrs William's office once before in the two years she had been at this college and she didn't really know what to expect. Her desk was covered in papers and she seemed to be looking for something through the half-moon spectacles perched on her nose. She gave up and looked enquiringly at Alice who was sat opposite her.

'So, you want to re-take your French A-level?'

'Yes, that's right.' Alice was wondering if she needed to put her case before the college would allow her to do the re-sit.

Mrs Williams looked over the papers on her desk again and sighed. 'Sorry, forgive me, would you remind me what grades you did get?'

Alice reeled off her results.

'Ah yes, I remember now; you want to go to Nottingham to do French.' She scribbled something on a note pad and then said, 'well it seems reasonable; of course there's a fee to pay.'

Harry walked into Fegos with Justin Sommerville and they found a discreet table in the corner.

'This should do the job.' Harry caught the waitress's eye and she abandoned the table she was clearing to go straight over to him. 'How can I help you?' She twirled her long black hair round her finger as she spoke.

'One cappuccino and one...'

'The same,' Justin added.

'Please.' Harry looked at her now.

'Right away.' The waitress hesitated, her eyes fixed on Harry, before moving away.

Harry's eyebrows flitted upwards and Justin laughed.

'Now let's talk about your portfolio.' Harry got down to business. 'Europe in particular. I want to explain what's going on there so we can fully understand your investment performance in recent months.' He spoke with a reassuring air of authority and Justin relaxed back into his chair.

'Bethan, what's going on? You've gone completely weird now.'

'I don't believe it. It's him! It's Harry! He's over there with some other guy.'

Miranda looked round.

'Don't do that!' Bethan screeched.

'Oh my God; I see what you mean.'

'What am I going to do?' Bethan was beside herself.

'What *can* you do? Looks like he's in a meeting or something.'

'Yeah, it does. How annoying. I wonder if I should wander over there... just to say hello or something. That would be okay, wouldn't it?'

'Subtle!' Miranda laughed.

'Well why not? I could ask him if he's spoken to his web developer friend yet.'

'I wouldn't. I just wouldn't. I mean from what you've told me he could just be helping you out to get an apprenticeship.'

'Let's get another coffee.' Bethan was trying to attract the attention of the waitress but finding it difficult.

'A *third* coffee! You must be joking; I didn't want the last one.'

'Oh Miranda, be a friend, please? We can't leave now!'

Alice decided to walk home. En route she was drawn to Highgate cemetery and found herself at her Dad's grave. She tidied it up, deadheading some of the flowers growing around it and wiping the headstone with her sleeve. Suddenly she checked herself and stood up. She looked at the sleeve of her blouse and wondered if it was stained. Her thoughts meandered to their last supper; her father remonstrating about how no daughter of his would not get anything less than an A grade. It was a double-edged sword of expectation over having so much faith in her. Her mother was simply on her side whatever life threw at her; she had certainly got that bit right. A tear rolled down Alice's cheek as she said out loud, 'I'm doing this for you Dad; I will get an A in French and I will make you proud.'

She looked around her; there was no one in earshot. An elderly couple added some fresh flowers to a grave and were walking towards Alice now. She could not decide whether to run away or wait for them to pass. Too late, they were there. 'Afternoon,' the man said lightly. They both offered a warm smile. 'Afternoon,' she managed before bursting into tears. The woman turned and said gently, 'you all right, love?' Alice somehow found the composure to say 'yes, I'm fine,' enough to convince the couple they could walk on before she fell to her knees and wept like a child.

The café had emptied somewhat now and Harry approached Bethan's table. Her heart was beating fast.
'Hello Bethan, how are you?' he said cheerfully.
'I'm okay thanks. This is my friend, Miranda.' Why did she say that? Did that make her sound foolish?
'Hi Miranda, I'm Harry.' He shook her hand enthusiastically.
'Good to meet you.' Miranda looked like she was enjoying this.
'By the way, Bethan, I spoke to my friend in web development and it seems they are looking to take on a Graphic Designer and would consider an apprenticeship.'
'Oh wow, that's great!' Bethan immediately wondered if she sounded too enthusiastic.
'Yes, so here's his card.' Harry pulled out a business card from his wallet and put it on the table.
'Oh right.' Bethan was surprised.
'Yes, just give him a call and I'm sure he'll be happy to interview you.'
'Right.' Bethan struggled to hide her disappointment. 'Thanks, thanks for that,' she said meekly.
'Tell you what,' Harry added, 'let's coordinate diaries and I'll take you over there and introduce you etc.. Would you like that?'
'Er, yes. Yes. That would be good.'
'Well if you'll excuse me, I'm just with a client of mine.'
'Of course.' Bethan felt confused.
'Told you,' Miranda was looking smug, 'he's just helping you to get a job.'
'Thanks Miranda; that's really helpful,' Bethan was red faced with annoyance.

Alice took pleasure in seeing Highgate village in the sunshine as she walked home. She imagined the scene when she got there. She would find her mother in the kitchen starting to prepare supper, a bottle of wine opened already. Alice would go straight up to her mum and give her an enormous hug; she would not need to explain why.

As she put her key in the front door she remembered Birch and thought that he wasn't part of what she had imagined and how he might spoil her dream and stop her getting what she needed right now. Like a self-fulfilling prophecy there he sat at the kitchen table but there was no sign of her mother.

'Oh hi.' She didn't hide her disappointment. 'Where's Mum?'

Birch was quick to get up from the table. 'She's just popped out to collect Bethan from a friend's house, won't be long.' He sounded apologetic.

'Oh.' Alice felt lost.

'Are you all right, Alice?' It was the second time she had been asked that, that afternoon. She sighed and said nothing.

'I was going to make you some tea but... perhaps a glass of wine would be more welcome?' He looked concerned.

'I've been to the cemetery; Dad's grave.'

'Ah.' Birch opened the fridge to find a bottle of Chardonnay and put it on the table. 'This okay? You'll have to tell me where the wine glasses are.'

Alice pointed and Birch efficiently got two glasses and poured them both a glass.

'Sorry your mum isn't here. I know I make a poor substitute.'

Alice looked straight at him now. 'It's okay. Not your fault.' She took another gulp of wine. 'You see...,' she looked down at the table, 'I think it's only just really hit me. My Dad.... he's gone.... gone forever.' The shock she was feeling was all over her face.

They sat in a sad silence and Alice let a tear roll down her cheek. She wiped it away.

'I cried. I cried at the cemetery.' She was looking at her father's grave in her mind. 'It's so difficult because I was so in awe of him, but now I know there was a side to him that none of us were aware of, not even mum, and so I wonder if I knew him at all.' She looked at Birch with an air of expectation.

'I'm sure he loved you.... and Bethan and your mum.' He smiled with tight lips. 'I'm sure all his intentions were good ones.'

Alice blew her nose and topped up their glasses. 'Yes.... you're right. Of course he loved us; what else matters?' She looked up and half-smiled. 'Thanks,' she said quietly.

'I've done nothing,' Birch said.

Chapter 21

Ross just had three more front doors to go and he was done for the morning. Number five had a dog and he was quite big and quite old but didn't bother to bark every time something came through the letterbox and hit the doormat. Number three had a racing green door which Ross particularly liked and he had often admired it on his round and wondered if he should paint the door of his flat the same colour but, being an internal door, it didn't seem worth bothering. His flat was small and he had furnished it from the second-hand charity shop in Archway.

    He had been down on his luck when his wife threw him out because she found out he was a secret gambler. He had lost his job working for the council just a week before. At the time just getting a roof over his head was the priority. David had been his saviour, gently pushing him into his first Gamblers Anonymous meeting. Then he lent him some money for the deposit for a flat and to set him up in his local magazine business. Three thousand pounds was not an amount that Ross could have even considered getting his hands on at that time. He felt guilty every time he thought about the money as he had not been able to pay David back before his untimely death. Ross pondered his growing and healthy bank balance since he had been running the My Mag franchise as he paced up to number one, the last house for the day. It was always a good feeling when the magazine was out for another month; the advertisers invoiced, the publication printed and delivered by his own fair hand. Some of the other My Mag owners paid their local paper to distribute it with the paper but Ross enjoyed the outdoors and he considered that the exercise did him good. He also had the time to do it. The business kept him fairly busy, drumming up more and more advertisers to make a bigger and better magazine, but there was always a bit of a lull for about a week from the moment the last one was delivered.

He made his way purposefully to the French bistro in the centre of Highgate village. This was the third month he had decided to treat himself to lunch to celebrate another successful edition. It was becoming a regular thing; something he looked forward to. He was also notching up the months in his mind since he gave up gambling. His last bet was placed almost eighteen months ago now and he hadn't missed a GA meeting since that first time when he met David, not one. He felt around for the coin in his pocket; it gave him comfort to feel its edges and to know it was still there. It was a pound coin like any other pound coin, but it was special to Ross as he had found it in his pocket exactly one month after he became a reformed character and said goodbye to the bookies. It may have been superstitious, but he had decided that as long as it was there, in his pocket, he would be okay and so it provided some small reassurance.

The waitress who normally served him was not around as far as Ross could see. However, the table he had sat at the two months previously was vacant, probably because it was rather small, and so he sat there. The waitress who came over was brash and business like and took no time for pleasantries and this left Ross realising that he had become rather fond of the other waitress who he had discovered was called Elaine.

'What will it be today?'

Ross wondered if she recognised him from previous visits. 'Duck confit, please, and a large glass of your house red wine.' Ross had said it in French to Elaine, 'un grand verre de votre vin maison rouge', but he didn't bother today.

'Right.' She was away.

Ross was just about to leave the bistro after his meal when he saw Elaine appear from the back. He smiled at her across the room and she smiled back. He put on his jacket and made for the door where she intercepted him.

'I hope you enjoyed your meal today.'

'Yes, yes, it was fine.' His tone gave away his disappointment at her not being there.

'Oh!' she sounded surprised and then she added cheerily, 'hope to see you again soon,' and Ross got the warm feeling back that he had felt at the end of his door drop run.

Ross headed up to the cemetery and noticed that David's grave had been tidied up recently so he simply stood there before it with his thoughts. He enjoyed the sense of calm that this place gave him. It felt like a peaceful, beautiful oasis far away from the noise and bustle of the City and it was somewhere he could easily walk to.

He had wanted to bring a few fresh flowers to leave at David's headstone but he was not sure if that would be a comfort to any family members visiting or an unwelcome intrusion, much like his presence at the funeral. But now he had met Katie and gone some way to explain how he and David came to know each other he felt better about these visits. There was just the matter of the three thousand pounds which left him uneasy.

Katie picked some cornflowers and some foliage from her garden to form an appealing bunch and found a small heavy vase to place them in. It was just a short walk up to the cemetery so there was no point in driving, especially as parking was difficult there. The weather was pleasant and she walked carrying the vase and flowers knowing there was a tap where she could get some water.

Her heart stopped momentarily when she saw Ross standing there but then she reminded herself how kind he had been and how he had revealed to her a secret part of David she had not known. It had helped her to make sense of it all. She walked slowly towards him; he was obviously deep in thought.

'Hello Ross.'

'Katie!' He looked startled. 'Sorry,' he said.

Katie was puzzled. 'Sorry?'

'I mean sorry if you don't want me here.'

'Don't be silly,' she said. He noticed her empty vase.

'Shall I find some water? I saw a tap somewhere. Over there, I think.' He pointed.

'Yes please.'

He took the vase from her. Katie turned to her husband's grave.

'Well, look where life's taking me since you left. I've met Ross and then there's Harry who's invested your winnings,' she hesitated before adding, 'and Birch.' She felt an undeniable twinge of guilt as she was growing fond of Birch and enjoyed his company so much so that she looked forward to their afternoon teas together.

'Well needs must,' she explained to her dearly departed, 'his rent pays the mortgage and what a mess I'd be in without that money.' She looked around her to make sure no one was in earshot. 'He's only a day time lodger.' Somehow that made it all respectable. She surprised herself; the hold David had over her even now.

Ross was hovering at a polite distance holding the vase now filled with water. Katie turned to him.

'It's okay,' she nodded to him and then to the thirsty flowers. Ross placed the vase and arranged the cornflowers and foliage clumsily.

'Oh, you'll have to take over now. Not my forte I'm afraid.'

'That's okay.' Katie fiddled with the stems until they looked neat and pretty. She stood up.

'Do you want me to go?' Ross asked.

Katie thought about it. 'No, no it's okay.'

'If you're sure.' They stood together in affable silence until Ross said, 'Katie, I've got something I need to tell you.'

Bethan was thrilled to see the text from Harry on her phone. She read it so quickly she had to read it again to make sense of it.

Hello Bethan, Just to say Paul Costelloe can see you on Thursday morning 10.30 – OK with you? If you get here for 10 we'll have enough time to get up there. Regards Harry

In her excitement she sent a text to Miranda.

Hi M, just had a txt from handsome Harry!! Seeing him Thursday!! Bx

Miranda's reply came through in seconds:
Wow! Great news. Where's he taking you?

Bethan re-read the text from Harry and now his formal tone was leaving her somewhat deflated. She immediately decided she would make sure she looked stunning on Thursday morning and replied to Miranda.

He's taking me for this interview with this web dev guy, Paul. Bx

Miranda came back with: Good luck x and it occurred to Bethan that Miranda had never really got excited about a boy, or a man for that matter. She had never had a boyfriend but then her parents were so posh and so old money she would probably have suitors at a coming of age party eventually.

Katie sat at the desk in what was David's study, but what she now tried to call *the* study, and took a deep breath to calm herself. When Ross first broke the news that David had lent him three thousand pounds, she was more upset that he had done this without her knowledge than anything else. Each new discovery, about the man she had been married to for over twenty-five years, left her bewildered and wondering how much more there was to know.

'You see, Katie, I was in a really bad way,' Ross had explained. 'No home, no job and when I had the chance to make a go of it with My Mag, well...' He had fixed his gaze on the distance throughout. 'Well I was desperate and you know I was *so* grateful...' Then he had glanced at her. 'So grateful that David actually believed in me. He believed I'd make a go of it with this new business venture and I'd be able to pay him back one day.'

She had felt weak at the knees and had made her way to a bench almost in a trance. Ross had followed her and they sat side by side.

'The thing is, Katie,' he took a deep breath, 'the business *has* gone well and I've got the money to pay you back now.'

'Right.' The whole story left Katie in shock. 'Right, okay then.'

Ross bowed his head in shame. 'I'm so sorry I didn't tell you about this before, but you see I didn't have the money then.'

'Oh,' she said still baffled by her husband's actions.

'Thank you,' he said. 'Thank you for understanding.'

'I'm not sure I do understand.'

'Perhaps what you should take from this,' Ross started hesitantly, 'is that David was a good man. He was benevolent and he helped me out and I'll be grateful to him, and you of course, for the rest of my life.'

Now Katie was home and sat down she thought about what she would do with the money. It was the sort of amount that wasn't going to solve their problems so perhaps she should add it to her investment managed by Harry. But then she thought about the unpaid bills piling up and the fridge freezer that desperately needed replacing, even Birch had commented on it playing up the other day. 'This milk doesn't seem terribly cold,' he had remarked and his tone was gentle but still made Katie's heart sink as it was just another reminder of how she was struggling with what little she had left of the cushion that was their diminished savings. No, she would use this money to help them get through the next month or two.

She picked up the phone and dialled Julia's number.

'Hello Katie,' Julia answered brightly.

'Hi, you doing anything?'

'What right now?'

'Yes, I need someone to talk to.' Katie scribbled patterns on a nearby notepad with a black biro.

'Do you want to pop round? I'll put the kettle on.'

That was what Katie wanted to hear. 'Yes, please.'

'Any clues so I can brace myself.'

'I need to set myself up in business as a Virtual Assistant and start making some money.'

'Ah, well you're coming to the right place!' Julia laughed at her own ineptitude.

'I just need some encouragement really.'

'That I can supply; I'll get some muffins out to go with the tea.'

Chapter 22

Bethan hated it when her alarm went off really early, but when she came to and remembered why, she smiled as she stretched herself awake. She knew for sure that Alice would still be in bed; she tended to work evenings and late too at the restaurant, so the bathroom they shared would be all hers.

She was back in her bedroom struggling into a black mini dress, which was tight on her hips despite the fact that she was very slim, when her mum knocked gently on her door.

'Yes?' She was annoyed as she would have preferred to have left the house unnoticed.

Katie appeared. 'I've just bought you a coffee.'

'Oh right. Thanks Mum. Can you just leave it there.' She waved her hand at her dressing table which was laden with makeup and beauty products and Katie had to move a bottle of body lotion to make a safe space for it.

'Will you be having breakfast?' Katie asked.

'No, no Mum. I'm out of here. Got an appointment at ten.'

'Oh? What's that for? Not the dentist judging by what you're wearing.' This comment met a scowl from Bethan.

'I've got an interview!' she responded, her tone harsh now.

'That's good,' Katie said, 'Who's that with?'

'Paul Costelloe.' She was concentrating on brushing a thick black mascara onto her eye lashes. 'You know, that web developer guy that Harry knows, he might take me on as an apprentice in graphic design. You seemed okay with it the other day.'

'Yes, I think it's a great idea.' Katie sat on her daughter's bed and Bethan threw her a stare.

'Mum, I'm trying to get ready!'

'Yes darling, I'm not going to hold you up. I thought this job was in Highgate anyway; you've got plenty of time. I'll drive you if you like?'

'No Mum! No! You're not driving me!'

'Why ever not?' Katie had raised her voice to match her daughter's.

'Because *Harry's* going to take me!'

'Ah.' Her mother had a knowing smile. 'That's why you're wearing that dress that's too tight for you.'

'Mum! Get out! It's not too tight!' She stood in front of her long mirror and tried to pull the dress down and to smooth out the creases. It *was* too tight; it was totally unsuitable for an interview. Frustrated now she said, as if blaming her mother, 'oh, bloody hell I'm going to have to put something else on!' She flung open her wardrobe doors and threw her hand across the garments hanging there. 'I haven't got anything else!'

'What about the dress I bought you the other day?' Katie said carefully.

Bethan calmed herself a little, 'do you think so?'

'Yes darling. You look lovely in it.'

'But do you think it's a bit dressy for an interview?'

'No, I think it's perfect.'

Bethan found it and held it up from its hanger. It wasn't as sexy as the black dress but it did reveal her long legs. There was no time to argue. 'Okay, I'll wear that.'

'I tell you what,' Katie said in that reassuring motherly tone, 'I'll drive you to Harry's office, then you will have time for a piece of toast. I read somewhere you can't concentrate on an empty stomach.' Without waiting for a reply she said, 'I'll see you downstairs.'

Bethan was gobsmacked by the audacity of her mother but actually pleased she was getting a lift; it looked like rain and she had planned to walk.

Celia put the phone down in the hallway just as Birch was gathering a few papers to take round to Katie's house for his day's work.

'It's all *your* fault!' She turned on him without warning. Birch noticed that she looked really upset.

'Are you all right darling?'

'Don't *darling* me! That was Jonathan's mother on the phone; he won't be coming for his violin lessons this term after *the nasty man shouted at him!*'

'Oh dear, sorry about that, but you must admit....' Birch stopped mid-sentence. The scowl on his wife's face told him to make a run for it or face fire.

'They are *children*!' She really was angry. 'They are beginners at the violin. You cannot expect them to all play wonderfully from day one!'

Birch decided to take the Fifth Amendment and stay silent. He put on a jacket, picked up his keys and headed for the front door.

'I suppose you're rushing round to be with *her* again!'

'Oh for goodness sake; this is getting ridiculous.' Birch turned to face her. 'I don't see why I should have to explain to you time and time again that it is simply an office where I can work in peace and quiet.'

Celia sobbed into a tissue. Birch approached her cautiously. 'Listen,' his tone now more sympathetic, 'I've got to review a restaurant over in Hampstead this evening. Why don't you come with me?'

Celia turned away. 'I'm busy this evening, going out with Jenny.' She would not look at him.

'Oh, okay. Well how about I put it back to tomorrow evening?'

She looked thoughtful for a moment. 'No, I don't think so.' She was staring down at the oak flooring they had had laid at her instigation and then she added, 'I'm watching what I eat at the moment; don't want to over-indulge.'

'Okay.' He put his keys in his pocket as he searched for clues on her face. Celia had always been slim as long as he had known her; but then he had never really fully understood her. 'I'll see you later then.'

She looked at him wistfully and did not say anything. He was puzzled but headed for the door anyway. 'Bye then,' he said meekly; still she didn't respond. He left with an uneasy feeling wondering if there was something his wife was hiding from him.

'Gosh you look nice,' Harry said before averting his gaze.

'Thanks.' Bethan could not have hoped for a better greeting. 'Hope I'm not late.' She knew she was early but she wanted to say something.

'No, on the contrary, we've got plenty of time.' Harry looked at his watch and then looked at Ben.

'Paul won't mind if you're a bit early,' Ben offered. 'Tell you what, I'll give him a quick buzz to give him the heads up.'

'Good idea, thanks Ben. Oh you two haven't met have you? This is Katie Green's daughter, Bethan.'

Ben got up to shake her hand. Bethan struggled to hide her disappointment at this form of introduction.

Harry grabbed the keys from his desk. 'Well, let's go then. Car's just out the back.'

Bethan slid her long limbs into the leather passenger seat of Harry's Mercedes convertible and decided that one way or another she was going to date this guy. Harry kept his eyes forward.

'Did you look up Web Dreams?' he asked.

'Yeah, I did. It looks like a fun place to work. They have some cool clients.'

'Yes, they do. Paul's done well. I'd say they are at the high end of the market price wise so standards are up there. Do you know how many people work there?'

'Er, not sure.' Bethan wished she did; this did not look good. 'Not particularly big, I'd say,' she guessed.

'There's about twenty five of them including a couple of freelancers.'

'Okay, thanks; that's good to know.'

He flashed her a smile. 'You'll be fine.'

Bethan suddenly felt nervous. What if she wasn't offered the apprenticeship; would Harry think less of her?

Birch arrived at Katie's house as she pulled up outside in her car. He opened her door for her. 'Ooh this is good,' she said, 'like arriving at a posh hotel!'

She stepped neatly out of the car putting her handbag over her shoulder.

'Where have you been at this early hour?' he asked cheekily.

'Oh, just dropped Bethan off.... at Harry's office would you believe! But it's okay, she's got an interview for an apprenticeship job.'

'Oh good, fingers crossed.'

'Yes, could be one less thing to worry about.'

'Oh dear, that doesn't sound good.'

'No, no it's fine.' Katie kept her fears to herself as much as she could where Birch was concerned. It was a confidence too far.

In the house Katie took off her jacket and headed for the kitchen. 'Do you want to take a coffee up?'

'That would be good. I'll make it,' he said. 'Didn't I promise that at the start of this arrangement?'

As he adeptly started producing two fresh coffees he asked, 'so what else is on the list of things to worry about?' and then he slapped his forehead playfully. 'Gosh that was a bit presumptuous of me!'

'It's okay.' Katie said and she meant it but then her financial worries did yet another whistle stop tour of her mind. She deliberately parked those woes and then said, 'I'm trying to set myself up as a Virtual Assistant but not getting very far. It's all the technology I'm struggling with.'

'Ooh, I wish I could lend a hand but the techie side of things is not my forte. Would Alice or Bethan be able to help you?'

'Yes, that's the obvious choice.' Katie was searching around for a notebook she knew she had had it last in the kitchen.

'Although they don't have much patience with me,' she said as she looked up at Birch.

He had finished making the coffee and passed her a cup. Then out of the blue he said, 'would you like to go out for dinner this evening to a restaurant in Hampstead?'

Katie stopped in her tracks and did not hide her surprise.

'I need to do a review for The Times,' he explained and Katie wondered if that made it okay.

He went on, 'the thing is, Celia doesn't want to go with me.' Raising his eyebrows he added, 'we could invite the girls as well if you like?'

That made it much more respectable, Katie thought but would they go? 'I think Alice is working,' she said with disappointment in her voice.

'Well that leaves Bethan; my greatest fan!' They laughed together and it broke the uneasy aura that had hung in the air. But still Katie was lost for words. He spoke. 'I tell you what, if you've made a start on setting up this VA business by six o'clock, we go to the restaurant and celebrate. What do you say?'

Katie would let herself be persuaded by this charming man; there were many reasons why she should not go but a strong desire to be reckless took over. She imagined this would be their secret; no one else would have to know.

'You're on.' As soon as she had said it she felt excited and nervous in equal measure. This was a bad idea; it was fraught with danger and yet... she wanted to go.

'Right well I better get on and...' he was thoughtful, 'so maybe you should make a plan? Write it down... and break it into bite size chunks.... so it doesn't seem so overwhelming?'

'Mm...' Katie dropped into a chair in a daze.

'What do I know?' He was in the hallway now approaching the stairs. 'I'm just a writer.'

Bethan's face gave nothing away as she emerged from Paul's office. She was pleased to see Harry had waited for her even though he had said he would and she had no reason to believe he would not.

'All okay?' He looked concerned.

'Yes, I think so.' Still she teased him with a straight face.

'Right.' Harry looked uncertain but lead the way to his car parked out on the street. Before reaching for his key fob he turned and suggested, 'Coffee?'

'Yeah, great.' Bethan's face lit up.

Fegos was almost full but they found somewhere to sit in the middle of the cafe. The dregs of the last customer's drinks were still on the table and after an awkward pause during which a waiter did not appear, Bethan decided to clear the table herself and took the tray up to the counter. She sat down again and arranged her long legs to the side of the table, her forefinger twirling her hair which fell in soft blonde waves down to her waist.

'So, how did it go?' Harry asked. 'I didn't want to ask you while we were still in Web Dreams' offices, it didn't seem right.'

'Oh, that's okay. It went well, I think. He's offered me a free trial for a week and if that goes okay he'll take me on as an apprentice.'

'Brilliant! That's great news. Your mother will be pleased.'

Bethan's smile disappeared.

'Isn't it?' Harry looked confused.

'Yes, yes it is. It's just that it's about me, not my mum.'

'Of course, I'm sorry. Well done you.' His eyes were on her now.

'That's okay.' Bethan said. 'Thanks. Thanks for setting it up for me.' Her large blue eyes were content now.

'Right, well let's see if we can get a drink.' Harry got some attention and managed to order.

'So you're starting this trial on Monday, are you?' He turned back to Bethan.

'Yes, that's right.'

'So just a few days to prepare yourself, do your homework as they say.'

'Right.' Bethan was bothered.

'I mean there must be some research you can do that will be helpful,' Harry explained, 'looking at the latest websites, finding out more about Web Dreams' clients, that sort of thing.'

'Yes, I suppose so.' She was reluctant to join in; this was not how she had envisaged this chat would go.

'You want to impress Paul next week to be sure of getting the apprenticeship, don't you?' Harry persisted.

'Yes, of course I do.' Bethan was beginning to wonder if she wanted this job at all.

'I remember when I started working in the City,' Harry relaxed back in his chair, 'I was working all hours, striving to be the best fund manager. It was hard work but great fun too. We knew how to enjoy ourselves and celebrate our successes.'

'And now?' Bethan asked, her frustration more obvious. 'Do you work all hours now?'

Katie sat at the desk in the study and looked at a blank screen. She wondered how on earth she would be able to concentrate enough to get this business idea off the ground. And yet she had promised herself she would. Today. She must not let another day go by. Her savings were disappearing; the wolves were nearing the door. She shut the door and as a knee jerk reaction to the impending struggle ahead she called Julia who answered straight away.

'Hello darling, I'm in the shop so I'll have to make it snappy.'

'Oh, sorry, should I ring back?'

'I'm okay at the moment, just one customer who looks like a serial browser,' Julia said quietly.

'Oh good,' Katie whispered.

'Where are you? Why are you whispering?' Julia asked.

'I'm at home in the study,' Katie said and then laughed to herself, 'I don't want Birch to hear.'

'Isn't he in the attic room?'

'Yes he is.' Katie raised her voice to a normal level.

'This is intriguing,' Julia said excitedly. 'What's happened?'

'Oh Julia, you won't believe what I've done.'

'Hang on a minute, customer alert.' Julia put her phone down and Katie could hear her serving someone. Moments later she was back. 'Why don't you come down to the shop and when Amanda gets here we can go for a coffee?'

''Trouble is I'm supposed to be working on setting up this business,' Katie explained.

'Oh bugger, another customer.'

'That's it, I'm coming down!' Katie gave up. 'I can't concentrate anyway!'

'This sounds fascinating; I need to know. Come down now!'

Chapter 23

There was only one other table occupied in the restaurant, a young family with a daughter who struggled to sit still, a boy more interested in a toy than eating, and parents who seemed to have a laissez faire attitude to parenting.

'That's the trouble with coming out at this time,' Birch said not bothering to lower his voice. 'Let's sit as far away as possible.' His look was that of a mischievous school boy. He picked a table for four.

'Will it be all right?' Katie asked.

'Oh yes!' He made himself comfortable and put his Dictaphone on the table in the spare place next to him. 'Everything becomes okay when they realise you're a restaurant critic; even the food sometimes,' he joked and Katie responded with a curt smile. She was quite pleased about the lively family; it put all notions of romance at bay.

'Sorry about this,' Birch said tapping the recording device, 'but it's a lot easier than making notes.'

'No problem.' Katie was too worried about being spotted to care about a silly Dictaphone.

Birch picked it up again, pressed a button, 'nil points for atmosphere,' he said simply and put it down again.

'It's a bit flat in here, isn't it?' he said and managed to catch the eye of a waitress. 'Any chance of some background music?'

The waitress looked discreetly at the recording equipment on the table.

'Maybe some jazz?'

'I'll see what I can do.' She had an air of confidence about her and handed them both menus. 'Can I get you a drink?'

Birch glanced up at Katie who was unsure as to what to order. 'We'll order some wine with our food if that's okay?'

'Of course.' She moved efficiently away.

Katie had a wry smile on her face. 'You're not difficult to please, are you? Maybe some jazz?'

Much to their surprise a Miles Davis track started up. At the same time another couple walked in.

'Phew,' Birch said, 'that's better. Suddenly we've lost the dentist's reception ambience.'

Katie laughed this time and started to relax. She then turned her attention to the menu, the Mediterranean style dishes sounded wonderful: sea bass with tomato and black olive salsa, grilled lamb chops with roasted garlic and goats cheese filo stack.

'Mm, this all sounds delicious.' Her face lit up.

'I'm pleased.' He looked genuine. 'I've heard good things about this place actually. Let's hope they deliver.'

Katie was noticing the high prices and as if he read her mind he said 'now remember this is all on me, as in The Times,' he waved a hand up and backwards as if The Times were behind him, 'and we should taste a number of dishes,' he continued as he grinned, 'to make a decent review.'

'Even better!'

Bethan checked her mobile for the hundredth time but there was no text from Harry. She was lying on her bed with her lap top looking up Web Dreams' clients and doing her homework as he had suggested. She'd told herself that if she did this, like a good girl, she'd be rewarded with a message from Harry, casually asking her out for a drink.

Tired of surfing, she decided she knew enough for Monday when she was starting her new job. Surely they wouldn't expect her to know everything on her first day, she reasoned. She started picking at the baby pink nail varnish from her thumbnail as it had already split. She looked at all her nails and decided they were a mess but she couldn't be bothered to do anything about it. She was startled by her phone ringing and quickly looked at the screen. It was Miranda.

'Hi you.' The disappointment was obvious in her voice and as if that was not enough she said, 'why can't you be Harry?'

'Hi you too! So sorry I'm not the gorgeous man!'

Bethan then realised she was actually pleased to hear from her friend. 'Do you fancy meeting up later?' she managed with more enthusiasm.

'On a school night? My parents won't let me.'

'Sooorry, forgot you're back doing you're A-levels.'

'How about Friday evening? I'm free then.'

'Yeah, let's do something. I'm so bored. Even my mum's gone out this evening to a restaurant. Can you believe it?'

'How about we try that new brasserie in Hampstead? I hear they have a bar there.'

Bethan immediately saw it as somewhere Harry might go, after all his office was in Hampstead. 'Great idea!'

'You're keen all of a sudden.'

'Oh you know,' Bethan closed her lap top and lifted it off the bed, 'anything's better than hanging around here.' She settled herself back into her pillows. 'Even Birch the lodger is not around.' There was still disdain in her voice as she spoke of him.

'Is he normally there in the evenings?' Miranda asked.

'Oh yeah, I hear him sneaking out around eleven o'clock sometimes. God knows what he's doing up there.'

'Shall we share, like in a Chinese restaurant?' Birch asked as their starters arrived.

'Why not?' Katie noticed that she had already drunk most of her first glass of wine. Birch was reaching for the bottle to re-fill her glass when she said, in reflex, 'oh, just a little for me,' and went to cover her glass with her hand.

Birch looked at her earnestly. They had come in David's Mercedes so either one of them could drive back but he had intended to drive. 'How about we get a cab back? The car will be okay where it is until the morning, I checked,' he admitted, 'and I'll come and fetch it first thing.'

Katie felt nervous. Her mind whirred, what should she say? Birch continued, 'I just thought it would be nice for you if you were able to forget your cares for one evening,' he said gently, non-judgementally and left the thought hanging.

Katie submitted, 'that's a lovely thought, thank you.' She signalled for Birch to fill her glass.

'It's been a tough few months....' There was so much more she could say but should she open up to this man? 'The girls keep me going.' She left it at that.

'What did you say to them about this evening?' he asked.

'Oh I just text them both and said I was going out and they would have to fend for themselves.'

'Good for you.'

'I think Bethan was actually in her bedroom at the time. It's ridiculous, isn't it? But I'd already been up to her room once today to find out why she was up so early. Every time I knock on her door she makes me feel like I'm the Spanish inquisition arriving!'

Birch laughed. 'Yes teenage years are certainly tricky ones.'

'It was easier when David was alive; he could get them to agree to anything. Mind you he spoilt them rotten.'

Birch pursed his lips and said nothing. She continued, 'the way he left things, well...' She stared at nothing in particular, 'it's not easy.'

'You seem to cope very well,' Birch said simply.

'Thank you,' Katie raised her glass to him. 'Anyway, I'm forgetting all my cares this evening, mustn't forget!'

He chinked her glass and looked admiringly at her as he said, 'For what it's worth I think you're a wonderful mother. You have two delightful daughters.'

'Hang on a minute!' Katie was animated now, 'After the way they've treated you!'

Birch laughed. 'Can you blame them! Some eccentric would-be barista called "Birch" of all names, turns up tapping away in the top bedroom of their beloved home all day! No wonder they are wary!'

'Well now you put it that way, you do have a point.' She looked down at the table, 'but I do hope they are realising now that you are...'

The waiter appeared to clear the starter plates away. 'Was everything all right?' he asked.

'Very good,' Katie was pleased to say.

The waiter gone, Birch said, 'I'm sure they're getting used to me.'

'Yes, I'm sure they are.' She wasn't at all sure.

'Right! Better not forget why we are here.' He picked up the Dictaphone to talk in his thoughts about the first course.

'The prawns were exquisite!' Katie chimed in, 'not to mention yummy!' she added and Birch repeated her words into the microphone.

Alice cleared away the coffee cups from her last table before the end of her shift. She'd been working since lunch time and was feeling a little weary. She had no particular plan for the evening and was surprised to see Jacob appear at the window pulling a silly face at her. She waved and held up five fingers to indicate that she would be five minutes. When she emerged from the back of the restaurant he was waiting for her open armed.

'This is a surprise!' Alice was all smiles.

'Yes, I managed to change my shift to match yours.'

'Ooooh!' She was secretly pleased.

'Hope that doesn't make me *too* keen?'

'Don't be silly,' she replied. He looked handsome in a blue shirt that matched his eyes and which he wore casually over his jeans.

'As it happens,' Alice said, 'my mum's out this evening; gone to a restaurant in Hampstead apparently.'

'Good for her!' Jacob said simply.

'But who with?'

'Didn't she say? Maybe, her friend, Julia?'

'It's not the sort of thing they do. Anyway we haven't got much money or so she keeps saying.'

'Maybe they've got a voucher for one of the chains?'

Alice stopped in her tracks. 'You don't know my mother.' She shook her head.

'Maybe she's gone with Birch?' Jacob suggested.

'Don't be ridiculous!' Alice was annoyed now.

'Anyway…' Jacob swung her round and grabbed her and before she knew it he was kissing her passionately. She emerged giddy.

'How about dinner at my place?' He asked with confidence.

'Can you cook?'

'Can I cook?!' He scoffed and then laughed. 'Well a bit. Come and find out.'

The restaurant had filled up around them and was buzzing now with lively conversation. Katie was very aware that she was more than tipsy but she was having so much fun she no longer cared. It felt like the first time since David's death that she'd laughed away and truly forgotten her troubles.

'What do you think of the lamb chops?' he asked, about to do his next recording.

'Delicious!' Katie said. 'I really must stop eating them!'

'Why? Surely you don't worry about your figure?'

Katie looked sheepish. 'It's because I worry that I don't put on weight.'

'I demand you eat the last chop!' Birch delivered the line as if in an amateur dramatics play. 'This evening is a care-free zone!'

Katie laughed yet again. 'Okay,' she submitted.

Birch spoke into his Dictaphone. 'Lamb chops with roasted garlic, excellent, according to my delightful dining companion.'

Jacob had put his ipod on shuffle and was dancing round his tiny kitchen in his first floor flat as he cooked pasta with a bolognese sauce. Alice looked on, glass of wine in hand.

'Listen, I hope you're not expecting the same standards as in the Green residence,' he had said as they entered his abode through a shabby looking hallway and up some stairs.

'Jacob!' Alice had protested, 'at least you've got your own place!'

She looked around the living room; the furniture looked like it was from Ikea and there was evidence of a hurried tidy up with cushions thrown into place if not plumped, and any flat surfaces cleared, if not dusted. More surprisingly there was a vase of bold pink lilies on a small dining table.

'These are lovely,' Alice admired them.

Jacob sniggered, 'not for your benefit of course,' and then his cheeks reddened.

'I see!' Alice rounded on him playfully, 'you planned this all along!'

'I took a punt more like! It's not every day I invite a posh girl round.'

'I'm not posh! Living on the breadline more like these days what with mum taking in a lodger. Whatever next.'

Jacob kissed her forehead. 'Okay, but none of it matters anyway.' He brushed a stray hair from her face and looked into her eyes, 'does it?'

'Of course not.' They kissed and Alice was thinking about her A-level re-take and what that might mean.

The pasta tasted good and Alice was impressed.

'Can't have been too bad,' Jacob said looking at her empty bowl.

'It was great, thanks, like I said, but you don't believe me.'

'Well I do now.' Jacob topped up Alice's glass.

'So what do you think of my place, then?'

Alice wondered why he was asking her. 'It's good. I like it,' she replied without enthusiasm.

'Your house in Bisham Gardens is lovely; I can't compete with that.'

'But why should you? You own this; we might get thrown out of ours! And I have to share a bathroom with Bethan.'

'Such hardships,' Jacob semi-mocked and then his face took on a serious look and Alice looked perplexed.

'What's the matter,' she asked sensing she should feel nervous.

'Well, I was wondering...'

'Wondering what?'

'I was wondering if you'd move in with me,' he said coyly.

Alice's eyes widened. 'Oh my God! Er... gosh... this is unexpected.' She looked down as she searched for an answer to his proposal.

'Is that a no?' Jacob asked sounding really offended.

'No, no! But the thing is..' Alice thought hard, 'the thing is I wouldn't want to leave my mum right now. I mean after Dad and everything. And also...'

'Also?'

'You know I told you a while back that I might re-sit my French A-level?'

'Er... yes.. sort of.'

'Well, the thing is, I am re-sitting it and I've decided I do want to go to uni next September.'

Jacob looked like his world had fallen apart. He spoke faintly, 'does that mean it's over between us?'

Katie could not manage another morsel of food but when she was offered coffee she said, 'yes', as she did not want the evening to end. She wondered if Celia knew that she had taken her place this evening and what the current state of their marriage was. He rarely talked about her.

Birch broke the amiable quiet between them, 'So, your virtual assistant business is about to launch?'

Katie immediately felt bad. 'Well actually, today turned out to be more of a planning meeting... with Julia, in fact... over coffee of course.'

Birch laughed. 'Ah, so you are here under false pretences!'

'Oh no, found out!'

'Well,' he said looking straight into her eyes, 'I'm so pleased you joined me. You've been excellent company, I've thoroughly enjoyed myself.'

'Me too,' Katie admitted.

The cab home dropped Katie first, at Birch's insistence, and he got out at the same time as she did and stood opposite her, his eyes looking straight into hers. And as he gently held her face between his hands and kissed her on the lips it felt like the most natural thing in the world.

'Goodnight Katie,' he said as he climbed back into the cab leaving her stunned on the pavement.

'Goodnight Birch,' she managed to reply and floated dreamily up to her door. She crept in quietly, not wanting to bump into either of her daughters. All seemed quiet, so she went to the kitchen for a large glass of water and sneaked up to bed like a naughty teenager.

Chapter 24

Harry was perched on the edge of Mrs Johnson-Sinclair's velvet sofa wearing his best suit and determined not to spill his coffee, when his client's daughter appeared.

'Mummy, I'm just off.....' She noticed Harry. 'Oh, sorry, I didn't realise you had company.'

Mrs Johnson-Sinclair rose to her feet.

'Darling, how opportune, I've been wanting to introduce you to Harry Liversage.'

Harry carefully placed his cup on its saucer and noticed his hand was not entirely stable. He stood up, somewhat relieved that he had managed it without incident and held his hand out to Natasha, who was a vision of loveliness.

'Oh hi, what's Mummy got you doing I wonder? You look like a City type. Investments may be?'

'Absolutely right.' Harry blushed.

'Well, take good care, that's my inheritance you're playing with.'

'Really Natasha!' Her mother admonished her.

'I think our track record speaks for itself.' Harry was pleased he had said something sensible.

Natasha swung herself towards the door and her long chestnut hair flew around with her. She turned back, the fingers of one hand now sweeping up the hair from her forehead.

'Nice to meet you, Harry,' she said sweetly, 'must dash Mummy, meeting Hannah for lunch.'

Katie awoke with a headache and a sense of doom. What on earth had gone on last night and what does it all mean? She decided instantly that she must put a stop to this nonsensical behaviour.

She was a widow of not much more than two months and Birch, a married man. Her daughters would most definitely be horrified at the prospect of anything between them.

She indulged herself in her shower, pressing the boost button so that lashings of silky warm water engulfed her body. She tried to think pure thoughts. Her role as a mother was paramount. Towelling herself dry, she reminded herself of her financial straits and the desperate need there was for her to start earning some money. This left her feeling depressed.

Dressed in jeans and a loose fitting blouse she sauntered down stairs and into the kitchen. She allowed herself a smile with a fleeting thought of the fun she had had last night, she needed to cheer herself up after the dose of reality she had dealt herself. As she walked straight into the kitchen and up to the kettle she heard, 'morning Mum,' behind her. She turned to find both her daughters sat at the table, their facial expressions were questioning and saying, what was going on with their mother?

Mrs Johnson Sinclair insisted that Harry called her Vicky.

'So Vicky, your portfolio is in good shape. Is there anything else we could be doing to meet your objectives?'

'No, I'm very happy with how it's all going but you know there is something you might do for me.'

'Oh yes?'

'Yes, my daughter, Natasha.' Vicky smiled broadly.

'Your daughter?' Harry felt a sense of foreboding.

'Yes, Harry. You don't mind me being frank with you, do you?'

'Er... well.... no, of course not.'

'She hasn't had a boyfriend for over a year now and I'm very concerned about her.'

Harry shuffled in his seat and realised his back was sore from having hovered for too long on the edge of the sofa. 'Right...,' he said, fearing what would come next.

'After all, she is not getting any younger, I mean, she's thirty-two already. In my day, you would be positively on the shelf at that age!' She laughed and Harry made some indecipherable noise suggesting he might be in pain.

'So what do you think?' She looked straight at him and he tried to position his features in such a way that would please his client whilst wondering if he should make excuses and run for the door.

'Perhaps you could ask her out for dinner? I'm sure she'd say yes,' Vicky continued.

'Right!' Harry said a little too loudly.

'She is a lovely girl,' Vicky added.

'Of course, I'd love to.' He tried to sound convincing; his golden rule of not mixing business with pleasure did not stand a chance.

'So you were just *helping him* to do his restaurant review?' Alice said the words slowly and deliberately as if she wanted to believe it.

Bethan still looked perturbed. 'But why doesn't he take his wife?' She was staring at her mother accusingly. 'Or a friend? Hasn't he got any friends?'

Katie took a deep breath. Her head was still hurting but she was not going to admit to a hangover. This was scary enough without letting on that she had drunk a little too much and actually had some fun.

'And why does Dad's car keep disappearing all of a sudden?' Alice looked intently at her mother.

'Oh well, I know the answer to that!' Bethan was vitriolic now.

'What?' Alice was baffled.

'Isn't it obvious? It's our lodger! I've actually seen him driving it!'

Katie thought her head might explode. 'More coffee?' She asked as brightly as she could, rising to her feet somehow feeling that she had to move at least. Bethan's expression went from confused to hurt child.

Both daughters stared at her in amazement. Katie was forced to speak. Being on her feet gave her some strength.

'Listen. Birch *has* used the Mercedes a couple of times; he paid for it to be serviced, taxed and made legal as *I* can't afford to and *you* won't let me sell it! I had little choice!' She was trying not to raise her voice but had to make her point.

Alice looked down at the table and sniffed.
'Well *I* think you should put a stop to it *now*!' Bethan raised her voice. 'That and the cosy meals out with the man!'
'Bethan, darling, it was just a meal out.' She tried very hard to lighten her voice before she said, 'can we drop this now?'
'What's the point? If Dad was here things would be very different!' Bethan shouted. She sprung from her chair and made for the door, but before she reached it she turned back, her face red with anger now. 'I think we should all go and visit Dad's grave!' Tears were welling up in her eyes. '*This evening*, in fact!'
Katie looked at her shocked and affronted.
'I mean,' Bethan continued speaking purposely, 'I haven't seen the headstone yet.'
'Well I have,' Alice was quick to retort, 'I was up there recently in fact and mum's been up too, haven't you Mum?'
'Yes darling, I have. But I'm happy to go up again with Bethan, and you Alice, if you wish. Anytime. Really.'
'Right, that's agreed then.' Bethan was halfway down the hall heading to her usual sulky retreat.
Alice turned to her mother and said with an air of formality, 'maybe it would be better if you didn't do any more restaurant reviews with Birch.'
Katie looked bewildered for a moment and then defeated. She shook her head and said, 'I think I'll make that coffee now.'
Alice's expression was solemn. There was an awkward pause before she said in a huff, 'right, well I'm going out,' and left.
Alone, Katie broke down in tears and decided she would be out when Birch arrived that day.

Chapter 25

Ross put the phone down and punched the air triumphantly.

'Yes!' he shouted. He had just signed up two new clients to advertise in his magazine and one of them had taken the premium back cover position for three months. His revenue for the October edition was looking very healthy. The good thing about this business was that you got your money upfront before you went to print so there were no cash flow issues. The phone rang and he was slightly disconcerted; he hoped no one had changed their mind.

'Hello, Ross Kirkdale speaking.'

'Oh Ross, it's Geraldine here.' There was an awkward pause while Ross tried to place her. 'From The Flask.'

'Geraldine, how are you?' Surely she did not want to cancel her advert after the full page feature he had done on their pub and restaurant last month.

'I'm great thanks. Just ringing to say a big thank you for the advertorial you did for us; we've had a really good response.'

'Oh fantastic! I'm really pleased Geraldine.'

The call from The Flask put Ross in high spirits and he decided to make himself a mug of tea. As he was boiling the kettle an idea suddenly came to him. He would offer some editorial space to Le Bistro, the restaurant he liked so much; it would be a good way of getting to know Elaine, the waitress, better.

*

It was about ten o'clock when the doorbell rang and Katie decided it could not be Birch as it was too early and anyway he had his own key. She had avoided him so far since their evening out even though it pained her to do so. She opened the front door to find a courier man holding a large box.

'Delivery for you.' His voice was strained.

'Oh?' Katie could not remember ordering anything. She was being so careful with her money; online shopping was a thing of the past. 'You'd better put it down here.' She pointed to a space on the hallway floor. She was looking for the address label, convinced it must be a mistake.

'Katie Green?' the man asked.

'Yes, that's me.'

'It's for you then.' He was dismissive and handed an electronic device with a plastic pen over to her. 'Sign here please.'

Ross wore an open neck grey shirt, his smartest trousers, a navy blue cord jacket and some aftershave he had treated himself to, as he strolled down to the centre of Highgate village with a spring in his step. It was a cool autumnal day but the sun shone through from time to time lighting up the gorgeous oranges and yellows of the leaves on the plane trees. When he reached Le Bistro he hesitated and tried to spot Elaine through the window but he could not see her. No matter, he would carry out his mission anyway. He walked in with a determination that surprised him, and asked to speak with the manager. The boy in front of him can only have been eighteen, a bit scruffy but was polite and helpful.

'She's in the office at the moment but I can tell her you called if you like?'

'I see.' Ross found this rather disappointing and it showed on his face.

'What's it about? Maybe I can help?'

Ross opened up his document wallet and took out a copy of My Mag. 'I own this local magazine which enables businesses like yours to advertise and we do a restaurant feature each month so I..'

'Oh right, well she might be interested, so how about I let her know you're here.'

'You're very kind.' Ross beamed at the boy.

'Do take a seat while you're waiting. Would you like a drink of anything?'

'That's very good of you; an espresso please.'

'Okay, won't be long.'

Ross sat with his espresso, people watching with his antenna programmed to spot Elaine but she did not appear. He decided it must be her day off and made a mental note to come back on a different weekday next time. Eventually the boy appeared and looked like he was coming over but then stopped to talk to another waiter. They swapped witty banter and the boy was still chortling as he came over to Ross.

'Well she doesn't like being interrupted but it must be your lucky day because she's agreed to see you.'

'Oh well thanks. Do I go up to the office?'

'No, no, she'll be down in a minute.'

Ross relaxed back into his chair. Just then Elaine appeared from a door at the back. He smiled and waved and was delighted when she came straight over to him.

'Hello Elaine.'

She looked puzzled. 'Are you the magazine man?'

'Yes!' Ross was confused now and then it dawned on him. 'You're the manager?'

'Of course.' She smiled and sat down opposite. 'Well I'm glad it's you and not some dreadful salesman,' she joked and they both laughed and Ross decided this was the best day he had had for a long while.

Katie had opened the box on the floor of the hallway as it was too heavy to move. Inside was a very expensive looking coffee machine, one that you might find in a restaurant. She pondered what this might be about and was soon convinced that Birch would be behind it. When she heard the front door go at ten past eleven her heart jumped and she froze in the kitchen where she stood. She heard someone walking down the hallway and then he appeared.

'Ah! Hello,' Birch smiled sheepishly. 'Didn't realise you were there.'

'Hello Birch.' Katie was nervous; it was the first time they had been face to face since that kiss. She wondered if he was thinking the same thing.

'You've received a parcel, I see.'

'Yes,' Katie said and no more.

'Yes, sorry to surprise you like that but I just thought you might... ...like it. I mean... you don't have one.... and well... they are quite useful.'

Katie was still wondering what all this was about but could not help smiling. 'So you've bought me a coffee machine?'

'Yes... indeed.' He looked awkward and then said, 'do you like it?'

'Well, it's probably not best appreciated on the hallway floor. Perhaps you could bring it in here?'

'Absolutely... and I'm glad you didn't attempt to pick it up.' He went to fetch it and came back with the machine extracted from its box and placed it carefully on the kitchen table.

Katie admired it. 'It looks great but perhaps one needs a lesson on how to use it.'

'Yes, well I'll work all that out and then I'll show you. Is that okay?'

'That sounds good,' and then Katie asked even though she was not sure why, 'do you have one of these at home?'

'No, no I don't.' Birch suddenly looked sad.

Katie wished she had not asked now. 'Well thank you. That's very generous of you,' she said to lighten the mood. 'It looks very impressive. Shall we make some coffee with it now?'

Birch's shoulders dropped and he looked more relaxed. 'You're very welcome and yes, I'll have a cup of cappuccino for you in... probably.... about...' He picked up the instruction booklet, flicked through it and tossed it over his shoulder. 'Half an hour.'

'Lovely, well I'll be in my study,' Katie said with an air of confidence that surprised even her.

'Oh right, things moving along with the Virtual Assistant business are they?'

'I'm making progress,' she said and headed off to her work with a new determination to make some money.

Ross was very pleased with how the meeting had gone with Elaine. He had made her a very generous offer so that she was getting a half page ad for less than rate card and a full page of editorial thrown in for free.

'Are you sure you can do this?' Elaine had looked suspicious.

'Yes, of course I can. It's my magazine, my business.' He straightened the collar of his shirt and decided he did not want to look like he was giving away too much. 'It's a first time offer I make to new clients sometimes, if I feel their business is the sort that's right for the magazine.'

'Okay,' she rested her chin on her hand and looked straight at Ross. 'Okay, let's do it.' She had a warm smile that was infectious and Ross smiled back.

When he got home he had an idea, picked up his phone and dialled Katie. She was surprised to hear from him but friendly.

'Katie, I've thought of a way I might be able to help you out.'

'Really?'

'Yes, are you still setting yourself up as a Virtual Assistant?'

'Er, yes, yes I am,' she said uncertainly.

'Right, well how about I put an advert in the next edition of My Mag? I have a space to fill. You can have it for free.' He was pleased with himself.

'Oh!' There was a pause before she said, 'I'm not sure if I'm ready for that.'

'You have to get started before you can be good,' Ross replied as if quoting someone. 'Who was it that said that? Anyway, what do you think?'

'Well, well, okay then, I'll do it.'

'Great!' He paused before he said, 'I will need some artwork from you.'

'Ah. How do I do that?'

'It's half a page but I'll email over the exact size. Do you have a logo? Some copy?'

'Er, well..' Katie hesitated before she said, 'how long can you give me?'

'Now let me see, I've got to go to final layout next Wednesday. So, if I could have it by last thing Tuesday, would that be okay?'

That gave Katie about five days. 'You're on,' she said and then, 'thanks Ross. I really appreciate this.'

'Katie, I'm so pleased to be able to help.'

Birch crept into Katie's study and placed the coffee he had made with the new machine gently on a coaster. 'Un cappuccino, Madam.' He stepped backwards politely as if he was going to back out of the room.

'Well it looks good.' Katie took a sip. 'Mmmm, I like.'

'Excellent Madam, I will leave you to your work.' He took on the air of a butler.

'Oh Birch, hang on a minute.'

'Yes?'

'I don't suppose you could write some copy for me for an advert in My Mag?'

Chapter 26

Bethan gulped when the bar man asked her for twelve pounds for two small glasses of white wine. She reluctantly handed the cash over and turned to Miranda.

'Bloody expensive, this place!'

'Yeah, I suppose so.' Miranda took her drink. 'Thanks and cheers! It's great though, isn't it? I love the shiny décor.'

Bethan looked around; it was full of shiny mirrors with silver trim and young beautiful people looking like they had just been to a fashion show and were celebrating the success of their latest collection. The only person she wanted to see was Harry.

'They've got a restaurant too at the back,' Miranda said raising her voice even though Bethan was stood right next to her.

'You can forget that! At these prices!'

'Oh yeah, I wasn't suggesting that...' She put a friendly arm around Bethan. 'Sorry, I forget you're strapped for cash these days.'

'Don't remind me! We even have to put up with a lodger but we still don't have any money – he just pays the mortgage. Still, at least mum seems to have forgotten about selling the house and moving to some God awful flat in Archway; can you imagine!'

'Doesn't bear thinking about. Poor you!' She looked full of sympathy.

Bethan kept her eye on the door. It was so crowded she reckoned her only chance of seeing Harry would be catching him as he walked in.

'You okay?' Miranda asked. 'You seem distracted.'

'Sorry, no, I'm fine.' To prove the point she added, 'I'm looking forward to my new job on Monday. I'm so bored at home.'

'It sounds great! You'll be a graphic designer! Much more fun than school. And you'll be earning some money.'

'Oh God, a pittance really. Minimum wage and all that. They said if I did well and make a real contribution to the business,' she said in a mocking corporate-style voice, 'they will increase my hourly rate.'

'Well that's something.'

'You sound like my mother!'

'She's lovely your mum; a lot less strict than mine. I had to agree to be picked up at eleven o'clock before they let me come out this evening! "And what sort of place is this," Dad asked.' Miranda adopted a haughty tone. 'I told him it's just a bar and it's new so I don't really know yet.'

Miranda followed Bethan's gaze to the door. 'Expecting someone?'

Bethan looked quickly back to her friend. 'No, not at all.'

'Oh… you've noticed those dopey looking guys over there!' Miranda laughed.

'No, no I haven't.'

'Let's move away from them before they come over.'

'They're not going to come over,' Bethan insisted.

'They are!' Miranda grabbed her friend's arm and steered her into the crowd.

Julia topped up Katie's glass with the Pinot Grigio they were drinking. Half way through the bottle, they were both very comfortable on Julia's sofa with shoes discarded and their feet resting on the coffee table.

'But what's the problem? I don't understand. You helped him do a restaurant review. Where's the crime in that?'

'I know, I know! But my daughters make me feel bad. They make me feel like I should be permanently dressed in black and never leave the house. I mean, of course I miss David terribly…'

She gazed ahead of her and then turned back to Julia, 'but I still have to deal with the mess he's left us in!'

Julia lowered her voice and leant towards her friend. 'Teenagers are difficult at the best of times but in their situation, they are bound to be easily upset.'

'You're right, of course, and actually I feel guilty for another reason.' Katie wore a worried frown.

Julia put her forefinger up to her mouth. 'Shh, Daisy's upstairs.'

'Oh okay, I won't say anything.'

'Don't be ridiculous. I need to know!' Julia whispered loudly.

Katie ran a finger round the rim of her glass, her expression now dreamy.

Julia looked astonished. 'You haven't slept with Birch have you?'

'No!' Katie was emphatic. 'Of course not!'

Julia looked carefully at her friend. 'So?' she asked simply.

'He kissed me goodnight.'

'On the lips?'

'On the lips.'

Julia's eyes were wide but then she seemed to shrug off the revelation. 'Well it's a free country!' she said and they both laughed. 'I think I'll open another bottle of wine.'

Bethan and Miranda had moved to the back of the bar, near the restaurant and were chatting unenthusiastically to two boys who were about their age. The better looking one called Dan was zoning in on Bethan.

'That's great that you've got a job. I've heard of Web Dreams, aren't they quite local?'

'Yes, they are.' Bethan was not about to give him the address.

'I'm doing A-levels. Bit of pressure from the parents. They want me to do accountancy and get a job in the City.'

Bethan managed a bored smile.

'You're lucky being able to do what you want,' he soldiered on.

'Actually, my Dad died recently and I don't have much choice.'

'Oh God I'm really sorry to hear that.' He shuffled uncomfortably.

'Not your fault,' Bethan said and then it happened. Harry appeared from the restaurant with a beautiful woman immediately in front of him. She turned to Harry as they shared a joke. There was no doubt they were together, they were holding hands.

'You all right?' Dan asked.

'No, I'm not feeling well actually.' Bethan's face was drained of blood. She felt giddy and grabbed Miranda's arm. 'Get your father to come now!'

'Thank you,' Katie said out of nowhere as she smiled at her friend.

'What are you talking about?'

'Just thank you for understanding.... and being on my side; it makes me feel so much better.'

Julia squeezed her hand. 'Don't be silly.' She looked thoughtful and then added, 'so are you worried about anything else?'

'Where to start!' Katie joked and then said, 'actually I've got myself in a bit of situation.'

'Not another!'

'Well this one's different. I need to produce some artwork, whatever that is, for a magazine advert in My Mag. I've got a free half page for my VA business.'

'Oh I see. Well that's good, that you've got a free advert.'

'Yes, but they need a logo which I don't have. Birch wrote the copy for me; I've got it here.' She rifled in her handbag and eventually pulled out a piece of paper and handed it to Julia who read it.

'Birch wrote this for you? It's really good. Was this before or after the kiss?'

'After. After the kiss and buying me an expensive coffee maker.' Katie was embarrassed.

'Goodness me! This is getting very interesting.' Julia refilled both their glasses.

'Hang on a minute, the point is I need to get this artwork done by Tuesday. I asked Bethan and she said she'd do it but it would be easier for her to do it at work next week.'

'In her first week in a new job; that's not good.'

'No, exactly. I want her to make a go of this apprenticeship; she's driving me nuts at home.'

'Daisy!' Julia almost shouted. 'She's good with computers.' She stood up and went to the foot of the stairs and called her. Nothing happened. She poked her head round the living room door. 'Just going up; she's probably got her headphones in.'

Miranda and Bethan sat side by side in the back of Miranda's father's car in silence. Bethan was staring gloomily out into the dark of the night.

'I was surprised to get the call so early after all that fuss you made about eleven o'clock,' Miranda's father said.

'Dad, leave it. Bethan's not feeling too good,' Miranda said.

'Not too much alcohol I hope. You're not going to be sick are you, Bethan?' he said with a disparaging air.

Bethan felt as if she could have vomited there and then but not because of the amount she had drunk. The prices in the bar had meant they had only had three drinks each. 'No,' Bethan replied feebly.

Miranda's father checked his rear mirror and seemed reassured.

'Dad, just let's take Bethan home, okay?'

'Okay!' he barked back.

They reached 12 Bisham Gardens and Bethan released herself from the seat belt and mumbled 'thanks for the lift,' as she got out. Miranda's big wide eyes looked up at her. 'You going to be okay? Text me.'

Bethan turned her key in the front door and noticed the house was quiet. She wandered into the kitchen and saw a note:

Gone to Julia's for the evening. See you in the morning.
Love Mum x

She then noticed the new coffee machine in the corner. How could she not notice this garish gadget that looked too big for its home? She could only assume that it was another blatant sign that there was a man living here who was not her father. She wanted more than anything to feel her Dad's arms around her. He'd always had a wonderful way of making any problem seem like nothing important. He would say something like, 'hey, who needs him; you're a stunning girl you can have the best there is!' She picked up her mum's note, screwed it into a ball and threw it across the room as she dropped onto a kitchen chair inconsolable with tears.

'So you see I've got the size and the copy,' Katie explained.

'But you need a logo and then for the artwork to be produced.' Daisy said. 'It's the logo that's the problem really. I mean what do you want? What's the business called?'

'Ah, forgot to say, Birch came up with a name: Virtual Magic.' Katie was not sure about it. 'What do you think?'

'Okay,' Daisy said rocking her head from side to side.

'I like it,' Julia said unequivocally as if to make up for her daughter's lack of enthusiasm.

'You think it's okay? Perhaps I should just call it Katie Green Admin Services or something like that.'

'No, no, no! Stick with Virtual Magic. It's much more memorable.'

'Yes, I think Mum's right,' Daisy agreed. 'And I could do something with that like add a few stars or a magic wand.' She grabbed a notepad and pen from under the coffee table and started scribbling ideas. 'What's your website address?' she asked.

Katie's heart sank. 'Darling, I don't have a website yet.'

'Oh, don't you,' Daisy said casually.

'Don't you have to build a website for your final year project at Uni? You were wondering what you could do.' Julia looked pointedly at her daughter.

'Er, yes.' Daisy sounded unsure.

'Well..' her mother prompted staring at her now.

'Mm..' Daisy looked deep in thought. 'The thing is..... with my uni project, it needs to be more than just brochure ware.'

'Well it could be, couldn't it?' Julia's eyes were wide.

'Oh, I don't want to be a nuisance,' Katie said concerned now that she was asking too much of Daisy.

'Mm..' Daisy said again. 'What about if I included an appointment setting widget so visitors to the site could arrange a time to call you if they were interested in your services?'

'Is that complicated?' Katie was bemused now. 'What's a widget?' she had to ask.

'Oh well it's just a bit of programming you put together to make something happen automatically. We need to include it in the website we build.'

'That sounds good, doesn't it Katie?' Julia looked excited.

'Well Daisy I don't want to put you to too much trouble.'

'No problem. I need to get this done in a week or so anyway if I'm going to meet my deadline. When does the advert come out?'

'Next month, Ross said. So that's a couple of weeks away.' Katie braced herself.

'Should be okay.'

'But darling,' Julia turned to her daughter, 'you know Katie will need it for when the advert goes out otherwise we'll have to leave the website address off.'

'Yeah Mum, it's cool okay.'

Katie stared at Julia, not wanting her to cajole her daughter any more.

'Great,' Julia relented.

'So will you be able to write the copy you want for the website and email it to me?' Daisy asked and Katie was pleased she had an amenable lodger who happened to be a writer.

'Yes, I will. Thankyou Daisy; you're a life saver.'

'That's all right. Actually, it's a load off my mind that I've got an idea for my project. I've been putting it off for ages.'

'There you are,' her mother said looking pleased with herself.

Chapter 27

Birch woke up just after nine feeling muzzy from his lie in. He slowly remembered that he had not dropped off until the small hours. After rubbing his eyes and persuading them to stay open, he stretched out his arm and felt the sheet across the bed with his hand; it was stone cold and unruffled; Celia's side of their king size bed had not been slept in.

He'd returned home from Bisham Gardens at around eight thirty last evening in the end. Helping Katie to write her advert had taken up a bit of time so when he finally got into the flow of his novel he did not want to stop. Eventually he had done a word count and decided he was on target to finish the draft ready for editing by the end of November. He could stop for the day.

When he got home Celia was out. She'd left a short curt message, devoid of affection, on the kitchen table.

Going for a drink with Rebecca. Don't wait up. C.

Birch had simply frowned and wandered over to the fridge to work out what he might have for supper. He quickly went for the easy option and brought out some eggs and bacon; he would have a fry up. Celia didn't like eating fried food so this was a good opportunity for him to have what he wanted.

Later he'd watched one of his favourite films, The History Boys, which he had on DVD and when he got to the end, and there was still no sign of Celia, rather than have to move from his sprawled out position on the sofa he started watching the Film 4 offering for the night. At the end of that he was too tired to wonder why his wife was still out – it crossed his mind he should send her a text message but based on the recent snappy responses he'd received he thought better of it – and dragged himself upstairs and into bed.

Katie had slept better than she had for a long time. She was surprised Bethan hadn't woken her coming in late; being quiet was not one of her strong points. She decided to go down to the kitchen and make some coffee and as she walked by Bethan's door she noticed it was wide open and the light was showing at the bottom of the bathroom door opposite. She knocked gently, 'Bethan, darling, is that you?'

'Yes Mum, it's me.'

To Katie's surprise she unlocked the door and peered round clutching a bath towel at her chest.

'Everything okay?' Katie asked.

'You making coffee?' Bethan ignored her question.

'Yes, would you like some?'

'Please. I'll be down in a minute.'

Katie wondered if her real daughter had been captured by aliens but headed downstairs anyway. It was still a surprise to see her brand new shiny coffee machine sitting in the corner of the kitchen and it still made Katie smile. Birch had been very good at explaining how to use it and she already had the hang of it. It did cross her mind, though, that neither daughter had commented on it. It was quite a presence in the kitchen, big, black and chrome.

Bethan appeared and Katie handed her a mug of coffee.

'Thanks Mum.' She sat at the kitchen table rather than dashing off to her room and Katie was both surprised and pleased, so she sat opposite her.

'Did you have a good evening? How was the bar in Hampstead?'

'Oh, it was okay, full of trendies and school boys.' Bethan was dismissive and Katie decided she must be hiding something; maybe a boy?

'Right,' she said simply and added, 'Miranda turned up, I take it?'

'Oh yes, of course she did, I told you I was meeting her.' Bethan seemed slightly annoyed now. 'How was your evening with Julia?'

'Actually,' Katie could not hide her excitement and was smiling broadly, 'it was great! Daisy was there and she's going to do the artwork for this free advert I've got *and* build me a website! Isn't that brilliant?'

Bethan sat upright in her chair and pulled her hair away from her face. 'I said I'd do the artwork for you.' She sounded miffed.

'Oh yes, sorry, I meant to say. The thing is, I didn't think it was such a good idea for you to do personal work in your first week in a new job. I know how much it means to you.'

'I suppose so.' Bethan's glum face bowed down to the table. 'Daisy's home from uni then?' she asked.

'Yes, she is. I'm sure she'd like to see you,' Katie said brightly, 'I told her about your new job and she was quite jealous.'

'You're joking Mum, jealous of me when she's at uni!'

'Well degree or not, getting a job is the important bit.'

There was an uneasy pause in the conversation. Bethan finished her coffee and placed her mug away from her but did not move. Katie decided she had nothing to lose.

'Did something happen last night?' she asked gently.

Bethan took a long time to reply. She wriggled in her chair, played with her hair and then said, 'You weren't here when I got home... and I was really missing Dad and I...'

'Oh darling, but I must have been here, I was home by eleven.'

'You weren't here! I got home early and so you weren't here!' Bethan burst into tears and through them she howled, 'I just needed a hug!'

At eleven o'clock it occurred to Birch that he'd not heard from Celia since Friday morning apart from the brief note she'd left him. For some time now he'd been vaguely aware of the cracks in his marriage but had adopted an ostrich mentality. He deluded himself that when his next book was published Celia would be so pleased with the lump sum he would get, that she would shop her way back to being the woman he'd fallen in love with.

He started to imagine that a dreadful fate may have befallen her and reached for his mobile to call her. Much to his surprise, she answered.

'Hello Birch,' she said with a serious tone.

'Darling, it's good to hear your voice, I was beginning to wonder where you are.'

'I did leave a note.'

'I know but that was for last night, I thought you'd be back at some stage.'

'Yes, I stayed at Rebecca's,' she said rather deliberately.

Birch was worried. 'Oh, I see.' He did not see but was not going to make a drama out of it. 'Well as long as you're okay. When will you be home?'

'Er...' There was a long pause. 'Not sure,' was all she managed.

'You're not sure how long you'll be? It's Saturday; don't you have some pupils this afternoon?'

'No. No, I cancelled them actually.'

Birch was surprised by that statement but had a more urgent question on his mind. 'Celia, what's going on?'

Katie was trying to focus on putting together a brief for her website to send to Daisy. She was looking at the sites of other virtual assistants for ideas and taking the bits she liked and ignoring the sections which didn't seem relevant to her or which scared her, for example, "*I will manage all your social media needs*". Katie was wondering how she was going to manage her own such needs and indeed what those needs actually were, let alone those of any client she might have. Some of the websites made her feel totally inadequate and she quickly closed them down. Most seemed to have a wealth of experience as a VA and all she could say was that she used to be a PA in the City.

She began to feel overwhelmed and started to wish that it was not Saturday and that Birch was likely to come round to do some writing and she could ask him for some help. She sighed and leaned back in her chair.

Spending time last evening with Julia, who was so supportive, and Daisy who was being amazing had put her in a really positive mood at the start of the day. But Bethan's outcry over seeing Harry with another woman had shaken her.

'But darling, it was not meant to be,' she had tried desperately to hug Bethan's tears away. 'I know there must be lots of boys who would find you very attractive; you're a lovely girl.'

She felt sorry for Bethan even though Harry was wholly unsuitable for her and she even dared to be secretly pleased he was dating another woman. But the fact remained, she had kept it from her daughters that Harry had invested some money for her and this was probably why he would not even entertain a relationship with her.

When Bethan's tears seemed to be subsiding Katie had had an idea. 'Why don't we go up to see your Dad's grave this afternoon? Remember you wanted to go the other day? We don't seem to have got round to it yet.' The truth was that after demanding they went that evening, Bethan had disappeared when the time came and Katie had decided to let it go.

'Yes, I want to.' Bethan moved away from her mum and grabbed a tissue from a box to blow her nose.

'Good, how about six o'clock? I'll buy you a drink at The Flask afterwards.'

Bethan had turned to her mother, 'thanks Mum,' and Katie had felt emotionally drained as she often did when trying to get it right with her youngest daughter and only ever partially succeeding.

Birch had felt an urgent need to leave the house and walk when Celia broke the news to him. He strode through the village at a pace and into the park where he could just keep going, speeding past any meandering dog walkers, not interested in passing the time of day with anyone, just wanting to walk away the blow his wife had dealt him.

He found himself thinking about the first time he'd laid eyes on her at a string quartet recital his friend, Bob, had insisted he go to. It was not his kind of thing but Bob was very persuasive. 'You should see the second violinist; she's a stunner!' he'd said. Bob had got seats in the second row and as the musicians were grouped in a circle he had a side profile of Celia. He'd been mesmerised during the whole performance, not because he cared too much for the music, but because he was simply spellbound by Celia's beauty. Her natural bountiful curls - a look that so many girls in the eighties struggled to achieve - cascaded down her back and her big brown eyes gave her a look of innocence he could not resist. Of course, now, she wore her hair short and used straighteners to keep it in a neat bob. 'But I like it like this!' she had protested, and Birch had learnt better than to argue with her. She was a strong woman, something that had first attracted him to her, but in recent years it was something that stifled him and stamped on any attempt he made to please her.

He began to slow his pace and realised he'd circled the park and was back near the entrance gates. He was not ready to leave and took a seat on a park bench with a gold plaque commemorating the life of Nicola Murray who came here for squirrel therapy, Birch noticed. The view from here stretched across the park to the City which today was shrouded in mist but the colour of the autumn trees brightened up the scene.

He leant back, closed his eyes and his breathing slowed. He finally felt strangely calm. It felt safe for him to take his head out of the sand now and come clean about what had been so obvious. He thought back over the last year and tried to remember one good time that he and Celia had shared; one joke imparted and laughed at together; one tender moment; one declaration of love. There was nothing.

One year. She had been having an affair for one year. The words fell from her lips so easily.

'Birch, I've got something to tell you. I'm having an affair. I've not been with Rebecca; I stayed with Alastair last night and I'm still at his place now.'

'How long?' he'd asked. Was it because if it had not been going on for long, he might be able to salvage their marriage, or did he just need to know how long she had been deceiving him.

'A year. About a year,' she replied without hesitation, in fact, sounding relieved that she had told him.

'Right,' he was still trying to take the information in. 'I see.' He had so many questions. 'So are you staying there now? Staying with this Alastair? Not coming home?'

'We've got a lot to talk about,' she said simply and he ended the call without another word. He had the right to cut her off, perhaps even to hurt her. He felt an overwhelming need to shut her up.

The sun came through the clouds now and he felt the warmth on his skin. He took a deep breath. The truth was that there was no joy left in his marriage and had not been for a long time. He'd managed to ignore the fact up until now but was actually relieved that he was forced to face the truth. He felt strangely free and a smile crept across his face when he admitted to himself in the cold light of day for the first time that he had feelings for Katie.

Bethan held some cut flowers she had picked from their garden and laid them on her father's grave. Katie had bought up a small vase and went to where she now knew there was an outside tap to fill it. As she walked back she watched Bethan who was stood very still staring at the headstone. Grey clouds were blowing over at a pace and managing to keep the sun out.

'All right darling?'

'He was a good Dad; he always made me feel better when things were hard. I don't just mean when he bought me presents and gave me money and told me that I'm beautiful,' her face was pained as she spoke. 'I mean when something went wrong and he'd drop everything and give me a hug,' she was smiling at the memory now, 'and make whatever it was seem like nothing at all. Like when I fell off my bike and he picked me up and carried me into the house in his arms. He asked me if it hurt anywhere, he even pretended that he was a doctor and I was his patient.' Bethan looked straight at her mother. 'Do you remember?'

'Of course,' Katie said and brushed a stray hair from Bethan's face.

Bethan's eyes were fixed on the headstone and she looked like she was deep in thought before she said, 'Mum, what was going on? With the money, I mean. What was actually going on? I don't understand.'

Katie put an arm around Bethan and pulled her close. 'Your Dad had an addiction. Gambling. It's like an illness for some people. Anyway, it got out of control and he lost a lot of money. He was trying desperately to win it back by gambling more; he really wanted to put things right for us.'

'Did you know about it?'

'No Bethan, I didn't know a thing.'

'So how do you know now?'

'Ross mainly. You know that man that came to the funeral and read that poem.'

'Oh him, the weirdo.'

Katie ignored that comment and went on to explain, 'He met your father at Gamblers Anonymous and your Dad helped him, became his friend.'

'I don't understand how Dad could help this Ross guy, but not give up himself.'

Katie sighed. 'No, nor do I,' and then she added, 'but strangely enough, it has helped me to talk to Ross.'

Bethan looked directly into her mother's eyes.

'Can I meet him? Where does he live?'

Katie frowned with concern. 'Let's think about this,' she said. 'Is that a good idea?'

'What's the worst thing that can happen?' Bethan asked, clearly agitated by her mother's response.

'Well okay, but first I must tell you something.'

'Oh God. What now?.

'Let's save it for the pub.' Katie thought that the news about the three thousand pounds that Ross had repaid to her, and what she had done with it, was best delivered sitting down with a drink.

'Is it something awful?'

'No, no. It's not awful; it's just something I haven't told you or Alice about yet.'

Bethan still looked worried.

'Stop it!' Her mother forced a smile and hugged her. 'We're going to be okay; that's the main thing, isn't it?' Every time she said that her stomach churned.

Bethan looked a bit happier. 'If you say so Mum.'

Katie once again felt weighed down with responsibility; three lives depended on her.

Chapter 28

'So what do you think?' Daisy had laid out three different options for the artwork for the Virtual Magic advert on the kitchen table. Katie marvelled at what was in front of her.

'Daisy, I think you're brilliant! Come here; let me give you a hug.'

'Oh, it's nothing really.' Daisy blushed. 'It's great to be able to help you after all you've been through.' She smiled at Katie and moved gently away. 'Now, do you like the logo?'

'I love it!'

'Great, so which ad shall we go with?'

Katie looked at all three carefully and then picked one up. 'I think this one.'

'Cool. Do you want me to email it to Ross for you?'

'That would be wonderful! Just think it will even be before his deadline!' Katie thought for a minute, 'and can you send it to me too? So that I've got a copy when you go back to uni?'

'Of course. Now,' Daisy was opening up her laptop, 'it's work in progress but I want to show you how far I've got with your website.'

'How exciting!' Katie was beginning to feel there was hope for this new business venture; it was starting to come together.

Alice had sent several text messages to Jacob over the weekend but he was resolutely not replying. As it was her day off she decided to go and find him. She went to the restaurant where he worked first. Henry was there but no sign of Jacob. He spotted Alice and acknowledged her and after serving one of the tables he went over to her.

'Hi Alice, how are you?' he said cheerfully. Perhaps Jacob hasn't said anything to him, Alice thought.

'I'm okay thanks. Is Jacob working today?'

'No, he's taken the day off. I was happy to cover for him as we're never busy on a Monday.'

'Right, okay.'

'I'm surprised he's not with you? Or do you have to work later?'

'No, it's my day off too,' she said and realised what he might deduce. 'Thanks,' she added and turned to leave.

'Everything all right with you two?' Henry asked. Alice turned back and looked at him not sure if she should say anything.

'Fine thanks.' She decided not to spill. Henry looked at her knowingly but didn't say anything.

Birch poked his head round Katie's study door when he arrived that morning. The first thing she noticed was that he hadn't shaved, possibly for a couple of days. He also looked very tired.

'Hi,' he said simply.

'Hi.' There was a pause while Katie wondered why he was saying hello to her as normally he went straight upstairs to start work. 'Okay?' she asked with a sympathetic tone.

Birch sighed and then pursed his lips. 'Bloody marvellous actually,' he said almost laughing apologetically and then he added, 'sorry, I can see you're working, I'll get out of your way.' He disappeared and Katie heard his heavy footsteps on the stairs. Before she had time to reflect on the incident her mobile phone rang. It was not a number she recognised.

'Katie Green,' she said.

'Ah, Katie, yes good. My name's Stephen Cardell. Harry Liversage gave me your number. I know him through our breakfast networking meeting. Saw him this morning as a matter of fact. He said you're a virtual assistant.' He cantered through his introduction alarming Katie somewhat.

'Yes, that's right.' Katie tried to hide her astonishment. She didn't feel anywhere near ready for this and felt like asking him to call back in a month's time but then she remembered her desperate need for money.

'Yes, well the thing is, I'm a business coach and I've just got so busy that I need some help with my admin. So, organising my diary, booking appointments and taking calls for me. Is that the sort of thing you do?'

'Er, yes! Yes, I can help you with that.'

'Excellent. And you're in Highgate village, Harry tells me.'

'That's right.' Katie was wondering what would come next.

'Shall we meet up to discuss this in more detail?'

'Yes, I think that would be best.' She grabbed a notepad and pen and wrote down his name. 'Do you know Fegos?'

'Yes, I could be there in an hour if that would suit you?'

Katie was taken aback by the pace this guy was going but at the same time she was really excited. He might be her first client.

'Well actually I could do that,' she said, running her hands through her hair and wondering what she would wear.

'Great. Well I'm sure we'll find each other.'

Jacob wouldn't answer the intercom for his flat. Alice was feeling desperate, almost tearful. Perhaps he was out and she should wait until he came back but that could be hours. Perhaps she should write a note and post it through his letterbox but that seemed a bit silly as he had ignored all her text messages. She sat on the low wall bordering the row of shabby terraced houses facing the street and sighed. Just then the front door opened behind her abruptly and she turned around to see a woman smartly dressed like an air hostess and carrying a small case.

She looked at Alice quizzically and asked, 'you okay?'

'Yes. Well...' her despondency showed in her voice.

'Is that, well *no*?' the woman asked rather directly.

'Oh it's just that I want to see Jacob. He lives at flat c and he's not answering his doorbell.'

'Yes, that's right, I saw you with him the other day.' The woman looked thoughtful. 'I tell you what why don't I let you in then you can go up to his flat and knock on his door. I'm pretty sure he's in, I've heard noises.'

Alice's heart lifted. 'Oh would you? Thanks! That would be great.'

Alice went up the stairs and stood outside Jacob's flat. She knocked gently and called his name.

'Jacob, it's me. Alice. I just want to talk to you.' She didn't raise her voice too much; she didn't want to make a scene. Nothing. A few moments passed. More nothing. Alice knocked again and then louder she called, 'Jacob, it's me. *Please* come to the door!'

She heard a scuffling sound and then footsteps and then the door opened and Jacob appeared looking unkempt, his hair dishevelled but he was still handsome in Alice's eyes.

'I'm sorry,' she said. 'I'm so sorry. Can I come in?'

Fegos was quite empty and Katie positioned herself at a table so that she was facing the door. Remarkably she was two minutes early despite a mad rush to change her outfit and then change again. She had looked at her trousers, blouse and non-matching jacket and thought this will have to do as she pulled a brush through her hair, put on some lipstick and rushed out of the house. As soon as she'd shut the front door she had realised she didn't have her notepad with her and was riffling through her handbag for her keys and thinking she must have forgotten those too. She rang the doorbell. Twice. The second time more persistently. Eventually Birch appeared looking confused at the very moment Katie pulled her keys out of her bag.

'Sorry, couldn't find these,' she said waving her keys around.

'No problem.' Birch said. 'Are you coming or going?'

'Going mad I think!' She composed herself. 'I'm just on my way out actually!'

She rushed into her study, grabbed her writing pad and shoved it into her handbag, deciding it was wholly unsuitable for client meetings but would have to do.

Birch looked even more muddled.

'Back later,' Katie said and flew out the door and down the street.

Stephen walked straight over to Katie with an air of confidence and Katie suddenly realised that this might be like an interview and felt a little anxious. She stood up and received his firm hand shake.
'Katie Green?'
'Yes, good to meet you.'
'Thanks for doing this at short notice. I'm really desperate to get someone on board to organise all my client appointments and seminars and well *me* really! Harry tells me you have experience of being a PA in the City?'
'Yes, that's right. A few years ago now but I worked for the CEO of Henderson Investments at one stage.'
'You sound perfect. Now if I may, I'd like to take you through my requirements so you can get started asap.'
Katie had her pen to the ready.
'Oh I suppose we should discuss your rate first,' he added. 'Do you have an hourly rate?'
'Yes, it's twenty-eight pounds an hour unless you have thirty or more hours a month in which case I would put you on a retainer fee.' Katie was so pleased she had done her homework on this point. She'd even emailed Nancy in America to ask for her advice.
'That sounds fine,' he said and before Katie knew it, she was taking her first brief.

Jacob handed Alice a mug of instant coffee and they sat down together on his sofa. Alice smiled at him with her lips closed.
'So,' Jacob said eventually, 'what's there to talk about?'
Alice frowned. 'I really like you Jacob. I mean, well it's more than that, I'm in love with you and I don't want to lose you and well... I've been thinking.'
'About moving in with me?' Jacob brightened a little.

'Yes, about that. The thing is, it's true what I said about my mum but now she's setting herself up as a VA and she's got a lodger I'm thinking it wouldn't hurt if I stayed here some of the time. Maybe semi move in and just go home for the odd night?'

Jacob smiled. 'Sounds like a plan,' he said and then he was thoughtful. 'So what about your A-level re-sit and the uni business?'

'Well,' Alice straightened her spine, 'I've been thinking about that too and...'

'You've decided you'd much rather be a waitress all your life!' Jacob had a cheeky grin on his face.

She laughed a little even though it wasn't funny. 'Not exactly. I am doing the re-sit and I do want to go to uni, at least I think I do. And what I was thinking was that we could still stay together while I was at uni. We could just see each other when we can, during the holidays and the odd weekend.'

Jacob looked surprised. 'Wow! That sounds serious.'

Alice was annoyed. She felt as if she had bared her soul and she was now vulnerable. 'Isn't moving in together serious?' she asked managing to maintain a passive tone.

'Yeah, of course.' He moved towards her and put his arms around her. 'Actually, I don't know why I said that because I do feel serious about you.' They kissed, a long slow kiss.

'You know we don't have to decide anything else until next September,' she said.

'Yes, you're right.' He looked like he'd won the lottery for a moment. 'So are you really going to semi move in with me?'

'Yes! I said yes, didn't I?'

Katie was feeling really pleased with herself when she got home. The meeting with Stephen went very well. She made a note to call Harry and thank him for the referral. She wandered into the kitchen and noticed it was very tidy and just as she had left it earlier that day which meant that Birch probably had not been in there for any reason. Their chats over afternoon tea had stopped abruptly after their evening out and that kiss. This was partly because Katie had deployed avoidance tactics and also because even when she was home, he didn't come downstairs.

She decided to grab a glass of water and go back to the study and start the work she had to do for her first client while it was all fresh in her mind. There were a lot of meetings to organise and she needed to create processes to manage this client effectively. It was all beginning to come back to her from her days in the City; the need for attention to detail and systems to ensure nothing was ever missed. As she worked she was thankful for the distraction.

Birch had re-read what he wrote on Sunday and changed a lot of it. He'd found it hard to focus at home even though he had been alone all weekend with no interruptions. His mind kept wandering off in different directions. He had re-played the last conversation with Celia on the phone over and over even though the message had been straightforward; there was nothing to analyse. He also thought back over his evening out with Katie and then reminded himself of the resounding fact that this woman was a widow of just a few months. Equally he could not deny his feelings for her and how much he enjoyed her company. He also had a strong suspicion that she felt the same way.

He forced himself to write another thousand words and read them back to himself. It was rubbish. He had lost his touch. He couldn't do it anymore. He looked out of the window and saw that it had stopped raining and the sun was coming through. He thought about going for a walk in the park. But then the last time he had done that he was reeling from the shocking revelation his wife had revealed to him and hurting badly, trying to make sense of it all. Would he be able to walk through the park today and find solace?

He snapped his laptop shut. It was no good. He picked up his mobile phone and found the number of one of his favourite restaurants, a French place in Primrose Hill, and pressed the call button.

Katie had completed the set-up she needed to do for her first client but she had a couple of questions. She was feeling much more confident now and decided to give him a call. He answered after just one ring.

'Katie! How's it going?'

'Very well thank you Stephen. I've put all the systems I need in place to manage your work...'

'Wow, that's impressive.'

'I just have a couple of questions about the dates for the monthly seminars.'

'Ah yes, they're always on the second Tuesday of the month so you can plan ahead.'

'Great. And at the same venue?'

'Yes, but can you check with them that they have all the dates because sometimes they can be a bit shoddy about diary keeping?'

'Of course.'

'Fantastic. I'm so pleased to have you on board Katie. It's such a load off my mind.'

'Thanks Stephen.'

'Call anytime.'

Katie sat back in her chair and smiled to herself. I can do this, she thought, I really can do this!

Just then Birch appeared with a tray, on it a pot of tea, a cup and saucer, a small vase with a few rich orange crocosmia in it (from her garden, but still...) and one of her favourite cookies. He found space on her desk and laid it down. 'Afternoon tea Madam,' he said in a butler-like voice and smiled at her.

'Oh Birch, this is nice. I was just about to make some tea.' His presence made her a little nervous since their evening out.

'Well I can see you've been busy. Your business empire building begins!'

'Hardly,' Katie laughed. 'But actually, I have just taken on my first client,' she added with her excitement revealing itself in her voice.

'Brilliant! Oh Katie, well done you!' He scratched his head and looked a little uneasy and then he said, 'It's a good excuse to go out and celebrate, don't you think?'

'I'd love to but I need to get paid first.'

'Well actually I have a dinner reservation at my favourite French restaurant in Primrose Hill... and no one to go with so far.'

'Oh,' Katie wasn't expecting this, 'another restaurant review?'

'Well... actually...' Birch was almost hopping from foot to foot now and looking slightly embarrassed, 'no.'

She was puzzled.

He continued, 'The thing is that I've had a dreadful weekend and well,' there was a pause before he went, 'I'd like to take you out to dinner.' He looked down to the floor his hand stroking the stubble round his jaw. 'I'll shave, of course, and smarten up. I've let myself go a bit in the last few days.'

Katie had a resounding feeling that something significant was going on and asked gently, 'what's happened Birch?'

'Celia's left me for another man,' he said simply and quickly but unable to disguise the hurt in his voice.

'Goodness!'

'Yes, it's a bit of a shock but I've had a few days to think about it. You see... it hasn't been the happiest of marriages in recent years.'

'Right.' Katie's mind was whirring with all sorts of scary thoughts.

'The thing is,' he sighed deeply, 'the thing is I like you and well...' Looking straight at her he said, 'the truth is... I can't write today anyway!'

Katie laughed. 'Oh Birch!'

'Will you join me for dinner?'

She wondered how she could possibly say no. 'Yes! Yes, I will!'

'Ohhh...' His heart lifted. 'Thank you.'

'But the girls must not know,' she added switching to a serious tone.

They looked at each other. She wasn't going to renege on this point.

'Of course, if that's what you want.'

Chapter 29

Bethan was hovering at Matt's desk. Matt was an account manager at Web Dreams which she understood was quite high up in the agency.

'Sorry.' She waited for him to acknowledge her which he barely did. 'Sorry to disturb but do you know anything about the website brief for the cup cake company?'

'Er...' Matt had big brown eyes, translucent skin and soft brown curls and Bethan thought he looked like a young film star. 'Short answer no,' he said looking up from his work briefly, and then quickly added, 'but what's your question? I might be able to help.'

'Right, well thanks. The thing is they want to show their range of cupcakes but I don't have any photos of them yet, just a few names, like,' she looked down at the paper she was holding, 'classic vanilla and... chocolate passion.'

'Oh, I see. Well you could just do placeholders for now for the images with the names on.'

'Oh, okay.' Bethan thought that wouldn't look very good when the website design was presented to the client. 'What about if I find some photos of cupcakes from another website and put them in for now?'

'You could,' he said glancing at her briefly.

'Cool,' she said and sidled backwards. 'Thanks,' she added and made her way back to the safety of her own desk. She looked again at the brief she had. There was a name and phone number for the client and, in a moment of bravery, she decided to call it.

'Hi, er, this is Bethan from Web Dreams.' She felt weird saying that; it was only her fifth day and she was still on trial.

'Oh, hi Bethan, you'll be wanting to speak to Carol,' the man said and then added, 'I'll hand you over.'

'Thanks.'

'Hi, Carol here.'

'Hi, I hope you don't mind me calling but I was just wondering if you have any photos of your cup cakes? I mean the ones you want on your website.'

'Oh yes, I told Paul I was going to get some for you. Didn't he say?'

'I see. No problem.'

'Thanks for reminding me anyway.' Carol sounded friendly. 'I shall get them over to you later today.'

'Would you like to send them directly to me?'

Katie was finding it very difficult to concentrate on her work. Daisy had sent her a link to her new Virtual Magic website for her to check over and she was totally unable to focus on the screen so she decided to print out each page. Her printer made a lot of whirring noises for a couple of minutes but failed to print anything. There was an error message but no way of getting rid of it. Exasperated she decided to re-boot her computer and anything else that would re-boot and sat back in her chair and waited for it all to open up again. She looked idly at a schedule for Stephen's coaching clients that was lying on her desk and realised he had a new one starting later that day, a Mark Tierney, and she hadn't had his coaching questionnaire forms back that he was supposed to complete. Stephen had been very particular in his brief about him having at least a few hours to read through his clients' answers before a session. She found the phone number she had for Mark.

'Hello, Katie here, Stephen Cardell's assistant.'

'Hi Katie, oh it's this afternoon isn't it?' He sounded as if he had forgotten about the call, let alone the forms.

'Yes, have you completed the questionnaire I sent you?'

'Oh damn! I knew there was something.'

'Would you do it now, please? And email it through to me?'

'Yes, of course. It's just quite difficult you know, all a bit soul searching for me.' And then for an unfathomable reason he asked, 'have *you* done it?'

Katie frowned as she smiled. 'No, I'm his VA.' It occurred to her that after the events of the last few days, she was doing enough soul searching without answering questions about her own goals in life.

'Right okay, I'll have a go,' he said and Katie wasn't convinced he was going to do it.

'Just do what you can and email it through in, shall we say an hour?'

'An hour?' He sounded horrified.

'Yes, Mark, an hour so that Stephen has it three hours before your call.' She remembered this assertive tone from her office days. Never forget who you're working for was her motto then, and she seemed to be adopting it now.

'Yes, of course,' he said.

'Thank you.'

Katie had just managed to get back to her website when a text appeared from Birch.

How's it going? X

In a moment of great resolve, she decided to leave it. She must focus on her work; it was vital that she started making some money. The last time she had looked at her bank account there was very little left. Luckily Alice was contributing to the household budget and now Bethan was working she would at least be able to fund her own social life. The stress of her financial situation threw her mind back to the romantic evening she had spent with Birch at the French Bistro. It had been an oasis of luxury, an indulgence that she dared not consider the consequences of.

She had had to lie to her daughters before making her escape. Luckily Alice was working and then staying at Jacob's place so that made life easier. Bethan was full of her new job and seemed to be enjoying it, much to Katie's relief, and she was arriving home exhausted each evening and more interested in slouching in front of the television than anything else. The lie she had concocted was that she was going out with Julia which, while rather lame, seemed like the easiest way forward.

'You're seeing a lot of Julia these days,' Bethan said with her eyes fixed on her phone and the added distraction of Big Brother on the television.

'Yes, well, Daisy's helping me with my website and...'

'I thought Daisy came round this morning?'

'Yes, that's right.' Katie decided she would go and get ready and sneak out without saying goodbye, that way she would avoid any more difficult questions. 'Anyway, there's left over risotto in the fridge if you want it.'

'Okay Mum.' Bethan looked up at her with a quizzical face now and Katie immediately felt a pang of guilt. 'See you later.' Bethan was back to the text message she was composing.

When she was finally sitting opposite Birch in the restaurant it felt like this was forbidden fruit territory. Katie's mind was oscillating from admonishment to what-the-hell and Birch sensed the turmoil she was in. He reached across and stroked her hand.

'Are we really so wicked?'

Katie thought about it. 'Julia thinks not. Go and enjoy yourself, she said to me. She even said she would cover for me if the girls were suspicious.'

'I like Julia and she's right, you should enjoy yourself, after all you've done nothing wrong.' He poured more wine into her glass and lifted his glass to meet hers, 'to us,' he said deliberately.

The food they ate was outstanding and once they both relaxed, they were perfect company for each other. Katie found herself opening up about all the recent ups and downs of the last few months, because it felt safe and she knew he was on her side. She even talked about her marriage to David and Birch was interested and had empathy for her late husband.

'And Bethan...' She stopped herself, deciding this was a subject to avoid this evening.

'What were you going to say?'

'It doesn't matter.'

'That usually means it does matter.'

'No, it really doesn't. I've decided I'm not going to let my daughters spoil the evening.'

'I'll second that,' he said with a wry smile.

It could have ended after the meal, after coffee. She could have gone home and convinced herself that they were just good friends and so she didn't need to feel guilty. They got a taxi and sat side by side, him caressing her hand. She could smell his pungent aftershave which had warm spicy notes. This time the car drew up at Birch's home first. 'Would you like to come in?'

'Don't be silly,' Katie said but didn't want to part from him.

'Celia's still at Alastair's. Just coffee?'

She suddenly felt madly attracted to him. 'Okay,' she said quietly.

He paid the taxi driver and as soon as they were inside they came together like magnets. He embraced her and kissed her over and over. They stopped only to rush upstairs, him leading the way and then made love ardently, like two lovers who had been kept apart for too long and the climax was such a relief. There would be no more pretence; their feelings for each other were strong and spoken.

After, he held her and they must have both fallen into a deep sleep because the next thing Katie remembered was waking up in a strange bed. It was three in the morning. She found her clothes and her handbag in the dark and stumbled to the bathroom. She got dressed and came out and there was Birch standing there in just his underpants.

'Are you okay? He took her into his arms. 'Why are you dressed?'

'I have to go home!' she whispered loudly.

'Oh, if you must,' he said and turned back to the bedroom. 'Wait a minute, I'll walk you home.'

'It's okay, it's not far,' she said but she didn't mean it. She wanted him to go with her.

'Don't be silly; I won't hear of it.'

Seconds later he had thrown some clothes on and they went out into the night again. They held hands and smiled at each other. There was no need to say anything. When they were nearing number 12 Katie stopped. 'I'd better leave you here.'

'Yes, I suspect Bethan has rigged up a surveillance camera outside your home. You can't be too careful.'

Katie laughed. 'Oh Birch,' she said with adoring eyes.

'Goodnight,' he said and kissed her once more. She turned and went up to her own front door. A quick glance back, he was waiting until she was safely inside; her lodger, now her lover.

Katie shook herself back to reality. So much for her determination to press on with her work, she thought. She might as well reply to the text.

Finding it difficult to concentrate. Any good at proof reading?

She knew it was dangerous to ask that question but the words just fell out. This man was her secret escape from an otherwise complicated world. She had just managed to print the first page out when Birch appeared at her door.

'What are you proof reading?'

'My new website.' She handed him the print out as she stifled a yawn.

'Bit tired?' he asked with a grin on his face. He grabbed a chair next to hers and stole a kiss before studying the print out.

She slapped his hand lightly, 'I've told you, we must be careful!'

He laughed and then turned to her computer monitor. 'This is good, isn't it? I like it. When's your advert out?'

'Next week, so it's got to be *live* then. That's Daisy's term, not mine!'

'Okay, why don't you print the rest out and I'll read through it all.'

'Birch that's really kind but what about your writing?'

'Well, amazingly, I've managed a thousand half decent words today already. Not enough, of course. Henry was on the phone earlier asking me for an e.t.a. for the first draft. I must admit my mind went blank. I was tempted to say some time next year but that wouldn't have gone down well.'

'No, especially as he wants it by the beginning of November,' Katie reminded him.

'Exactly. Anyway he wants to have lunch with me tomorrow down in Covent Garden so I'll have to make something up before then!'

They laughed simultaneously like young lovers playing truant; how easily they had gelled together and how arduous it was for Katie to live with such a guilty secret.

Paul Costelloe burst from his office door. 'Bethan!' he shouted across the room. Bethan felt something heavy in her stomach. She looked round to face him.

'Bethan, have you got a minute?' His eyebrows arched up.

'Yes, yes of course.' She walked obediently into his office and stood opposite him.

'Sit down,' he said and he sat too.

'Listen, I've just had a call from Carol, Mrs cup-cake herself.'

'Oh!' Bethan wished she hadn't called her, what a silly mistake to make. She should know her place. Matt hadn't suggested it. Why did she do it?

'She's very impressed with you.' Paul said simply and his eyes widened.

'Oh.' Bethan wished she hadn't said that again.

'Yes, she said you've shown initiative.'

'Oh good.' Bethan's shoulders dropped to where they normally reside. 'Great, cool,' she added.

'Yes, anyway..' Paul looked down at his desk and shuffled some papers around apparently for no reason. He looked up. 'It's the end of your trial week and basically, we'd love you to stay and do your apprenticeship.'

'Oh good.' The relief was immense.

'Have you settled in okay? Everyone being helpful I hope?'

'Yes, yes, it's all fine.' She had spent the week trying to fit in and making sure she did everything she was told. She had decided by the end of her second day that she wanted to make a go of it; they were a young team and seemed to have some fun together along the way.

'Good, well that's all good then.' He smiled at her and she smiled too.

'Listen, we tend to go to The Flask on a Friday about sixish, first round on me, just an end of the week kind of thing; it would be good if you joined us.'

'Yes, I'd like to.'

'Good. Well done Bethan.'

It was ten past six and most of the agency had headed off to the pub. Matt wandered over to Bethan's desk and stood there looking at her properly for the first time. She could feel his eyes on her.

'Coming to the pub?'

'Yes, okay,' she replied. 'I'll just shut my computer down.'

'No rush,' he said. 'I'll wait for you.'

'Thanks.' Bethan was pleased to be going with someone and not walking into The Flask on her own. Their eyes met and he smiled at her.

'I hear you're staying on. That's good.'

Chapter 30

Alice was tired after her shift at The Lemon Tree and was pleased to be going home at six o'clock. Jacob had sent a text earlier to say he was working late and she was looking forward to some home cooking and a night in. She poked her head round what had become her mother's study door.

'Hi Mum.'

'Hi Alice.' Katie's eyes were fixed on her screen; she seemed to be deep in thought.

'Mum!' Alice raised her voice as she vied for her attention.

Katie frowned as she turned to look at her daughter.

'What is it, darling?'

'When's supper? I'm starving.'

'Oh, I don't know; I'll have to look in the fridge,' she said vaguely.

'Great!' Alice said sarcastically, feeling somewhat aggrieved.

Katie stood up now. 'Listen, why don't we both look in the fridge and decide.'

'If we have to.'

Alice was staring at a few vegetables, half a packet of cheddar cheese and two eggs.

'God Mum, there isn't even enough for *another*,' her voice dragged for emphasis, 'omelette!'

'Sorry, darling. I'll maybe pop down to the shop in a bit; although I haven't really got any money. I don't suppose you've got some?'

'So, I have to do the food shop now? I'm not even living here half the time; this is ridiculous!'

Katie sighed. 'Leave it to me; I'll sort something out,' she said and went back to her study leaving Alice bewildered.

Ross was surprised when Elaine had agreed to meet him for a meal at The Flask on her day off. He was sat alone at a table for two, nicely tucked into one corner of the restaurant and carefully positioned away from the door to the kitchen or the one for the toilets. He looked at his watch. He was still early, now ten minutes early. He had already read the menu and decided what he would order. Feeling rather warm he took his jacket off and sat there in his t-shirt but then he had a change of heart and put the jacket back on again as he thought he looked smarter with it on. He was trying to achieve a smart casual look and it didn't really work without the jacket.

Elaine came through the door and looked around. She spotted Ross and went over, her pace quickening and a broad smile on her face.

'Am I late?' She looked at her watch.

'No, no, it's me, I'm early!'

'Oh okay, that's all right then.' She was wearing smart jeans and a red tunic which set off her short chestnut hair and emphasised the redder streaks she had.

He handed her a menu. 'I've already chosen,' he confessed.

'Right.' Elaine scanned the menu and then put it down. 'Actually, I've eaten here before. The sausage and mash is really good so I'll plump for that again even though it's boring.'

'Well you might as well have what you want,' he said. 'And as a matter of fact that's what I'm having too. Shall we have a bottle of red with it?'

Alice was staring at the takeaway food with amazement. 'I don't understand it; how come we can suddenly afford take-aways but our allowance has been stopped and I am forced to contribute to the household budget?'

'Birch paid for it,' Katie said in a tone suggesting she was not inviting further comment on it.

'Oh! So, he's eating with us now, is he?'

'No,' Katie said quietly, 'no he's not.'

'Well why the bloody hell has he paid for it then?'

'Don't swear!' Katie paused for a moment and composed herself. 'He'll take it out of next month's rent money,' she said, knowing he wouldn't, but she would say anything to keep the peace. Alice opened her mouth to protest further but Bethan walked in.

'Something smells good,' Bethan said. 'Is that a Chinese take-away?'

'Yes, it is.' Katie started putting cutlery on the table and took some plates out of the oven. 'Now, shall we sit down to eat?'

Alice pulled a chair out noisily and plonked herself down, a deep frown of disapproval etched into her forehead.

'What's wrong with you?' her sister asked.

'Nothing!' she said loudly and as if the whole world was against her.

'Shall we enjoy this now?' Katie said looking pointedly at both her daughters. 'It's a long time since we had a Chinese take-away, isn't it?'

Alice sulked and Bethan tucked in. 'Thanks for getting a veggie dish Mum, ooh and prawns, yummy.'

'Prawns are not veggie,' Alice said confirming her bad mood, as if she needed to.

'Lots of vegetarians eat fish,' Katie said and Bethan looked at her sister as if she was the elder of the two, certainly the more grown up at this moment in time.

'How was work today?' Katie asked no one in particular.

Bethan replied. 'It was good. We did the presentation to Carol for her cup cake website and she really liked it.'

'And did you design it?' Katie asked.

'Yes, I had some help but it was basically my design.'

'Well done you! How's it going at The Lemon Tree?' Katie made a point of asking Alice.

'It's all right.' Alice stared at her plate as she wound a noodle onto her fork. 'I might... leave soon.'

'Oh really? Why's that?' Katie was pleased that Bethan had asked that and not her.

'Well I'm doing my A-level re-sit so I'm going to have to do some study.'

'I'm sure you can find time for both,' Katie said and then added, 'we need the money at the moment.'

'But that's just not fair! Anyway, you're going to be earning soon. You've already got your first client.'

'Yes, I am but the money won't come in for a while, I'll be billing monthly, and anyway it won't be enough.'

'Oh great, so I'm expected to support all three of us! What about Bethan, she's earning now!'

'Minimum wage!' Bethan raised her voice.

'Oh, and what do you think I'm earning waitressing? Slightly more than the minimum wage!'

'Listen,' Katie tried to calm everything down, 'we all need to pull together at the moment. What little money we had left has just about gone...' her speech met two incredulous faces, '...and so until I've got a full practice of clients on board, you're going to have to help me out. Anyway, as long as you're living at home I don't see why you shouldn't contribute, do you?'

'Oh marvellous, so does that mean *I* have to pay you as well?' Bethan asked.

'It's not *paying me*; it's contributing to the food we all eat and the bills for running this house!' Katie was trying not to lose her temper.

'Well I think it sucks!' Bethan said angrily. 'I've had virtually no money from you since Dad died and now you're saying I've got to *pay* to live in my own *home!*'

Katie took a deep breath. Alice pushed her plate away from her and announced, 'I'm moving out actually. I'm moving in with Jacob so I won't be contributing anymore.'

Katie felt like crying and decided she couldn't eat any more either.

'I thought you said you were only semi moving in with Jacob,' Bethan piped up.

'Well, yes I am, but I'm sure it could be permanent. Jacob wants me to live with him.'

'You've only known him a few months; don't you think it's a bit rash to move in with him?' Katie resorted to becoming the voice of reason.

'No! No I don't think it is! Anyway…' The red on Alice's neck spread up to her cheeks as she stood up fuming, 'it's got to be better than living here!' She stomped out of the kitchen and up to her room.

'Oh great,' Bethan said acerbically, 'so that just leaves me. How much do *I* have to give you, just so I can *eat* in my own home?'

Ross re-filled Elaine's glass.

'Ooh not too much! I've got to work tomorrow… and I'm sure I'm talking too much. I must have given you most of my life history by now!'

'Don't be silly. Anyway, I'm interested.' Ross put the bottle of wine down.

'Mm.' She sounded sceptical. 'Anyway, what about you? Your turn to spill the beans.'

'Ah…' It occurred to Ross at that moment that his was not a pretty story. Of course he'd known that all along and at least he had discovered that Elaine had some baggage: a divorce behind her, a six year old daughter and she lived with her mother as it made it easier to hold down a job. Elaine was waiting and trying to get his attention.

'Hey, it can't be that bad,' she said.

'No, well,' Ross sighed, 'at least I'm doing all right now with My Mag.'

'And?' she stared at him with her big hazel eyes.

'Okay, here goes.' Ross took a large gulp of wine.

Katie sat alone in her living room. The television was on but she wasn't watching it. She sipped some coffee wishing she had poured herself a glass of wine. Her thoughts turned to David and how he had always spoiled his daughters; nothing was too much money or too much trouble for his little angels. His answer to any of their problems was to throw money at it. He often gave them fifty quid to cheer them up for the slightest reason. 'Buy yourself a new dress,' or thirty quid for a day out; 'go and enjoy yourselves,' he'd say. Was it any wonder that they were selfish and struggling to deal with today's reality. And, of course, it was David who had left her in this financial mess. Up until his untimely death she was living oblivious to the facts and thinking, what with the rent from the York house, and the mortgage paid off well before David was due to retire, money would never be an issue for them. She had felt safe and secure in that knowledge; that knowledge which turned out to be a lie.

She was crying now and let the tears come, reaching for a tissue to dry her face. All evening she had held it together; she didn't want to cry in front of her daughters, she wanted to be strong. Just then her phone bleeped and there was a message from Birch.

Hi Katie, sitting here and thinking about you so I've come up with an idea. What about a day trip to Sandgate; fabulous antique shop and lunch by the sea? We will wear dark glasses and head gear to avoid being spotted. What do you think? B x

It brought a smile to Katie's face, even a murmur of a laugh. She blew her nose and thought how lucky she was to have found him.

Fabulous idea. I need cheering up actually. Dreadful row with both daughters; will tell more tomorrow. Total fall out. Which day for trip? K x

Oh no! Must be soon then; how about Friday? B x

Perfect! K x

Until then, don't worry about the girls. All teenagers are frightful so they tell me. Be happy for me. B x

Katie was touched by his understanding. She decided she would spend the rest of the evening in bed, and this time she would watch one of her favourite programmes on her ipad until she fell asleep. Her daughters could wallow in self-pity if they wanted to.

Chapter 31

Harry insisted on buying Katie lunch.

'It's just The Flask, I thought we should have a catch up,' he had said.

Katie put on a coral tunic, dark leggings and brown knee length leather boots. It was an ensemble she hadn't worn before even though all the items were from her wardrobe. It was the sort of outfit that, in the past, she would have thought made her look older for trying to look younger. Today she looked at herself in the mirror and was pleased with what she saw. She felt younger; she felt great; she was falling in love.

It was a lovely autumnal day with a bright blue sky and the trees were colouring the landscape beautifully. She decided to walk to the village and when she arrived at The Flask she looked around for Harry but couldn't see him. Just then he appeared behind her somewhat breathless.

'Sorry, Katie, sorry I'm late.'

Katie looked at her watch. 'You're not, I've just got here.'

'Oh good,' Harry said and then, 'you look well!' He smiled at her.

'Thank you,' she said, even more pleased with her chosen attire.

He found them a table and ordered drinks in his usual efficient manner before turning his attention to Katie.

'So, how are things with you?'

'Good,' Katie said unequivocally and realised she meant it. 'Life is not without its challenges,' she added thinking about her daughters' maddening behaviour, 'but I'm pleased with the progress I've made with my VA business.'

'Oh good. Excellent. Actually, I spoke with Stephen just this morning. He said you're a marvel and doing exceptionally well. He says he's never been so organised!'

'That's great. I'm so pleased I'm doing a good job. It's funny, but even though it's a long time since I've done this sort of thing, I seem to have fallen into my old ways easily and it's all come back to me.'

'Well done you,' Harry said sitting tall and trying to catch the eye of a waiter. 'Now, let's get the menu bit over with and then I have an update for you on your investment,' he said tapping his laptop.

Birch emerged from the tube at Leicester Square and walked up to Browns Bar and Restaurant with a spring in his step. It was lovely to feel the sun on his face and he always enjoyed the busy and fun atmosphere of Covent Garden. He reflected on recent events and was amazed at how easily he had adapted to life without Celia. He was now free to do all the things she didn't like him doing and, of course, it was a green light for his relationship with Katie. Every time he thought about her a grin spread across his face and his eyes glinted. He got to Browns about ten minutes after he was supposed to meet Henry and considered that not too bad. His publisher was sitting in front of a kentia palm looking relaxed in his colonial surroundings and taking in the menu.

'Henry! Good to see you.' They shook hands.

'Yes,' Henry grimaced, 'reliably late as usual.'

'Oh, just a little.' Birch sat down and picked up a menu.

'I'm having the special,' Henry said almost as if he expected Birch to have the same.

Birch looked at the specials board. 'The steak?'

'Yes.'

'I think I'll have the fish.' Birch was thinking it was the healthier option.

'There's a first.' He looked enquiringly at Birch and then said, 'you look different. In fact, you look like a kid in a sweet shop! What's going on?'

'Celia's left me,' he said almost cheerfully.
Henry was taken aback. 'And that is good because?'

Harry was showing Katie some performance figures for the funds he had invested her five thousand pounds in.

'You see they've all done pretty well over five years.'

Katie was trying to stop her eyes glazing over but struggling. 'But you only invested my money three months ago.'

'Ah yes, so I have the overall performance since the day I bought the shares and it's up twelve percent.'

'That sounds impressive,' Katie sat back in her chair. 'It's funny isn't it, I never used to be superstitious in any way; all a lot of mumbo jumbo I thought. But I can't stop remembering the name of the horse that David bet on the day he died, Forever Lucky. It was that horse that won me the money. And I know it's purely coincidence but we live at number 12.'

Harry laughed. 'Thank goodness you don't live at number 42!'

'Don't be silly!' Katie giggled. 'And do you recommend I leave it where it is?'

'Absolutely! Your shares are growing nicely. Don't worry, I'll keep you up to speed.' He was looking straight at Katie. 'You did say you were in this for the long term?'

'Oh yes, until I retire, anyway.' Then she smiled to herself. 'That sounds funny to me. You see it was always until David retired and I only did voluntary work.'

'Well that's all changed now,' Harry said gently.

'It certainly has.'

'How's Bethan getting on?'

'She's really enjoying that job at Web Dreams. We can't thank you enough for that.'

'Oh good. Yes, I spoke to Paul the other day. And how's the lodger, Birch, is it?'

'A life saver,' Katie replied without hesitation as her face lit up. 'I mean in terms of the rent covering the mortgage.'

'Yes, very sensible solution.' Harry's eyes sparkled as he smiled back at her.

'So you're having an affair with your landlady, which her daughters don't know about, and you wonder why you're distracted from your writing?!' Henry topped up both their glasses.

'It was Celia! She was the one that dropped the bombshell that she's been having an affair for a whole year and was leaving me! "We've got a lot to talk about," she had the audacity to say to me.' He mocked her voice. 'Huh!'

'The thing is, Birch, we really want this in the shops before Christmas and it's not looking good, is it?'

'Don't worry. It will be fine. I will get it to you by mid-November.'

'Listen mate, I do understand and I appreciate you're having a difficult time. How about you hand over what you've done so far to the editor so she can get started?'

Birch thought about this. Did he want to go back and change anything? 'Well, yes, but let me have a final read through and check it's all there or there abouts and then I'll send you what I've got.'

'Sounds good.' Henry seemed satisfied but then he said, 'so when can you send the first lot over?'

Birch considered the next few days. He was taking Katie to Sandgate and nothing would get in the way of that but his weekends were pretty empty these days so he could do it then. 'I'll send it over next week.'

'Great. Monday?' Henry asked looking hopeful.

'Thursday.' Birch said emphatically. A waiter came over with their bill and hesitated, looking for a sign that one of them was willing to pay it, before placing it in the middle of the table.

'Henry's paying.' Birch sat back in his chair.

Henry laughed and picked up the bill. He looked at his dining companion in a considered way.

'You know I think this change in your life, I think it's going to be a change for the better.'

Birch looked puzzled. 'Why's that then?'

'You've got more fight about you, more energy; you always seemed a bit deflated before. Well, in recent years anyway.'

The phone was ringing as Katie arrived home. She took her jacket off and flung it over the newel post before diving in to her study. The answer machine had already clicked in and Nancy was talking to her. She grabbed the handset, 'Nancy! Sorry about that, just got in.'

'Katie! I'm so pleased I've caught you. I hope you don't mind me phoning you on your home line? I got it from Harry.'

'Not at all, it's lovely to hear from you.'

'Oh thanks. How's it going?'

'Well pretty good actually. I've got my first client and my website is now up and running.'

'Brilliant!

'How are things with you?' Katie wondered why she was calling, had Harry prompted her.

'Well good also, yeah, actually that's kinda why I'm phoning.'

'Oh?'

'Yes, it's nothing bad, don't worry.'

Katie sat on her chair at her desk and braced herself. 'Okay.'

'The thing is, Harry doesn't know this, but I'm seven months pregnant.'

'How wonderful.'

'Yes, I am pleased. Elliot has always wanted a playmate. But the thing is, I'm expecting twins!'

'How lovely.' Katie thought that twins would have finished her off.

'Yeah, yes it is, but I'm gonna have my hands full! Anyway, I've managed my work with childcare up until now but I've decided to take a year out from about when they're born, maybe a little earlier if I get much bigger.'

'Yes, I can totally understand that.'

'So, I was wondering how you would feel about taking Harry on as one of your clients?'

'Gosh! Er, yes, well, what sort of work is it?'

'Well it's pretty easy really; I would be happy to train you up on all the things I do for him.'

'Well, assuming I can do it, I'd love to. But have you asked Harry about this yet?'

'No. No I haven't. The thing is, I wanted to have a solution in place before I drop the news if you see what I mean.'

'Yes, yes I do.'

'So, you up for it?'

Katie was thinking back to the graphs Harry had shown her over lunch. 'I tell you what, why don't you take me through what you do for Harry and then, if I'm comfortable with it, we'll tell him.'

'That's a good idea,' Nancy said. 'Oh Katie, it's such a relief. I was dreading telling him.'

Chapter 32

Katie opened the car door and the wind from the sea blew it wide. She stepped out onto the pavement while Birch got out carefully on the road side holding the door to him. Everything was flying; hair, scarves and wraps and Katie let out a giggle.

'I hope the restaurant's not too far!' she said hanging on to her hair and her handbag.

'Right here Madam.' Birch gestured up to the Sandgate Hotel which was a splendid, tall, white-washed Georgian building with a stained glass window above the double doors at the entrance. They rushed together across the road and Katie smoothed her hair as they arrived in the lobby.

They had been in the car for two hours but the time had flown by as Birch had entertained her with amusing anecdotes from the time he was a struggling writer. He'd also asked her lots of questions about herself and it felt as if he was eagerly soaking up her life history. The one question that had crossed her mind, but that she hadn't asked yet, was why Sandgate?

Birch recommended they had the seafood platter which could be shared between two with a side order of chips and a glass of Pinot Grigio.

'Sounds perfect,' Katie said and pushed her unread menu away from her. He was looking at her and her expression was curious now.

'So why Sandgate?'

'Ah!' He attracted the attention of a waitress and gave her their order and then turned his attention back to Katie. 'Well, the thing is,' he started.

She had never seen him even slightly lost for words before now.

'I was born here actually.'

'Oh!'

'And well, I know it's not as scenic as Cap D'Antibes, but I rather like the ruggedness of the sea and the elegant architecture. It's somehow.... stuck in time.'

Katie nodded and smiled. The restaurant overlooked the road they had parked on and beyond that a pebbly beach and the grey sea swirled with sparkles of blue where the sun hit it further out.

'And...' He hesitated again. Katie's eyes widened.

'And well, my mother still lives here.' Then he added very quickly, 'not that that matters today.'

'Oh!' Katie was taken by the coy delivery of this fact. 'Are you going to call in and see her? I can always make myself scarce for an hour or so.' She was genuine in her offer and thought it might be quite nice to wander the streets of this little coastal town.

'No, no! Definitely not!' Their food arrived and Birch changed the subject. 'Anyway there's a wonderful antique shop I want to show you after lunch.'

Harry liked Natasha. What was not to like? She was a beautiful woman with a wonderful figure and they enjoyed lively conversation together over dinner. He decided he would not sleep with her. It was so much easier to extract yourself from these relationships if things hadn't gone that far, especially as her mother was his client. But on their last date *she* had insisted the night was still young as they came away from the restaurant and she'd love to see his pad. He had barely turned the key in his front door before she pounced. There wasn't even a futile discussion about coffee. The sex had been energetic and fulfilling. After she had got up and walked naked into his kitchen to find a bottle of very decent Chianti and two glasses. She came back and handed a glass to Harry who sat himself up and wondered what he had let himself in for.

'Hope you don't mind?' she asked even though it was too late. 'I just felt like a drink.' She smiled seductively at him and brushed his cheek with the back of her hand. Harry was beginning to feel like his precious bachelor flat had been invaded. He smiled despite himself.

'Of course I don't.' He put his glass on the bedside table. 'It's just that I've got a bit of an early start tomorrow.' He was trying to sound apologetic.

'Really?' she said it as if she didn't care.

'Yes, so...' Harry was attempting to work out what would get through to this woman but was struggling for ideas. It was clear Natasha didn't do subtle.

'So?' She looked at him and he wished she'd get dressed.

'Shall I call you a cab?' He almost hated himself for asking.

She had gone eventually, but not until he promised to take her out again soon. Harry decided the whole situation was a disaster now. He even contemplated the damage it would do to his client relationship with her mother if he just dumped her.

Katie looked in amazement around her. The antique shop was like a home in dire need of de-cluttering. On elegant white painted French furniture lay candle holders, jugs, lamps, vases, wine racks, lanterns, kitchen paraphernalia, ornaments, clocks and much more. The owner, Julia Fraser, had her hair in a sleek white grey bob and despite her diminutive size and advanced years (Birch reckoned she was about eighty-five) she was most certainly in charge and her young assistants ran around her, afraid to do anything that might annoy her.

Birch led the way at first to the back of the shop where a sky light provided a conservatory feel and the theme changed to garden furniture with lots of wrought iron and basket ware. They then made their way upstairs as the owner shouted after them, 'do help yourselves to coffee' and sure enough on the first floor there were coffee making facilities with a pint-sized glass bottle of milk. One room was made up as a children's nursery while the other was an adult boudoir, still every inch of floor space utilised, yet more hanging from the ceiling. Birch turned to Katie and said excitedly, 'pick something! What would you like?'

Katie took a sharp intake of breath. 'But I can't!'

'Please! I want to buy you something.'

'But you've been so generous already and I can't reciprocate right now.'

'Well I'm pleased you said *right now*.' His eyes were mischievous. 'I look forward to receiving my gift when you are a successful VA with high paying clients!'

They laughed together. Katie looked around her and then she said, 'actually there was something downstairs that caught my eye.'

Alice was hungry and trying to find something she wanted to eat in Jacob's fridge. She picked up some sliced bread in a plastic bag and was considering toast when she saw the lurid green mould across the bottom of the loaf. Grimacing she dropped it all in the pedal bin. There was a black cherry yoghurt pot but it was past its use by date and a piece of cheese which was very smelly and not to her taste. She sighed and put the kettle on. She knew for a fact that Jacob had some coffee, even if it was instant. The shiny fresh coffee machine in her mother's kitchen came to mind and, even though it was further evidence of their lodger becoming firmly ensconced in the house, it was also a reminder of the stark disparity between her family home and Jacob's student-like flat. She looked at her watch while the kettle boiled. It was only eleven in the morning. Jacob wouldn't be home until this evening. Suddenly the day ahead of her seemed very long.

Her coffee made, and luckily the milk she added was fresh, she went into the living room and sat at the table where her text books were laid out for her A-level revision. She looked at them, then again at her watch and sighed as her stomach rumbled. It was no good; she was going to have to go to the village shop to buy some food. Actually, if she was honest with herself, she welcomed the distraction. Her original idea to cut down her hours at The Lemon Tree so that she would have more time to study for her re-sit was not working out well. She had less money and, with Jacob working all hours, too much time to think.

They were laughing as they got back into the car having fought the wind again as they struggled to hold on to their purchases and get them safely into the boot. Birch was giving her a long lingering look and she was drawn to him like a magnet. The kiss was long and slow and sent a shiver down her spine.

With a mischievous smile she asked, 'Do you want to go and see your mother now?'

Birch didn't answer for a while and then he said, 'I suppose we could call in for a cup of tea.'

'We?' Katie was surprised but not unnerved by the idea.

'Yes, well...' he was hesitating again, 'I'll just tell her you're a friend.'

Katie was amused.

'A good friend.' He smiled back.

'Does she know about Celia?'

'Not yet,' he said gently and started up the engine.

Sylvia opened her door to them. She looked startled. 'This is a surprise! How lovely!'

Birch embraced his mother. 'Sorry Mum, we were in the area and...'

'You didn't bother to let me know.' She smiled and raised her eyebrows.

'This is a friend of mine, Katie.'

'How charming to meet you, I'm Sylvia.' She showed them in to the sun room at the front of the apartment which overlooked a garden which went down as far as the beach.

'This is a lovely home.' Katie was admiring the scene before her.

'Yes, it suits me.' Sylvia smiled and then asked, 'would you like some tea?'

Katie looked around the room, the walls were light and the floor tiled with slate. A large cream sofa and a brown leather armchair were both angled to take in the magnificent view. A palm tree was centre stage in the garden and there were incidental patio areas leading down to the beach.

Sylvia returned with a tray and having served tea, in bone china mugs painted with flowers, she sat back and her eyes fell and lingered on Katie.
'So how do you two know each other? Are you a writer, Katie?'
'Oh no!'
Birch intercepted. 'Mother, I told you that I'm renting a room in Katie's home as a sort of office for my writing.'
'Ah yes. And does that work well? I suppose it must if you've brought her to see me!' Her eyes twinkled.
'Well actually I wanted to show Katie Sandgate and well, Mother, I have something I need to tell you.'
'Oh yes?' Sylvia sat forward in her chair and looked really pleased.
'The thing is, Celia has left me.'
'Oh good!' Sylvia exclaimed. 'I never did like that woman.'

Chapter 33

Katie was deliriously happy. She didn't have a care in the world. They got back to Bisham Gardens so obviously together after what had been the perfect day. Birch parked outside the house in the Mercedes that had been David's car.

'Coming in?' she asked knowing that this was reckless behaviour but thinking, in a vague sort of way, what could possibly go wrong?

'Love to,' he said.

The path from the front door to the kitchen was clear and Birch started making coffee for them both. Katie unwrapped the Clarice Cliff teapot Birch had purchased for her and admired it. She loved its bright colourful design and the fact that you would never actually use it to make tea in.

'Thank you,' she said, 'I love it!' And she swung round to kiss him and they folded into each other's arms and didn't notice Bethan walk into the room.

'What! What the bloody hell?' The red from her neck flooded her cheeks. Katie stepped away from Birch and her face could not have been more serious.

'Bethan,' she said trying to take in what was happening, 'hello,' she said meekly in an attempt to be normal.

'Hello?' Bethan looked horrified and demanded, 'what's going on?'

'Now calm down,' Katie said and added, 'let's sit down and talk about this.'

'Talk about it! Are you bloody joking?' She was shaking now. 'Don't you *care* about Dad?' She turned and stormed upstairs. Her bedroom door slammed shut.

Katie put her head in her hands. 'Oh my God, what have we done?'

They looked at each other. Katie was in a state of shock and confusion and at a complete loss as to what to do next.

Birch spoke first. 'Shall I go?' He held the cup of coffee he had made for her in his hand. 'Do you want this? Probably not.'

She took it from him. 'I'm not sure what I want right now. Do you think I should go to her?'

'Yes,' he nodded his head, 'if you think it will help.' And then he added, 'she's very angry.'

'Yes, perhaps I should wait a moment for her to calm down. Oh, I don't know.' Katie ran her fingers through her hair in despair. 'What were we thinking?'

It was only a moment later that Bethan decided for them. She'd packed an overnight bag alarmingly quickly in a slapdash fashion and almost ran down the stairs. She appeared at the kitchen door and shouted,

'I'm leaving! I can't live here anymore!'

'Bethan, I am so sorry you've had a shock. I'm sorry that I haven't handled this better but...'

'You're sorry! You're not sorry! What about Dad? Are you sorry he's *dead?*'

Katie felt faint and became unsteady on her feet. Birch took her elbow to steady her.

'Perhaps you should sit down,' he almost whispered.

'Yes, I think I need to.' Katie reached for a chair.

'Oh *look* at you *two*! Very cosy in *my Dad's kitchen*! I can't believe you!' She turned to leave.

'Where are you going?' Katie managed to ask.

'What do you care?'

'I need to know where you're going,' Katie said as Bethan marched down the hallway and furiously banged the front door shut.

'Oh my God.' Katie collapsed now onto the chair.

Birch sat next to her and took her hands in his. 'I'm so sorry,' he said. 'I feel responsible.'

'Don't be silly. It's me she's angry with. Her father has only been dead a few months. It must seem like a betrayal to her. She doesn't fully understand. I can't explain it to her.'

Birch sat and listened.

'They both adored their father... and he them. He spoilt them rotten and they can't see, or won't see, what he actually did to me, to all of us, through his gambling.'

He put an arm around her and kissed her and she responded finding consolation in his arms.

'She'll come back eventually. Probably stay with a friend for a night or two.'

'Yes.' Katie needed to believe that. 'Maybe she's going to Miranda's house. I could call her mother.'

Alice was lying on the sofa watching a property programme when Jacob get back from work at seven fifteen.

'A-level revision going well?' he asked.

'That's a nice greeting.' Alice said sarcastically. She switched off the television and got up.

He walked over to her and took her in his arms. 'Did you miss me?'

'Yeah I suppose so. I'm bored with my revision already. And there was nothing to eat in the fridge.'

'Right, well I'll go to the shop,' Jacob said picking up his keys again.

'No need, I've already been.'

'Oh good. Thanks. Get anything for supper?'

'Yeah, I got pasta and a tin of tuna.'

'Makes a change,' Jacob said as his eyebrows flitted upwards.

'Well I don't have much money!' Alice raised her voice to emphasise her point.

He looked at her but said nothing. And then he said, 'Just getting changed. Do you fancy going to the pub?'

'I can't afford it!' Alice was exasperated now.

'Okay, I'm buying.' He kept his cool.

'Well actually.. ,' she thought about it, 'I would like to go out. I've been stuck here all day apart from going to the shop.'

'Right, well I'm going to have a quick shower.'

'Ah, the thing is, I'm not sure if there's any hot water after my bath.'

Katie felt better after a large brandy. 'Thanks for making me drink that.'

'Don't be silly,' Birch held her closer as they sat spooned together on the sofa in her living room. 'Do you want another?'

'No, that's fine. The fact is that both my daughters have left home of their own accord and at least I know where they are.'

'Yes, that helps a lot,' Birch agreed.

'Mind you, Alice's text message was a bit concerning.'

'Oh really?'

'Yes, she sounded really fed up.'

'Did she say what with?'

'No, but I can guess it's probably having to live like a student when she thinks she's some kind of princess.'

Birch laughed. 'Sorry,' he said sheepishly.

'Don't be. I'm under no illusions where my daughters are concerned.'

'You're a wonderful mother.' Birch kissed the top of her head.

'How can you say that? I feel like a failure.' She sighed.

'You *are* a wonderful mother. You have endless patience with them. You creep around their sensitivities like you're walking on eggshells. They don't appreciate you! Are you sure you don't want another brandy?'

Katie smiled. 'Sure. You have one.'

'I know what I'd rather do.' He held her closer.

'Oh yes?'

'I'd rather take you to bed.'

She lifted her head to his and they kissed. It still made her spine tingle.

'Not here,' she said. 'It would be awful if one of them came back and found us.'

'You're right. My place?' He looked hopeful.

Katie hesitated.

'Listen,' Birch looked straight into her eyes now, 'they are both safe. Bethan is at Miranda's and Alice is at Jacob's and they both have your mobile number.'

'You're right.' She lowered her eyes. 'Okay.'

Alice had only eaten half her pizza.

'You finishing that?' Jacob asked.

'I don't think so.' Alice looked down at her plate. She thought coming out would cheer her up but it hadn't.

'What's the matter?' Jacob asked. She knew he hadn't got a clue.

'Oh, I don't know. I just hate not having any money.'

There was a pause before he said, 'Why don't you increase your hours at The Lemon Tree again? I mean you don't seem to be getting much revision done anyway.'

Alice was surprised by this. 'Maybe not today, but I need to do it! I don't know; I felt restless today.'

Jacob looked puzzled. 'When's your re-sit exam?'

'End of January, some time.'

'So, you've got a couple of months at least.'

'Yeah, s'pose so.' She felt uneasy and played with her cutlery.

'So how about it then? Increasing your hours again?'

'I think they've taken someone else on now.'

'Alice, restaurants are always taking people on.' He sounded frustrated; probably because he'd said this before. 'Anyway, they had to get someone when you reduced your hours. But, I'm sure they'd prefer to have you back, you being more experienced.'

'Maybe.' Alice tossed her hair back and continued to stare at her half-eaten pizza.

'Oh cheer up will you!' He was staring at her in disbelief.

'What have I got to be cheerful about?' She looked affronted.

'I don't believe you! You expect to have everything handed to you on a plate. Since when did I agree to keep you in the style your mother was trying to?'

'I got some food in today.' She was defensive now.

'A tin of tuna and packet of pasta! Great! And you used all the hot water up!'

'Oh, you know, you can forget it!' Alice stood up and threw her napkin at Jacob. 'I'm getting my stuff and moving back home!'

Jacob lowered the napkin to his lap, picked up the remaining piece of Alice's pizza and started eating it and then said, through a mouthful, 'good!'

Birch turned the key in his front door and held it open for Katie to walk in before him. Celia suddenly appeared in the hallway her eyes wide with bewilderment.

'Celia!' Birch look horrified. 'I wasn't expecting you.'

'Clearly not!'

'Well you have been staying at Alastair's flat for a while now,' he said in his defence.

'This is still my home!' She was staring at Katie. 'Well you didn't take much time did you?'

'I think I better go.' Katie turned and Birch followed her out onto the street. They looked at each other. She didn't know what to say. It was an awful moment. Katie felt like she was being punished for finding a little happiness. Birch had a pained expression.

He held both her hands. 'I'm so sorry but I'm going to have to talk to her.'

'Of course,' Katie tried to pull herself together. 'I'll go.' She was close to tears.

'Look, I'll call you as soon as I can.'

'Thank you,' she said knowing she would be going home to an empty house.

She walked away slowly her head turned down and thought of her life, at that moment, what a mess.

Celia was in the living room, standing at the French windows looking out onto the garden. Birch sat on the sofa in a pose of mock relaxation and looked up at her back. 'So, what do you want?' He didn't hide his fury at what felt like a gross intrusion.

'What do you mean? This is my home, isn't it? Am I not allowed to be in my own home?'

'Possibly not after you've had an affair for a whole year and practically moved in with your lover.'

Celia turned towards him, 'Oh and what have you been up to since you moved in with *that* woman!'

'My relationship with Katie developed *after* you left me.'

'You honestly expect me to believe that?'

'Well that's the truth. You've certainly been lying to me for a whole year so I don't know why you're trying to blame me for all this.'

'What do you expect when you behave the way you do!' She said angrily. 'What kind of a husband are you? You don't care about me!'

Birch looked baffled. He took a moment before he said, '*What do you want* Celia? Why are you here? Alastair kicked you out, has he?'

'No, he hasn't!' Celia twisted her pearls around her fingers, her eyes fixed on the floor.

'So?' Birch was irritated by her very presence.

'I'm going to be living here for the meantime, until we've talked properly and decided what we're going to do with this house.' She looked calm but her voice was quivering.

'And where am I supposed to live?' Birch was outraged now. How could she do this to him?

'Well, you can move into that woman's house; you practically live there now anyway.'

'No I don't! For the last time it's my place of work! Anyway, it's not possible for me to simply *move in* as you say. You don't know what you're talking about.'

'Well I'm moving back in here, for now, so you'll have to find somewhere else.'

'You've got to be joking! You go swanning off to live with this Alistair chap and then expect to come waltzing back into my life and demand that I move out of this house! This house that I paid for! Huh! You must be mad, woman!'

'I'm not mad.' Celia was shaking. 'I simply want to live in my own home.' She turned back to the window and stared out.

'You are incredible! You really are!'

Katie had made herself a mug of tea and was sat in front of the television in her living room, not watching it, her mind whirring from what seemed like the longest day of her life. The time in Sandgate had been so wonderful, she'd been so happy. It had been such a huge come down when Bethan walked in on them. And as if that wasn't bad enough, being confronted by Celia was truly horrible. All Katie could remember was this fearsome woman, full of anger and judgement. It was hard to believe that she was Birch's wife. Try as she might, Katie could not find comfort in any of her thoughts, even looking at her Clarice Cliff teapot brought tears to her eyes.

The front door opened and Katie dared to hope it was Birch, having let himself in with his key, for although she knew it would be dangerous she longed for him to comfort her. Alice appeared red faced at the door carrying a large holdall.

'Hi Mum,' she said looking morose as she dropped the bag, walked over and sat on the sofa next to her. 'I need a hug.'

Katie held her daughter close and tried to hold it together so she didn't have to explain her tears. She daren't say anything.

Alice pulled away and looked straight at her. 'You okay Mum?'

'Yes,' Katie sniffed, 'yes, I'm okay.' She reached for a tissue and blew her nose trying to shake herself out of her fragile state. 'Are you back?'

Alice looked down as she replied. 'Yes. Yes, if that's okay?'

'Well it is your home,' was all Katie could manage. She wasn't sure if she was pleased or not.

'Mum, I can't live at Jacob's, it's awful. I can't settle there and he doesn't understand me.'

Katie could easily guess what had gone wrong but said nothing.

Alice looked worried. 'Mum it's all right if I move back, isn't it?'

'Yes, of course.' She was saying what she needed to say but the right sentiment wasn't behind the words.

Alice moved away from her mother and perched on the edge of the sofa. She was looking vaguely at the television when she said, 'I'm going to increase my hours at The Lemon Tree again, if I can, and then I'll be able to give you some money each week.'

'Thank you,' Katie said simply and decided that it would be best if she didn't say anymore. A text message appeared on her mobile and she grabbed the handset. It was from Birch. She looked up at Alice. 'I expect you'll want to unpack?' She kept her eyes on her daughter.

Alice looked puzzled. 'Yeah, I suppose so.' She left the room reluctantly.

Katie read the text message:

Hello my love, I'm so sorry about all this. My wicked wife is insisting on moving back in here. Any chance I can come round tonight? Bx

Her heart sank.

I'm so sorry, darling, Alice has turned up, fallen out with Jacob. I long to be with you. Katie x

She turned off the television and decided to go to bed. At least she felt tired; in fact, she was exhausted after such an emotional day.

Chapter 34

Bethan was finding the bed in the guest room of Miranda's house very uncomfortable. She fidgeted around moving limbs and sighing. There were two narrow single beds in the room and she had thought about pushing them together as she was used to a double bed at home. But Miranda's mother, Stephanie, had made it quite clear that she would only need one bed and it would only be for a couple of nights.

'But it's all right isn't it Mum?' Miranda had pleaded to her mother on her behalf. 'I mean Bethan has had a difficult time recently, losing her father.'

'Yes, I'm sure she has,' Stephanie said holding her pink rubber gloved hands in the air before turning back to the sink where she was washing up. 'And I'm sure her mother has too,' she added.

Miranda sighed and smiled at Bethan. 'I'll show you,' she said and lead the way up the stairs. The hallway and stairwell were carpeted in a slate blue and the walls were stark white making it feel cold. The colour scheme in the guest bedroom was no less forgiving. The bedspreads were the old-fashioned type and navy blue giving no relief to an overall gloomy theme. There were small framed pictures dotted along the wall with cameo paintings of wild flowers which could not have interested Bethan less.

'Well this is it.' Miranda sat on one of the beds and Bethan sat opposite her.

'Are you sure this is okay?' Bethan felt unwelcome.

'Yeah, don't worry about Mum, she's fine really.'

Bethan turned down the bed she was sat on. There was no duvet, just a sheet, one blanket and the bed spread. The room was chilly and Bethan hugged herself against it.

'I'll put the radiator on tomorrow,' Miranda said and Bethan was confused.
'We don't have the heating on upstairs after eight o'clock. Mum says it's better to sleep in a cool room.'
'Right.' Bethan tried to brighten up. 'Any chance of a hot drink?'
'Of course. I'll make you one. Let's go down to the kitchen.'
Now in bed, despite having left a pair of socks on and wearing PJs, which she was so pleased she'd thrown into her bag, she was still cold and couldn't sleep. She re-lived the moment she walked into the kitchen to find her mother in Birch's arms and was repulsed by it once again. It felt like her mum had changed so much since her Dad had died and that she didn't know her anymore. She forced herself to change the record and deliberately considered if she fancied Matt at work, as he was beginning to show an interest in her. But her thoughts quickly turned to Harry, who she knew she adored, and the scene of him coming out of that restaurant with an attractive woman began to haunt her. Tears ran down her face. Her life was unbearable; how could she carry on?

The following morning Katie was sitting in her study but not achieving much apart from the pretence that she was working. She saw Harry's number come up on her mobile when it rang and she felt slightly nervous as she knew Nancy had told him that she was pregnant with twins and would be taking at least a year out from her VA work.
'Hello Harry.' She tried to keep her voice even, giving nothing away.
'Katie, how are you?' He sounded as friendly as ever.
'Good, thanks.' She tried to lift her voice despite her low mood.

'It's turned really cold hasn't it?' He sensed he might have caught her at a bad moment.

'Well it's to be expected isn't it?' Katie wished he'd get to the point now.

'Yes, of course. Listen, I'm in your neighbourhood this morning, any chance I can drop in?'

'Erm.. .' Katie was trying to remember what state Alice had left the kitchen in. 'Yes, okay.' And then she added because she couldn't stop herself, 'something important?'

'Yes, I suppose so,' he said in a cheery voice, 'something *good* I hope.'

'Oh right.' Katie decided that must be a sign of what she was expecting. The session she had had with Nancy, when she took her through Harry's workload, had been pretty comprehensive and had left her feeling confident she could handle it all.

She tried again to focus on her work. Servicing her one client, Stephen, was the easy bit. That was very much on the lines of what she had done years ago. It was working out a strategy to attract new clients that was the big unknown. She was finding all sorts of advice on the internet. Just putting a profile on Linked-in had led to numerous emails from people, professing to be experts in their field, with top tips and suggestions. It was too much information and she felt more overwhelmed than guided. And so her thoughts turned to Bethan who surely was fine at Miranda's, or was she? Although her mother had sounded terse on the phone and had emphasised that it would only be a couple of nights. What would happen after that? Then there was Birch apparently at home with his wife. He had not turned up today but often didn't on a Saturday. But then again, what on earth would be going on at home with Celia there? Alice was a bit of a mystery; was she heart-broken about Jacob, or was it simply the realisation that the perfect life is not easily come by.

Katie found herself navigating to her online bank account and there was the balance: a minus number in red staring at her. It was only over by ten pounds and forty-two pence, but she wondered how overdrawn it could go before they started slapping all sorts of charges on her and making things even worse. She knew the sensible thing would be to call the bank and find out, or indeed arrange an overdraft, but she really couldn't face that right now.

Alice appeared at Katie's study door looking dressed up. 'I'm going out, Mum,' she said.

'Okay.' Katie replied rather feebly wandering where and why but not daring to ask.

'I rang The Lemon Tree and they need someone for the lunch shift so I'll be back around five-ish.'

'Oh good.' Katie remembered about Harry's imminent visit. 'Is the kitchen tidy?'

'What?'

'Have you left the kitchen tidy?'

'No! I mean... I don't know! Why the hell does the kitchen have to be tidy all of a sudden?'

'Because Harry's coming round,' Katie said simply.

'What on earth is *he* coming round for?' Alice found her keys in her shoulder bag. 'Mum, I've got to go! I'm going to be late.'

Katie said nothing. As soon as the front door had closed she went into the kitchen. She put all the dirty dishes in the dishwasher and wiped away breadcrumbs, bits of cereal and coffee mug rings thinking that Alice must have had a substantial breakfast that morning. She had just finished when the doorbell rang.

She opened the door to find Birch standing there looking awkward.

'Oh! Hello.'

'Is it safe to come in?' he whispered.

'Er yes, actually, Alice has just gone to work.'

He closed the door behind him and took her in his arms. 'I'm so sorry about all this.' He kissed her and she held back. 'What's the matter?' he asked.

'Nothing, it's just that Harry's coming round about now. I thought you were him.'

'I see! What's Harry coming round for?'

'Well...' The doorbell interrupted her. She opened the door for him. 'Harry, do come in.'

'Hello Katie. Ah, I see you have company.'

'Er yes, this is Birch.' Katie was trying to think if it was okay if these two met and couldn't think of a reason why not.

The two men shook hands. 'Nice to meet you, Harry,' Birch said with a friendly smile, as he spotted Harry's briefcase.

Harry looked uncomfortable for a moment and Birch picked up on it. 'Listen, I see you two are having a meeting so why don't you park yourselves in the living room and I'll bring through a couple of delicious cappuccinos!'

'Oh thanks,' Harry said bemused. 'You didn't tell me you had a butler, Katie,' he teased.

Miranda knocked on Bethan's door at eight thirty with a cup of tea. Bethan was still asleep but her friend persisted.

'Bethan, wake up, it's morning. I've brought you a cup of tea.' She put her hand on Bethan's shoulder and rocked her gently.

Bethan squinted her eyes open. 'What time is it?' she said yawning widely.

'Er,' Miranda looked at her watch, 'eight thirty.'

'You are joking?'

'No.' Miranda seemed put out. 'There's a cup of tea here for you. I made it especially. Anyway, mum says it's about time you were up.'

Bethan sighed. 'Right well, thanks then.' She looked at Miranda hoping she would leave her alone.

'Probably best if you sit up and drink your tea or you might fall back to sleep again.'

Exasperated Bethan heaved herself up and put a pillow behind her. She decided she would do as she was told, even though it seemed ridiculous and beyond unreasonable. She certainly hadn't had enough sleep and it was Saturday. Normally she'd stay in bed until at least ten o'clock.

Miranda smiled at her. 'I'll see you downstairs for breakfast in ten minutes,' she said as she made her way back to the door.

Bethan had a look of total bewilderment on her face. '*Breakfast* in *ten minutes*,' she stammered. Miranda was gone. Bethan groaned as she acted out throttling someone, probably Miranda's mother, with her hands.

'Great, I'm really pleased you'll be taking over from Nancy.' Harry closed up his notebook and put his pen down.

'Thanks Harry. I won't let you down.' Katie felt a bit more cheerful now.

Birch appeared with the coffees and placed them on the little table between them.

'So, Birch, I hear you're a writer?'

'Yes, that's right. I'm usually up on the top floor tapping away at the keyboard.'

'Even at weekends?' Harry raised his eyebrows.

'Ah, well, the thing is I have a bit of situation at the moment.' Harry looked blank.

'Not sure how much I should say?' Birch slid into the nearest chair trying to read Katie's mind.

Katie decided to come to his rescue. 'Birch has a bit of a domestic problem.'

'Ah.' Harry left it at that but then added, 'lovely coffee, by the way.'

'Yes, the new machine is really good,' Birch enlightened him.

'You've bought yourself a coffee machine, have you Katie?' Harry grinned at her.

'Actually,' Katie blushed, 'Birch bought it for me.'

'Oh, I see.' Harry was beginning to put two and two together. He looked over at Katie and Birch. 'So are you staying here full time now, Birch?'

Birch opened his mouth and shut it again.

'Sorry, I didn't mean to pry.' Harry hid behind his coffee cup.

Birch looked at Katie. 'Is it okay if I tell him?'

Katie felt that things couldn't get any worse if Harry knew about them and actually it felt quite good letting someone know. 'Why not?' Katie said.

'The thing is, my wife, Celia left me for another man and moved in with him, which was fine until she decided to come back yesterday. She insists that she lives in our home until matters get resolved, whatever that means. Would you believe I spent last night in the car.'

'Oh dear,' Harry downed the last of his coffee, 'so why don't you sleep in the top room here, as well as write; surely that's the perfect solution?'

There was an awkward pause. The lovers didn't have to say anything. Harry added, 'ah, perhaps things have moved on between you two?'

'Yes, and I have my daughters feelings to consider which makes it all very difficult.' Katie managed a smile.

'More coffee?' Birch offered.

Bethan was finding Stephanie's home-made muesli, which was full of whole dried apricots and whole nuts, hard work and her jaw was beginning to ache. She regretted being persuaded to add more to her bowl having sprinkled in a small amount.

'Have some more, Bethan, it's very good for you. Lots of fibre and vitamins. You're looking a bit peaky if you don't mind me saying; in need of a pick me up.'

Bethan soldiered on and asked hesitantly, 'would it be okay if I had a cup of coffee?'

'I'll make it.' Miranda sprung to her feet.

'It's not good to drink too much caffeine, Bethan, I'm sure your mother has told you that.' Stephanie was stood at the kitchen sink in her apron, a place that she seemed to rarely move from.

Breakfast over, Bethan was relieved to be back in her room. She had been given permission to have a shower and she prayed it would be hot. But first she checked her mobile and to her surprise there was a message from Matt.

Hi Bethan, how's your weekend? Just wondering if you fancy meeting for a coffee at Fegos? Matt

Bethan decided it would be the perfect escape.

Hi Matt, sounds good. I could be there at 11. Bethan

Harry was beginning to find out what had been going on in the Green household.

'Oh Katie, I don't envy you having to cope with your daughters. It's all rather delicate, isn't it?'

'That's one way of putting it.' Katie was becoming increasingly impatient with them.

'I tell you what, Birch,' Harry said turning to him, 'I think there's an apartment in my building that's come up for rent. Might be a temporary solution?'

'Oh really. Yes, well I'm rapidly coming to the conclusion that I need to rent somewhere until I can make Celia see sense.'

Katie turned white at the thought of losing the money she was getting from Birch. She had never been totally honest with him about how dire her financial situation was and she certainly didn't want to say anything in front of Harry.

'You okay, Katie?' Birch put a hand on her knee.

'Yes, I think I'll get myself a glass of water,' she said as she darted from the room before anyone could offer to get it for her.

In the kitchen she downed some water, took some deep breaths and felt a little better. She was half hoping Birch would follow her but he didn't so she braced herself and went back into the living room. Both men watched her as she sat back down.

'Actually Katie, we've come up with a much better solution,' Harry said looking pleased with himself. 'I have a spare bedroom and Birch is more than welcome to stay with me while he sorts things out.'

'Yes,' Birch added, 'and of course I would still like to rent your top room for my writing.'

Katie gulped. 'Oh, well, if you're sure.'

'Yes, yes,' Harry was smiling now, 'you know the funny thing is, this could also be a solution to a little problem I have.'

'Oh?' Katie was surprised.

'Yes, you see one of my clients, well, her daughter... well I've been dating her.' He sat back in his chair. 'The thing is, it was at the client's suggestion that I took the girl out.'

'Ah! Tricky.' Birch looked interested.

'Exactly! You see I have a golden rule about mixing business and pleasure. Anyway, to cut a long story short I'm now in a bit of a predicament. But if you were to move in with me temporarily, I will have the perfect excuse not to bring her back to my place. And, as she's living with her mother...'

'I see,' Birch said. 'Good plan.'

Bethan had sneaked out of Miranda's house without a word. Miranda was doing homework in her room and her mother had made it very clear that she was not to be disturbed for at least two hours.

'Oh you've left school now haven't you? You'll just have to amuse yourself!' Stephanie had said in a patronising tone and Bethan wondered if she even had a de-frosted bone in her body.

The windows of Fegos were starting to steam up as it was so cold outside and Bethan walked into a blanket of warm which felt heavenly. Matt was already seated and waved to her. He stood up as she went over to him and they looked at each other. He hesitated but then kissed her cheek. 'Hi,' he said.

'Hi.' Bethan sat down.

'What can I get you? You look like you need warming up?'

'Tell me about it! Miranda's home is like a fridge!'

'No! Don't they have heating?'

'Yeah, they just don't seem to have it on.'

Matt beckoned a waitress over. 'What are you having?'

'Cappuccino, please.'

'Two cappuccinos, please.' The waitress nodded to Matt and went away.

Matt gave Bethan his full attention. 'I take it you were just staying the one night?'

Bethan thought about her overnight bag still in the guest room. 'We'll see.'

'But I thought you lived at home with your mum?'

'Yes, well I did, until I saw my mother kissing our weird lodger.'

'Oh, that doesn't sound good. Are they erm...?'

'I knew my mum fancied him right from the start but she didn't admit it.'

'Hang on a minute; didn't your Dad pass away *recently*?'

'Yes, exactly.'

'Oh Bethan, you poor thing.' He reached over and touched her arm momentarily and then pulled his hand back quickly.

She smiled at him as if to say it was okay. 'And I'm sure mum's forgotten but it's my birthday on Tuesday.'

'Right, well that's okay. We know how to do birthdays at Web Dreams, just name your bar!'

She looked more cheerful. 'Where do you guys normally go to celebrate? Not The Flask I presume?'

'Oh, I think we can do better than that.'

The drinks arrived and Bethan cupped her hands around hers.

'You're still not warmed up, are you?'

'Getting there.' She raised her eyebrows.

'Listen, there's a spare room at my place at the moment, for a few weeks in fact. Rob's gone to America, that's where his family is, and he's so bloody rich he could afford to keep the room on.'

Bethan looked interested but didn't say anything.

'We're pretty good, you know, I mean we keep the place clean and do a weekly food shop and stuff. Actually Jake, my other flat mate is a really good cook.'

'Where is it?' Bethan asked.

'Pond Square.'

'Oh!' Bethan didn't hide her surprise at hearing it was at such a desirable location in the village.

'Yeah, it's okay. You wouldn't be slumming it.'

'Sounds great.' Bethan hesitated before she said, 'Would I be able to come and see the flat?'

'Of course.'

Chapter 35

Katie had finally found a parking space in the pay and display car park near Kenwood House and was trying to get out of her car without damaging the car parked selfishly in the next space. Once free from metal entrapment, she peered around for the nearest pay and display ticket dispenser. She spotted one quite a distance away and quickened her pace wishing she hadn't chosen to wear stiletto heels. A hasty look at her watch told her she was five minutes late for the meeting already. The machine rejected her first pound coin. Twice. She selected another which was accepted and then found the right change to make up to two hours. She considered that the meeting would only last that long and didn't imagine she would want to stay any longer than she had to. With the car park ticket in her hand she breathed a sigh of relief and rushed back to her car to display it in on the passenger side of the window where there was a bit more room for manoeuvre.

She had walked across Hampstead Heath many times and admired the outside of Kenwood House and its Georgian magnificence but had never been in it. The entrance was grand and lavishly decorated. That, and the fact that she was attending her first business networking event there, left Katie feeling more nervous than when she had woken that morning and her fate had dawned on her.

She looked at her watch. It was ten past seven, a ridiculous time to be putting oneself through such an ordeal, Katie thought. The woman at reception didn't even bother to look up.

'Excuse me, would you tell me where the business networking meeting is, please?'

The woman blinked at the screen she had been staring at and then looked at nothing in particular and waved a hand to her right. 'Down the corridor, second door on the left.'

Katie headed off with a purpose and found an open door onto a melange of male suits and the odd woman having lively exchanges whilst balancing cups and saucers and document wallets. Katie looked at the scene before her and thought seriously about making a run for it when a short, grey-haired gentleman approached her.

'Hello, I'm Ralph. This is your first time?'

'Er yes. Katie Green.'

'Welcome Katie,' he said and walked a short distance to a table with papers on it. He looked down a list and found her name. 'Ah yes, here you are.' He looked up and smiled. 'No need to worry,' he said, 'we're all quite friendly. Now let me introduce you.' He moved in on two men and interrupted their conversation.

'James, Chris, this is Katie Green; it's her first time,' he said and left her.

Katie smiled and wished she hadn't been introduced as the new girl. Wasn't it obvious enough?

'Katie.' James had discarded his coffee cup and so had a free hand to extend to her. 'I'm James Mongford. Mongford Accountants.'

'Ah, nice to meet you.'

'Chris Lingford, photographer,' the other one said.

Katie shook hands with both. 'Katie Green, VA,' she said following suit even though it felt totally unnatural. Did her business define her?

'And what area do you specialise in, Katie?' Chris asked.

The answer that popped into Katie's head was on the lines of any work at all right now, I'm desperate! But she managed to say instead, 'I've only just started out really,' and as she did she was looking at two facial expressions of unease. This is not going well, she thought but then she added, 'but I have two clients already, one is a business coach and the other, a fund manager.'

'Oh well done,' James said encouragingly. 'That wouldn't be Harry Liversage, the fund manager I mean?'

'Yes, that's right. It was him that told me about this meeting.'

'I think he's over there somewhere.' Chris, who was just shorter than Katie, stood on tip toe to see if he could spot Harry but to no avail.

Katie remembered the first rule of networking that she'd read on a website she had come across and asked them both about what they did. Business cards were handed over promptly as they spieled out their much-practiced elevator pitches. Katie tried to look interested even in the importance of having an accountant which frankly horrified her, given the financial mess she was in.

'Have you got a card?' James asked.

'Oh yes!' Katie remembered that they were in her handbag and reached for a couple to give to them.

'Virtual Magic, I like it,' Chris remarked and Katie thought two down, too many to go. Just then Harry appeared at her side.

'Hello Katie.' He kissed her cheek. 'James, Chris.' He nodded to them both before turning his attention back to Katie. 'There's someone I'd like you to meet.'

'Oh, yes okay.' Katie was pleased to see a familiar face.

Harry steered her away and when they were out of earshot he said, 'I hope those two weren't boring you too much.'

'They were perfectly nice,' Katie said with a wry smile, 'I must say it's good to see you though.'

'Yes, I'm glad you're here. Charlie Butcher is actually looking for a VA and I've already sung your praises. He's a good guy. Property developer. Could be interesting work.'

'Alice, can I have a word at the back.' Margaret was the manager at The Lemon Tree and spoke discreetly before heading to the kitchen.

Alice was wondering what she had done wrong. She finished serving the table she was at and made sure they had everything they wanted before heading for the back of the restaurant. She straightened her apron. 'Yes?'

Margaret smiled. 'No need to look so worried. I was just wondering if you wanted to do more shifts? I've had to let Jenny go.'

'Really.' Alice feigned surprise but actually Jenny's treatment of the customers left a lot to be desired.

'So?' Margaret said impatiently.

'Yes, yes, I'd love to do more hours.'

'How about six shifts a week? I know you're studying for your A-level re-sit, so let me know if that's too much. I don't want to be messed around.'

Although Margaret had stopped short of saying it, Alice knew she was referring to the time she'd asked to reduce her hours which was only a few weeks ago.

'Six is fine for now. I might need to reduce them to five in January when I do my exam.'

'Good. Well let's talk again in January.'

'Thanks Margaret.' Alice sounded truly pleased.

'That's okay. You're a good worker. Now you better get back to your customers.'

'Of course.' Alice went away happy that she was appreciated and she had the extra work. Anything to keep her mind off Jacob.

Bethan was presenting three alternative website designs to Tom Frobisher who ran a film making business. Matt and Paul were also in the meeting and they were making her more nervous than the client.

'I like option three the best,' Tom said, nodding at Paul. 'It shows our work off to best advantage.' He sat back looking thoughtful and picked up one of the boards he had just been presented with. 'But I do like the home page of option two. I like the way it draws you in.'

Bethan employed some quick thinking. 'Right, well, I'm sure we could use elements of option two with option three as the basis for the website.' She wasn't sure really but this was her first client meeting and she needed it to go well.

'Yes, we could do that,' Matt added encouragingly. 'We could use this graphic device and slot it in here,' he said demonstrating by pointing at the boards.

'What do you think?' Paul asked Tom directly.

'Yes, well yes, that would be perfect.'

Paul beamed at Bethan and Matt. 'Good. We'll have the revised option, shall we say option four, over to you tomorrow,' he said looking enquiringly at Matt, even though it was a statement and not a question.

'No problem,' Matt said and avoided Bethan's gaze.

After the client had left, Matt turned to Bethan. 'Are you okay with that? We could maybe work on it a bit this evening at the flat?'

'Yes, okay.'

'I tell you what, I'll get a take away in for us. I don't think Jake's about tonight.'

Bethan was finding it strange working and living with Matt but they were just good friends, as far as she could tell, and she felt comfortable with that. Convincing her mother of this was harder. She had phoned on Wednesday and Bethan decided to answer even though she had ignored several of her text messages.

'Mum, hi.' Her voice was cold.

'At last! Bethan are you all right?'

'Yes, I'm fine.'

'Still at Miranda's? I don't think her mother's very happy about you staying for any length of time,' Katie blurted out rather carelessly.

'No, well that's okay because I moved in with Matt, one of my work mates, yesterday.'

'You what?' Katie could not hide her alarm.

'It's okay Mum, we're just flat mates. Jake lives there too. I'm in Rob's room while he's in America with his family.'

Katie tried to take it all in. 'So you're living with two men?'

'Mum, I've got my own room. I work with Matt; it's all fine.'

'Bethan you're only seventeen.'

'Oh! So you remembered my birthday then?'
'Of course I did. Did you get my card?'
'No!'
'Well I sent it to Miranda's house.'
'Oh, well her mum probably tore it up.'
'What? Don't be silly.'
'Mum, I've got to go.'
'Okay but when am I going to see you?'

There was a long pause and then Bethan said in a disgusted tone, 'I'm not coming home while you're with.. I can't even say his name.'

Katie sighed. 'Listen Bethan, I am sorry about how you found out but we need to talk about this. I need you to understand.'

'Not interested,' Bethan said abruptly and ended the call.

Charlie had outlined what he was looking for in a VA and asked Katie what experience she had. Having worked for Stephen, and now Harry, and getting good feedback her confidence had grown.

'I've been organising events and doing the admin for a business coach and my work for Harry includes putting together all the research for any new investment opportunities and helping to manage his clients. Before that I worked in the City as a PA for CEOs.' She no longer referred to this latter experience as being a long time ago. As Julia had pointed out, even though it was decades ago, the experience was still relevant and it wasn't as if she had forgotten it.

'Sounds impressive. I think you and I need to talk further. Do you have your diary handy?'

The time flew by for Katie in the end and when she realised her car park ticket had expired ten minutes ago she wished she had put in extra coins. She found Harry so she could say a quick goodbye. Rushing out of Kenwood House she suddenly noticed Birch stood to one side of the entrance.

'Birch, what are you...'
'I hope you don't mind. I just wanted to see you.'

'Mind! Of course not. But my car parking ticket has run out. Silly me, I thought two hours would be more than enough!'

'Oh okay.' He quickened his pace and the two of them ran across the road and found her car. Birch checked the windscreen and then looked furtively around. 'I think we've got away with it this time,' he said mimicking Cary Grant. Their eyes met and she melted into his arms.

After a long kiss he said, 'it's strange isn't it, being in the same house but not being allowed to be together?'

'Strange, yes, but perhaps crazy is more appropriate. I mean it's like we're being held to ransom by my own daughters. But what do we do about it?' Then a thought struck her. 'Where's your car, by the way?'

'I walked. I knew you had your car here so I thought the exercise would do me good.'

'Impressive,' she said.

'How about brunch? You can't have had time for breakfast,' he said and his eyes lit up.

'Well no, I didn't but...'

'Come on, let's be spontaneous. There's a place I know, not far from here. They do a great full English.'

'Okay but I must be back in the office this afternoon. I've got to prepare for a meeting tomorrow morning with a potential new client.'

'That's brilliant Katie, well done!' They kissed again and as they drove off it occurred to her that David's reaction would have been different. He would have said: are you sure you're not taking on too much? What's this Charlie like anyway? Sounds like a wide boy to me. Katie would put it down to jealousy up to a point, as it would mean she had less time for him, and would be flattered in a funny sort of way. But she also knew that such a reaction would have made her think twice about what she was doing. Question it. The reaction she got from Birch helped her to believe in herself.

Harry saw Natasha's name light up on his phone. He had been avoiding her for a week now and decided he needed to face the music, so he answered.

'Natasha, how are you?' There was no hint of guilt in his voice.

'I'm fine,' she said as if she was not. 'Where have you been? Somewhere with no mobile signal maybe?'

'Oh Natasha, I remember now you sent me a text the other day. I'm so sorry I've been extremely busy and...'

'I've sent more than one text message!' She interrupted him, annoyed by his dismissive tone.

'Have you? Well I can only apologise,' he said knowing this was likely to make her angry.

'Okay, apology accepted, but how about supper at your place this evening to make it up to me?'

'Ah, well, the thing is...'

'I don't care if you've got plans; cancel them.'

Harry was beginning to find the situation amusing. This woman was not going to give up easily. He came straight to the point. 'Natasha I've got a friend staying with me at the moment, Birch. His wife is being difficult and he needed somewhere to stay so you see the situation is...'

'Well can't you tell him to go out for the evening? After all it is *your* flat!'

'Look, the guy's down on his luck.' An image of Birch and Katie together flashed into his mind and he had to wipe a smile from his face, 'and a bit fragile if I'm frank. I really don't want to be flaunting such a beautiful woman as you in front of him. But you know he's not staying long; just until he gets fixed up with a flat.'

'That could take weeks!'

'Yes, just a few weeks I'm sure,' he said not responding to her exasperation.

'Oh for goodness sake!' Natasha screeched down the phone.

Harry waited. She was obviously infuriated with him now; all she needed to do was to tell him to get lost, no doubt in more colourful language than that, and this conversation would have gone to plan for him. If *she* finished it he might even be able to keep her mother as his client.

'Harry, are you trying to end this relationship? Are you really not man enough to say?'

'Natasha, I hope we'll always be friends,' he said in a conciliatory voice which just served to make her more furious.

'You are incredible! I can't take any more of this!' She ended the call.

Harry squirmed. The outcome had gone his way but it was a shame she had got so angry with him.

The Deli looked quite shabby in a trendy sort of way and the blackboard outside was promoting that day's breakfast specials. Katie was pleasantly surprised at how comfortable it was despite the student feel to the place and the staff certainly looked friendly.

'This is different,' she said.

'Er yes, I know it doesn't look much but the food's good.' Birch was almost apologetic.

'I'm sure it is.' Katie scanned the menu.

They ordered and then Birch sat back in his chair looking very pleased with himself. Katie felt a little nervous.

'What's all this about then?'

'I told you,' he said, 'I just miss you. I figured this was one way we could spend some time together away from the beady eyes of...'

'Yes, let's not talk my daughters today.'

Birch nodded appreciatively. 'So, this VA business is going great guns. Well done you!'

'Thank you. I am quite surprised myself. But you know I have Harry to thank for a lot of it. He's been putting a good word in for me left, right and centre.'

'Only because he knows you're good. He has his own reputation to think of as well.'

'Yes, I suppose he does. What's it like sharing a flat with him?'

'Better than I thought, actually. He's a very considerate chap. Just wants to live the life of a confirmed bachelor and work hard to be a very successful fund manager.'

'Well I suppose if he's open about not wanting a long term relationship, that's okay.'

'I'm not sure how honest he is with Natasha, but then she was foisted on him by his client!'

Two full English breakfasts arrived and Katie suddenly realised she was ravenous. 'This looks good.'

'Yes, it's not bad here. Not somewhere I frequent very often but at the moment needs must.'

'That sounds ominous.'

'Yes, well I found out yesterday that my dear wife has cleaned out our joint account.'

'Oh Birch, that's awful. And she has the house; it seems a bit unreasonable.'

'A bit! Huh! I'm beginning to realise I've been deluded for many years now.'

'So what are you going to do?' Katie tried to hide her alarm.

'Well first off I've got Henry to re-direct all my royalties to a new bank account I've opened. And I've given the Times the new account details, although they said they probably wouldn't be able to do anything for this month.'

'Oh dear.' Katie was wondering how this was going to affect their arrangement. Perhaps he'd brought her here to soften the blow.

'Don't look so worried,' he reached across and held her hand.

'Sorry. I'm sorry it's just that..'

'I know. There's no need to be concerned. It will all sort itself out in time and meanwhile Mother has kindly lent me some money to tide me over.'

'Oh that's good. Thank you Sylvia! What a star.' Katie felt relieved.

'Yes, she's a good sort. Anyway, when I spoke to her I asked her about the family lawyer she has used for many years, a guy called Jonathan Taylor; he's based in Sandgate.

'Oh?' Katie braced herself.

'Anyway I've spoken to him and on his recommendation I'm filing for divorce.'

'Right,' Katie said feebly trying to take it all in.

'I hope you're pleased,' Birch said all bravado know gone from his voice.

'Yes, yes of course I am.'

'Oh phew. For a minute there..'

'No, no I'm really pleased.' Katie tried to stay calm. 'Divorce, gosh.'

'Yes well, as Jonathan said, it will force the issue of the house. I mean I'd be homeless if it wasn't for Harry and I can't count on his goodwill long term.'

'No.' Katie had to agree but hoped it would be long enough to avoid Birch having to rent somewhere.

'Jonathan reckons that I can go for half. We sell the house and I get half the proceeds. Celia doesn't earn much but she comes from a wealthy family. A lot will rest on whether or not she moves back in with this Alistair chap. Let's just hope he can keep her in scatter cushions and objet d'art!'

Katie smiled at his joke but was thinking about all the headlines in the papers about ex-wives ripping off their ex-husbands. 'I hope it all works out for you.'

Birch looked at her quizzically, 'I hope it all works out for *us*!' He raised his coffee cup towards hers.

'To us,' Katie smiled and suddenly felt warm and loved.

Chapter 36

Katie was in her hallway with her coat on, rifling through her shoulder bag to make sure she had everything she needed for her meeting with Charlie.

Alice appeared on the stairs, 'Mum, before you go...'

'Alice, I'm in a hurry; I've got a meeting.' Katie looked at her watch.

'Yes, I know, but I just wanted to give you this.' She handed over some cash.

'Oh, what's this for?'

'My contribution for living here,' she said surprised.

'Oh right, thanks. Would you leave it on the table. I'll pick it up later.' Katie waved towards the kitchen.

'Mum, it's a hundred pounds.'

'Great. Thank you.' Katie's tone was flat. 'On the kitchen table will be fine.'

'But Birch might take it.' Alice looked upset now.

'Don't be ridiculous.' Katie opened the front door.

'But why can't you just put it in your handbag?'

'I'm going to be late if I don't leave *right now*!'

'But that's my wages from two shifts at The Lemon Tree.'

'Bye, see you later.' Katie ran to her car and jumped in leaving Alice stunned and offended.

Charlie Butcher's business resided in a block of serviced offices in the centre of Hampstead. Harry had told Katie where the best place to park was and she found it easily. She arrived just in the nick of time and made a mental note not to cut it so fine next time; her heart was beating fast and she was short of breath.

'Katie, good to see you.' Charlie shook hands with her and turned to a man sitting at the only other desk in the room. 'This is my partner, Adam.' Adam was on the phone so Katie simply smiled and nodded towards him.

'Sit yourself down.'

She sat on the only vacant chair in front of his desk, crossed her legs and calmed herself. She reached for a notepad and pen out of her handbag and looked up at Charlie. He was a middle aged, apple shaped man who had what was left of his greying hair cropped short. The ruddiness of his complexion suggested not the healthiest of lifestyles but he had a warm smile.

'Now I've thought about this and the problem I have is that I'm trying to manage several developments at once and there's a lot of chasing up to do. You know, builders who suddenly disappear half way through a job, electricians who are running late. I hope I'm not putting you off but that's the reality of the situation and the result is that properties get completed late and that's my cash flow slowed right up.'

'I see,' Katie looked enthusiastic, 'so what you need is a project manager who draws up schedules and chases all the tradesmen to make sure everyone sticks to the deadline.'

'Bang on! Yes, that's exactly what I need.'

'Okay,' Katie was thoughtful now, 'so what happens when a particular plumber, for example, proves very unreliable? Would you want me to try and find someone else?'

'Yes! We need to find reliable people.' Charlie sat back in his chair, 'I mean there's plenty of work for them if they are dependable so that should motivate them. But some of the guys I use, well you just want to put a rocket up their arses. Excuse my French.'

Katie smiled suggesting she didn't mind his language; she actually found him quite amusing. 'What area do your developments cover?'

'Ah, good question. I keep it reasonably local to keep the leg work down. Had a house refurbish' going on in Balham once. Well, it might be the gateway to the South but trying to drive down there was a nightmare. Yes, so it's Highgate, Hampstead; had a nice job in Golders Green once, good earner, but no, I keep it local on the whole.'

Alice went into the boutique in Highgate village. She justified the decision because they were having a sale and she had been working so hard she felt she deserved to treat herself. The fact that the shop was very near Chez Pierre where Jacob worked was just one of those things. There was only one other customer when she walked in and the sales assistant greeted her from behind the counter. Alice browsed at the front of the shop where the discounted clothes were and decided to try on a grey silk dress which was half price.

With the dress on, she looked at herself in the mirror from every angle, and was pleased with how it fitted her and how it complimented her auburn hair. She looked at the price label again and decided it would be irresponsible to buy it, but as she walked out of the changing room and up to the counter she thought about what Jacob's reaction might be if he saw her in it.

'I'll take it,' she said and felt cheery for a moment.

Out on the street she sauntered slowly towards Chez Pierre but stopped when she saw Jacob standing outside the restaurant speaking to someone on his mobile phone. She hesitated. Perhaps she should turn away but then he spotted her and waved. It would look odd now if she turned round so she walked up to him. He ended his call.

'Jacob, hi,' she said casually.

'Been shopping?' He spotted the bag from the boutique and she was pleased.

'Yes, just thought I'd check out their sale.'

'Anything nice?'

'A dress actually.' She opened the bag a little to show him.

'Good for you,' he said, 'and how are you?'

'I'm okay. Working six shifts at The Lemon Tree now.'

'Ah, I told you they'd have you back.'

'Yes, you were right.' She smiled at him and looked into his eyes. He looked away so she asked, 'and you?'

'Great.' He paused kicking at the leaves on the pavement. 'Actually I've started seeing Emma. She works here now,' he blurted out and then looked up to see her reaction.

Alice was stunned that he had moved on so quickly but tried to hide it. 'Oh, I see.'

'Yeah,' Jacob pursed his lips, 'no more Chardonnay girls for me.' He let out an embarrassed laugh.

Alice looked confused and hurt. A tear welled up in her eye and she turned away from him. 'Bye then,' she said feebly.

'Alice, I'm sorry. I mean I'm sorry it didn't work out.'

Alice quickened her pace as more tears came. She told herself she would get over him but she knew it would be so much easier if she had someone she could turn to for comfort, that someone being her dad.

Katie was on a high as she left Charlie's office. She knew the work would be demanding but he was paying for thirty hours of her time a month and she felt sure she would enjoy working with him. Back in her car she reached for her smart phone to do a simple calculation that she could not do in her head because she was too excited. Nearly two thousand pounds per month she would now be billing with all three clients. 'Brilliant,' she said out loud and started up her engine.

Katie walked into her home feeling sure, for the first time since David's death, that she would be able to keep the house. It was a wonderful feeling. Being a VA was challenging but the more she got into it the more she enjoyed it. She was blessed with great clients and she made a pact with herself, there and then, that she would never work with anyone she didn't like. What would be the point?

Alice, her face still red from crying, was sat at the kitchen table with a text book in front of her. Katie was so happy that she did not notice straight away.

'Hi darling, you'll never guess, I've just taken on my third client!' She was jubilant as she spoke.

Alice sniffed. 'Oh,' she said indignant.

Katie looked at her. 'Alice, are you okay?'

'Yes,' Alice shook her head, 'I'm fine.'

'Right.' Katie considered that she might have been crying over Jacob or her father's death. 'I'll put the kettle on,' she said softly. She made a pot of tea and put it on the table with two mugs and a jug of milk and then sat opposite Alice.

Alice looked up from her book. Her mother could see now that she had been crying and had not bothered to fix her makeup. Mascara was smudged under her eyes.

Katie spoke. 'Do you want to talk about it?'

'I've just had a crap day.'

Katie remembered the cash her daughter had tried to give her earlier. She looked on the table for it but could not see it. She poured the tea and handed a mug to Alice.

'It didn't help that you wouldn't even take that money I tried to give you. You couldn't even be bothered to put it in your handbag. I mean, what could be so vitally important?'

Katie sighed. 'I'm sorry but I was on my way to meet a new prospective client. It would have given a bad impression if I'd been late.'

'Well, I hope it was worth it.'

'Yes, it was.' She kept her tone even. 'As I said, he's taken me on. You know, Alice, I'm doing this so we can keep this house. What's more important than that?'

Alice sipped her tea thoughtfully before she said, 'Jacob's got a new girlfriend already.'

'So you've both moved on,' Katie said trying to diffuse the tension. 'You're doing your A-level re-sit and going to university and he'll probably be still waiting on tables when you graduate.'

Alice looked surprised at first but then she said, 'yeah, you're right Mum. I'm too good for him.' She smiled but then she burst into tears, 'but you see Mum..'

Katie got up and went round the table to hug her. 'I know darling, it's tough.'

'I just miss Dad so much!'

Chapter 37

Matt emerged from Paul's office beaming. He looked handsome dressed casually in jeans and a t-shirt which was the permitted dress code of Web Dreams on days that they didn't have client meetings. Bethan caught his eye and he went over to her.

'You're looking very pleased about something,' she said. His smile was infectious.

'Well!' Matt couldn't stop grinning. 'I've just been promoted to Account Director,' he whispered.

'Oh excellent!'

Matt had his forefinger up to his mouth. 'Shhh, Paul's announcing it later.' He turned to go back to his desk but changed his mind. 'You doing anything this evening?'

'Er, no.' Bethan didn't want to sound as if she was boring but as she was sharing a flat with Matt there was no point lying.

'Fancy going out to celebrate?'

'Are we all going to the pub after work?'

'No, actually.' He shuffled from one foot to the other. 'I meant just the two of us.' He was trying to read her expression. 'But if..'

'Oh yes. Yes, that'd be cool.'

'Great.'

Harry called Birch on his mobile.

'How's it going at Bisham Towers?'

'Well, apart from being confined to my room and not allowed to show any affection towards Katie, not bad. Let's see, three thousand words and counting.'

'Ah well my friend, I might have some good news for you. You see I have to go away tomorrow night; it's a conference up in

Edinburgh. Anyway I thought maybe you and the lovely lady might want to enjoy a night in, chez moi.'

'Wow, that's sounds great. Thanks mate.'

'No problem. But make sure Katie's not shackled to one of those daughters of hers won't you?'

'Don't worry, that will be the first thing I do.'

'Excellent. And you know where the take-away menus are?'

'Certainly do,' Birch said as he let out a laugh.

'What's funny? You're not going to cook for her are you?'

'Well it crossed my mind. But if you'd rather I..'

'No, no, you go ahead. You can teach me how to work the oven when I get back. I looked at it once. It's pretty hi-tech. In fact, I think it comes with a magic wand which they forgot to include with my delivery!'

Birch was laughing. 'You are such a bachelor boy!'

'That's me. Right, well let me know what the lady of the house says.'

Birch picked up his phone to text Katie but then decided to go and find her. She was in her study. He knocked.

'Hello, any chance of a minute of your time?'

'Oh Birch, come in.'

'Is Alice out?' he whispered.

'Yes.' Katie whispered too even though she didn't need to.

'Busy?'

'Yes, just getting to grips with Charlie's work. There's a lot to set up. Before now they seem to have worked in complete disarray.'

'Good job they've got super woman on the job then!'

She laughed.

'Now come here,' he said, 'I've got something to ask you.'

'Ooh!' She stood up and he put his hands round her waist and pulled her towards him. They kissed.

'What are you doing tomorrow evening?' This was quickly followed by, 'and the answer is spending it with me.'

'Mmm, I like the answer. What are we doing?'

'Harry is playing cupid and letting us have his flat for the whole night!'

'Oh gosh, yes, that's right, he's going up to Edinburgh. I booked the flight for him.'

'So is that a yes I'm free to make love all night after a delicious supper cooked by me?'

'Sounds wonderful.'

'And your daughters can spare you?'

'Well, as you know one has left home and the other works most evenings. Anyway, I shall leave some sort of note just in case they are even curious as to where I am.'

'Perfect!' They kissed again.

Katie emerged feeling distinctly distracted from her work. 'Got time for a cup of tea?'

'Most definitely, but is it safe in the unguarded territory that is the kitchen?'

Katie was amused but then she said with a serious tone, 'this ridiculous situation has to change.'

Matt took Bethan to a trendy gastro-pub which was walking distance from the flat. Bethan looked at the prices on the menu.

'The burgers are good here and the steak,' Matt said.

Bethan looked as if she was hesitant to order anything. Living at Pond Square was proving expensive on an apprenticeship wage.

'Oh whoops I've just realised you're a veggie or have you given that up now?'

Bethan let out a giggle, 'I'd say I'm a lapsed veggie!' She was looking over at another table where they were tucking unashamedly into red meat. 'I think I'll try a burger.'

'Great.' He was taking in her expression which was still one of concern. 'Oh and by the way this one's on me. Sorry, I should have said before.'

'Oh thanks. I'd love to go halves with you but my mum doesn't give me any money these days so it's all a bit desperate.'

'Don't worry about it. You're dining out with an account director now!'

The waitress appeared and Matt let Bethan order first.

'Do you want red or white wine? Just asking,' he said thoughtfully.

'Oh red please.'

'Great a bottle of the house red it is.'

Bethan looked distracted.

Matt was beginning to wonder if this was a good idea. 'Is there something wrong?' He decided to go for the direct question, especially with what he had planned for later.

'Well, no, but the thing is, well, I saw the postcard from Rob. Sorry, it was on the kitchen table. Anyway, I see he's coming back next week.'

'Yes, yes that's right.'

'So, I guess I'll have to give up my room.'

'I'm afraid so.' Matt looked apologetic.

Bethan sighed. 'Oh well, it's been great, I've really enjoyed it.'

'Good, I've enjoyed it too. Actually I thought it might be a bit much working together and flat sharing but it hasn't. I mean, well, what I actually mean is, I really like you Bethan. A lot.' His eyes were wide and full of hope.

Bethan was amazed and flattered by his declaration. She felt wanted, desired even, which she had not felt for a long time. 'Well I like you too.' She was blushing now and she smiled as she looked back into his eyes.

'More Champagne?' Birch reached for the bottle on the bedside table and Katie pulled the sheet up to cover her nakedness.

'Yes, please.' She was luxuriating in the moment. 'Isn't it wonderful to know I don't have to go home and we have all night?'

'Heaven.' Birch gently stroked her cheek with the back of his hand. 'And what's even better is that you are the most relaxed I've ever seen you.'

Katie let out a delighted giggle. 'Now I wonder why that is?' She turned to Birch. 'I know we said we wouldn't talk about the girls this evening but I need to tell you; I've made a decision.'

'Okay.' Birch sat up and re-filled his own glass.

Katie was finding the right words. 'I've decided..' She noticed he looked anxious. 'Oh darling you have nothing to worry about. Quite the opposite.'

'Phew!'

'What did you think I was going to say?'

'Never mind that! What have you decided?'

Katie took a deep breath. 'That I'm going to talk to them and tell them about us. I want us to be able to be open about our relationship.'

'That's brilliant.' He kissed her. 'Thank you.'

'Goodness, it should be me thanking you for putting up with so much from them.'

'I've come across friendlier sorts. But I always justify their behaviour with the fact that they've lost their father so recently.'

'Yes, me too. But the fact is that I didn't just lose him, I lost any financial security and even worse,' she took a gulp of Champagne, 'in a way, I lost the happy memories I had; they're all tainted with this dreadful gambling that he kept from me. I think back on times when I didn't really understand him and now I know why.'

He looked concerned.

'Sorry,' she said, 'I'm spoiling our evening together.'

'Don't be silly. I want you to feel you can talk to me about it.'

She smiled. 'Anyway, I'm going to talk to Alice and Bethan as soon as I can get them together.'

'And what sort of reaction are you prepared for?'

'I've thought about that. Let's face it, so far they've both left home even though Alice came bouncing back. All I can do is try and make them understand.'

'You're right. Do you want me to be there? Maybe hiding upstairs?'

'I think I need to do this on my own.'

'Of course.'

'But after, when they've both stormed off,' Katie laughed at how she was making light of what their response might be, 'a big hug would be lovely.'

He kissed her. 'Now, we still haven't had dessert. I have two beautifully light, calorie-free, of course, chocolate mousses courtesy of a well-known store.'

'How indulgent!'

They were not far from the pub when Matt turned to Bethan, took her in his arms and kissed her. Her head felt dizzy and she realised she'd had too much alcohol to drink but she enjoyed the kiss. They walked on, him with his arm around her now. When they got back to the front door of the flat he joked, 'At least I don't have to ask you in for coffee!'

Bethan squealed with pleasure. 'Go on, ask me! Ask me if I want coffee?'

He took her in his arms again, and they enjoyed a long slow kiss.

'Bethan Green,' he put on a more formal voice now, 'would you like to come to my room for coffee?'

'Mmm, sounds good.'

They kissed again and started undressing each other in haste.

'On the other hand...' he said in her ear as they fell onto his bed.

Chapter 38

Katie had rung Bethan the evening before and got her voicemail. She decided to try again the following morning even though she assumed Bethan would be at work. She had checked with Alice and she was not working that very evening and so it was a good opportunity to get the three of them together.

'Mum, I'm at work.' Bethan had at least answered her mobile.

'I know darling but you don't return my calls so I thought I'd try again. Are you free this evening?'

'What? What for? Probably not,' she said in a dismissive tone.

'I'd like to meet up with you. Alice is coming too.' That wasn't strictly true but Katie knew that her other daughter would be more pliable.

'What for?'

'I'd like to see you apart from anything else, I haven't seen you for weeks.' Katie realised that this was avoiding the issue.

'Is that all?'

'No,' Katie primed herself, 'I've got something I want to tell you.'

'Well, why don't you tell me *now*. If it's about that Birch I'm not interested anyway.'

'I've booked a table for three for dinner at The Flask at seven thirty; I expect you to be there.' Katie was pleased with this assertive stance. She knew her daughter well enough to know she was likely to turn up out of curiosity if nothing else.

'Sounds like I have no choice.' Bethan was sulky now.

'Oh, you have a choice,' Katie said calmly and ended the call.

Birch was sat opposite his wife in Fegos. Celia hadn't touched her cappuccino. She looked around the cafe in disgust and made sure she didn't touch anything.

'What kind of a place is this? Is this the best you can do?'

'It is, after you cleaned out our bank account,' he said smugly and added, 'in fact you're paying as you're the one with the bulging purse.'

She looked embarrassed now. 'It was Alistair's idea, he's convinced you're going to leave me high and dry.'

'Out of work, is he, your Alistair?'

'No, don't be silly, he's an accountant actually.'

'Oh wonderful! Huh, my wife's left me for an accountant!' Birch realised straight away from Celia's face that this kind of talk wasn't going to get him very far. 'I'm sorry; I shouldn't have said that.'

'I just want what's owed to me,' she said quite offended.

'Ah yes, what's owed to you for being the dutiful wife for, what was it, twenty years?'

'This isn't helping,' she said and carefully took a sip from her cup, her elbows hovering above the table.

'No, you're right. Well, as you may know by now, I've spoken to Jonathan at Taylor Woodshaw and he is proposing that we put the house on the market and split the proceeds fifty fifty. As he rightly points out, the simpler and more amicable we keep this, the less it's going to cost both of us.'

Celia was thoughtful. 'And what else does Jonathan suggest?'

'Well, he says the easiest way of doing it, in our position, is to get the divorce on the grounds of living apart for two years.' He stopped short of mentioning adultery, even though it seemed to him the most obvious way to go but, as Jonathan had said, that route tended to get messy.

'And are you happy with that; I mean waiting two years?'

Birch replied with a very controlled, 'yes,' before taking a deep breath and telling himself to leave it there.

'Let's sit here.' Katie chose a table in a corner where they would hopefully be able to have a discreet conversation.

'Okay.' Alice was still looking surprised. Since her mother had asked her for this meeting she had been imagining all sorts of scenarios.

'I still don't understand why we're not doing this at home? I mean, I thought money was so tight that meals out were a complete no no.'

'Now I've got a few clients I can afford to buy a meal at the pub every now and then,' Katie said avoiding her first question.

Alice looked confused. 'So what are we waiting for now?'

'Bethan,' Katie said simply, 'I'm hoping she'll be here soon.' She looked at her watch. Bethan was already ten minutes late.

Another twenty minutes passed and Katie was finding it increasingly difficult to keep the conversation no deeper than small talk. She was about to give up on Bethan when she walked in, clearly in no hurry.

'Hi.' Alice looked pleased to see her even if it was only so they could order some food.

Bethan looked at her mother accusingly as if blaming her for having to meet them in this way.

'Hello darling.' Katie tried to keep it normal.

'Hi.' Bethan was barely audible. She looked at the menu briefly. 'I'll have a pizza. Margherita.'

Katie was offended by her rudeness but decided to ignore it for now.

Having ordered, and all three of them with a drink in hand, Katie thought about her wonderful evening with Birch at Harry's flat. She knew they had strong feelings for each other and she tried to draw strength from that.

'The reason I wanted to talk to you is that I'm now in a relationship with Birch and I want to be open and honest about it.'

'Well making out in the kitchen isn't exactly hiding it!' Bethan said in disgust.

'No, and I regret you found out that way Bethan, as I have already said.'

'Hang on a minute!' Alice was shocked. 'Why have I been kept in the dark?'

'I'm telling you now.' Katie went on with steadfast determination to make her well-rehearsed point. 'We haven't been together long and I've chosen to tell you now.'

'But, but isn't he married? You told us he was married.' Alice was struggling to come to terms with this revelation.

'Yes, he is married, but they have separated.'

'Because of you! Poor woman!' Bethan took a large gulp of wine.

'Actually, Birch discovered that Celia had been having an affair for a year or so. And we didn't get together until after that.'

'I don't believe this is happening to me.' Alice looked bewildered.

Katie looked at Alice. 'Am I not allowed to find happiness? Have you not had a relationship since your father died?'

'That's different!' Alice raised her voice.

Katie looked around the pub. No one seemed to have noticed. 'I know your dad hasn't been dead long but I've had an awful lot to contend with since then.'

'Oh, and we haven't!' Bethan was angry.

Katie continued regardless, 'what you don't fully realise, because I have sheltered you from it, is the whole truth about your father.'

'Oh this just gets worse,' Alice said as the waitress appeared with an inane grin on her face and delivered the food.

'Any sauces?' she asked oblivious to the tense atmosphere at the table.

Katie looked at both her daughters and said, 'no thanks.'

They both seemed to have healthy appetites despite the trauma Katie was apparently causing them. She, on the other hand, was struggling to eat anything.

She decided to plough on with what she wanted them to understand. 'Your father left us in a dire financial state and I've had to deal with that. His gambling eroded our savings down to nothing but still, I don't blame him. I'm not angry with him and I'll always love him. But the fact is that I've had to get in a lodger and set myself up in business in order to secure our futures.'

'You didn't have to sleep with the lodger,' Bethan said with a mouthful of food.

'I'm with Birch because I love him.' Katie met the glare of both her daughters and held it until they had both looked away.

'I've heard it all now,' Alice said quietly, the wind out of her sails.

'Well you can do what you like. I'm staying at Pond Square,' Bethan said.

'I thought it was just until Rob gets back?' her mother asked.

'Yes, well things have changed. I'm going out with Matt now so we're sharing his room.'

Even though Katie had guessed as much she still felt a thud to her stomach as Bethan delivered the words, pitched to hurt her. She finished her glass of wine and poured another from the bottle.

Alice considered everything she was hearing, 'Just *me* living like a nun then.'

Katie stifled a laugh as she put her hand over Alice's and was amazed when her daughter turned her palm towards hers and held it tight.

'Mum, I'm happy for you. Really, I am. But it's all happened so quickly; we must never forget Dad.'

'Of course not, my darling.' Katie smiled and stroked Alice's cheek. 'He was a massive part of our lives. I visit him regularly at the cemetery.'

'Next time you're going, let me know. I'd like to come with you.' Alice smiled back at her mother.

Bethan looked appalled at the display of affection before her. 'So you're living back at home now, Alice?' she said, her tone scathing.

'Yes, it didn't work out with Jacob,' Alice replied bravely.

'She's too good for him,' Katie added before turning to Bethan. 'You know you'd be very welcome to come home any time; it must be hard for you on an apprenticeship salary.'

Bethan had finished her pizza and drained her glass. 'Yes, well it is but I'm not coming back. I can't share a house with that man.'

Katie was hurt by every biting remark she made but her unconditional love forced her to say, 'perhaps I can help you out now my VA business is going well. I can't promise anything long term but at the moment I can afford to give you something each month.'

'I think that's only fair as Alice is living at home.' There wasn't an iota of gratefulness in her voice.

Katie could see that Bethan was hurting inside but her defences were so high she wasn't going to let anyone in. It pained her to know what a vulnerable position she had put herself in, relying on a young man for a roof over her head.

'Right, well I'll sort something out. And however you might feel now, I want you to know that I love you and would always welcome you at home.'

Bethan grabbed her coat and bag clumsily and with tears falling down her face she said, 'I'll *never* come back while *he's* still there,' and Katie knew she could do nothing but let her go, as her daughter rushed out into the cold night air.

Chapter 39

Birch placed a large tray laden with croissants, jam and fresh coffee on the bed next to Katie. She smelt the delicious aromas and opened her eyes.

'Ooh, you've been busy.'

He opened the curtains a little and a blue sky brightened the bedroom.

'Happy Christmas,' he said, and then lent over to kiss her.

'Certainly is.' She sat up and rearranged her pillows to make herself comfortable.

'Now tuck in.'

'What's the time?' She reached for her watch. 'Shouldn't I be doing things in the kitchen? How many will there be for lunch again?'

'Don't worry. I told you yesterday, leave it all to me.'

'Oh bliss.' She took a sip of coffee. 'You know what, I think I might even enjoy today.'

'Good, well that's the idea isn't it?'

'I don't think so.' Katie had a wry smile on her face. 'As a mother, you're just supposed to suffer and work hard all day and be unappreciated!'

'Well, today will be different.'

'Yes.' Katie looked around her and felt truly blessed. 'It would be perfect if Bethan appeared having transformed into an angel. Let's lay a place for her at the table just in case.'

He said nothing but kissed her cheek. He wasn't actually sure whether Bethan turning up was a good thing or not, given that all his attempts to get on with her had failed.

'At least Alice is here,' Katie said tucking into her croissant.

'Actually her room is empty; but didn't she say she was staying with a friend after their pub crawl?'

'Oh yes, she'll be back soon.'

Birch brought out an exquisitely gift wrapped box from under the bed and put it on Katie's lap. 'And now for the best bit,' he said with a grin on his face.

Bethan woke up alone in Matt's bed. He had left really early to drive to his mum's house in Surrey and had only woken her briefly.

'It's just a few days. And it's a family tradition,' Matt had said when he told her he was going. 'The whole family always meet at mum's house. She says they'll be fourteen of us this year.' It was as if he was asserting his right to go. To Bethan, a few days seemed like an eternity.

'My brothers will be there, and Gramps. He's still going strong,' Matt continued regardless.

Bethan forced a smile.

'So will you go back to yours?'

She squirmed in her chair. 'Not sure.' Miranda had said that she was welcome to spend Christmas with her family but Bethan knew that Miranda's mother would have only agreed under duress. When Bethan had left their house abruptly to move to Pond Square, Stephanie had only feigned concern that she would be okay. It was obvious she was very pleased to see the back of her. It made Bethan realise that her home life with her mother had been very free and easy in comparison to the strict homework and early night regime that Miranda endured.

Matt put his arm around her. 'But you'll be all on your lonesome if you don't go.'

'Yeah, I know. I'm just not sure I can cope with Birch being there. And let's face it, he will be.'

Katie opened the door to Sylvia just after eleven o'clock. 'Oh Sylvia, it's so good to see you. Thank you for coming all this way.'

'Don't be silly; it's a joy to be here! Let's face it, it's this or some depressing lunch with the old folk of Sandgate, half the men dribbling down their fronts.'

They giggled as they hugged. 'Now where's that son of mine?'

'In the kitchen I'm afraid; he's insisted on doing it all!'

'How wonderful! Makes a change doesn't it?'

'It certainly does,' Katie agreed but then she remembered that David had often taken over in the kitchen and she felt a moment of sadness and had to brush a tear away.

No sooner had Katie got mother and son together than the doorbell rang again and Julia stood there with Andrew and Daisy behind her, laden with bags.

'Happy Christmas darling!' They hugged.

Andrew said, 'pud' holding up one bag and 'presents' elevating the other. 'Where shall I put them?'

'Oh, but we said no presents!'

'It's only token gifts,' Julia explained. 'It's nice to have something to open isn't it? Even though we're grown-ups!'

Daisy raised her eyebrows. Katie hugged her. 'Daisy you've been my saviour in helping me set myself up as a VA. There's definitely a pressie for you.'

'And I see you're wearing an exquisite new bracelet!' Julia admired the new addition on Katie's arm which was her gift from Birch.

'Oh yes.' Katie looked a little embarrassed.

'It's gorgeous!' Julia inspected it closely.

Katie ushered them all into the living room. 'Now shall we start with coffee?'

Alice appeared. 'Hi everyone,' she said and made a beeline for Daisy.

Sylvia emerged from the kitchen and raised her voice over the general chatter. 'I've been instructed to make drinks for everyone.'

Bethan was beginning to realise the full enormity of her decision to stay home alone on Christmas day. She had sent Matt a text but he hadn't replied. She imagined him immersed in family life, not even bothering to look at his mobile.

She opened up the fridge. Apart from some chicken curry left over from the other night there wasn't anything particularly appetising. This had crossed her mind the other day when she was in the local shop; perhaps she should buy something nice to eat but the thought of being on her own was so miserable that she hadn't been able to bring herself to do it. Her mobile bleeped. It was a text from Alice.

Happy Christmas Beth, missing you. Why don't you come over? Alice x

Bethan burst into tears and thought about how much she missed her father. If he was still alive, she would be at home with her family and he would make it a lovely day. Eventually she decided to pull herself together and showered, put on her favourite jeans and a new top she had bought with the money her mother was now giving her. She used her hair straighteners and put on some make-up. All dressed up she looked back at her reflection in the mirror. Perhaps she'd walk up to the cemetery first. The doorbell rang and although she had no idea who it was she felt quite excited and rushed over to the intercom.

'Hello?'

'Bethan, is that you?'

'Yes!'

'It's Harry.'

'We're on the first floor,' Bethan managed to say her heart beating faster. Was this really happening?

She flung open the flat door to see him standing there looking as stunning as he always did.

'Happy Christmas Bethan,' he said cheerily.

Bethan could have melted into his arms but kept her poise. 'At a loose end?'

He laughed. 'Actually, I'm on my way over to your mum's house. She's got quite a crowd going for lunch.'

'Oh?' Bethan imagined that Birch diluted by others wasn't such a dreadful prospect.

'Anyway, I wondered if you'd like to walk with me?'

'Yes, yes I was going to go round there myself; just been getting ready.'

'So I can see,' Harry said grinning unabashed.

Katie was pleased with how it was all going so far. She went into the kitchen.

'Anything I can do?'

Birch went over to her and was about to put his arms around her when she pointed to his messy apron.

'Not on my new dress!'

He kissed her with his hands in the air as if surrendering to a gun pointing at him.

'It's all under control. In fact, we could open the Champagne now if you like,' he said.

'Oh yes, lets, although Harry's not here yet.'

Right on cue the doorbell went. Katie opened the door to find Harry standing behind her daughter.

'Picked up a stray on the way over,' he said with a knowing look.

'Oh how wonderful! Oh Bethan, it's so good to see you.'

They hugged and Harry sidled past them and into the living room to join the happy throng.

'Perfect timing darling, we're about to open the Champagne.' Katie beamed at her daughter. 'And there are presents for you under the tree.'

'But Mum, I haven't got you anything!'

'Don't be silly. That doesn't matter. All that matters is that you're here!'

Alice appeared at the doorway. 'Bethan! I knew you'd come.' She held her sister close. 'It's been ages! Come on in. Daisy's here.'

Lunch was a frenetic affair with lots of laughter and Katie didn't even mind that Bethan was making eyes at Harry and he was flirting back. The dining room was very tastefully decorated by Alice with gold ribbons, green foliage from the garden and white fairy lights running down the centre of the table. Birch was complimented on his excellent roast beef by Julia and they all agreed it was a welcome change from turkey.

By the time they had finished their Christmas pudding they were all tipsy and relaxed in each other's company. Birch offered to make more coffee and suggested they adjourn to the living room. As people heaved themselves out of their chairs and made their way, Katie took the opportunity to grab her coat and scarf and slip out of the front door unnoticed.

Once outside she took a moment to take in the view. It had snowed just enough to cover the ground and now the sky was clear and Bisham Gardens looked very pretty with the street lights coming on as the daylight faded. As she set off down the road it was eerily quiet but somehow very peaceful. Despite having the most unsuitable shoes on she enjoyed every step of the walk to the cemetery and wasn't surprised to see others had had the same idea on this significant day.

Katie reached David's grave and stood for a moment. She remembered last Christmas when he had entertained them in his own inimitable way. He had cooked goose even though Katie had commented on how expensive it was, 'nothing but the best for my family,' he had said. Katie smiled at that. She thought perhaps they should have engraved those words on his head stone, *nothing but the best for my family*. He meant it too. It was what he strived for; she believed that now.

Just then she felt warm arms around her. She turned around. 'Birch! How did you know?'

'You were missing and I guessed.'

'You got here quickly.'

'I was in a hurry.' He held her close and kissed her. 'Do you want some more time alone with him? I'll wait for you by the gate.'

Katie turned back to the grave. 'No, no it's okay. We're both at peace now.'

They looked down at Katie's shoes which were sodden with snow. She let out a giggle. 'I've just realised, my feet are freezing!'

'Well there's nothing else for it; I'll just have to carry you back!' And he picked her up so that she lay across his arms and she laughed with delight as they made their way back to Bisham Gardens.

∞ ∞ ∞

Read on for an extract of the sequel:

Birch & Beyond

A testing time for Katie leaves her
uncertain about her future...

'Happy New Year, darling,' Birch said with a subdued tone but Katie still had to gulp back a tear. It was her first New Year without David and it was moments like this that were a poignant reminder.

'Yes, happy New Year,' Julia echoed leaning over the dining table to squeeze Katie's hand.

'Shall we go through to the lounge?' Katie suggested and she felt three sets of eyes on her as she tried to shake away the memories that saddened her.

'Yes, we could turn on the telly and watch the fireworks,' Andrew suggested in an attempt to lighten the mood. They went through and the contrast from the warm dining room made Katie shiver and wrap her arms around herself. Birch quickly stoked the fire and added a couple of logs to raise the temperature in the room. Katie turned on a standard lamp in the corner which gave off a warm mellow light and sat on the edge of the sofa warming her hands against the fire.

'David always made a big thing about the fireworks.' She smiled at the recollection but then she thought of him lying in Highgate cemetery in his willow coffin, unable to enjoy anything anymore.

'Shall we put them on then?' Andrew asked picking up the TV remote from the glass coffee table.

'If you like; I'm not bothered. We could have some music on – maybe some jazz.' She looked up at Birch who was a big fan of Miles Davis and Thelonious Monk, while she only tolerated them. Before they decided one way or another their conversation was interrupted by the doorbell ringing loud and shrill. Twice.

Julia turned to Katie, 'Alice, maybe – forgotten her key? Seems a bit early for her.'

'Maybe it's some drunk,' Andrew suggested laughing.

'I'll go,' Birch said, a serious frown on his face. 'You stay here.' He was nodding pointedly at Katie as he backed out of the room and closed the door behind him.

The amount of champagne he had drunk had lightened his mood, but nothing could have prepared him for the sight before his eyes.

'Is this a private party,' Celia slurred, lunging towards him, 'or can wives join in?' She put great emphasis on the word wives and was now close enough to him that he could smell alcohol on her breath. She was wearing a bright red, low cut party dress, which was completely out of character, her black mascara was smudged messily around her eyes and her vibrant lipstick was marking her front teeth.

'Well?' Her expression demanded an answer and she spoke loudly enough for half the street to hear.

'Celia, you know you're not invited.' He spoke quietly in the hope that she would too. 'You left me for Alistair, remember? Why aren't you at his party?'

She threw a dismissive hand around in the air. 'Turns out he's not the one for me.' She started fluttering her eyes at him in a feeble attempt at flirtation.

Birch suddenly felt very sober. 'Well, I'm sorry to hear that but as you know I'm with Katie now and what's more you and I are going through a divorce.'

'Ah!' Celia cried triumphantly. 'Ah yes, but no!'

'What are you talking about?' She was beginning to worry him.

'What I mean is,' she was staggering from foot to foot and looked like she might topple over at any moment. Birch grabbed her wrist to stabilise her.

'What you mean is?' He tried to hurry her. This interruption of his evening had gone on long enough.

'I mean that I don't want a divorce anymore!' She was standing uncomfortably close to him now, looking wide-eyed up at him with her blue grey eyes. In her inebriated state she was convinced that she was appealing to her husband, when actually she looked a mess.

'Don't be ridiculous,' Birch tried to keep his voice steady and was trying to steer her away from him. She pulled her wrist back in protest and immediately fell backwards on to the path.

'Oh my God, are you all right?' He crouched down and peered at her. She lay there motionless with her eyes closed for a few seconds before bursting into a giggle and lifted her head in an attempt to stand up.

'Whoops!' she shrieked delighted that Birch had taken her hand and was helping her up. 'Silly me!' She put her head on his chest. 'You see I need a husband to look after me, otherwise I might get into all sorts of trouble,' she squeaked in a little girl voice.

Birch sighed deeply. 'Celia, you had better go home.'

'What, before Katie finds out I'm here?' She raised her voice as loud as she could.

At that point the lounge door burst open and Katie stood there looking hurt and confused. Birch immediately told Celia she should go home and closed the front door on her but she banged with her fists repeatedly crying, 'I want my husband back! Give me my husband, you money grabbing bitch! He's mine! We're still married you know!'

'What on earth is going on?' Katie asked and Birch went straight over to comfort her.

'I'm so sorry, my love. This is outrageous. I can't believe she's stooped so low.'

'What happened?' Katie still didn't understand what was going on.

'She just turned up. She's drunk.'

'And she wants you back?' Katie blinked disbelieving.

'The woman is delusional. She's too drunk to know what she wants.'

'It doesn't sound like that to me,' Katie said shivering. The opened front door had let in an icy cold wind. Julia appeared with Andrew close behind.

'Everything okay?' she asked her voice deflating as she saw her friend upset.

About the Author

Gill Buchanan is a business graduate who worked in marketing before writing her first novel. Having lived a little herself and experienced the ups and downs of being a woman in the 21st century, Gill decided to create female characters who blossom in the face of adversity. She uses modern day dilemmas which resonate with her readers and humour to add a lightness to the story. She has written four novels to date and her latest work, The Disenchanted Hero, is inspired by the true story of Molly and Guy who met during World War 2 with enormous hurdles to overcome before true love could run its course. It's a family saga with tragedy and heartbreak at the centre of the tale.

Gill lives in rural Suffolk with Tony, her husband, and Gracie, her cat. She loves to hear from her readers.

Please email her at: words@gillbuchanan.co.uk

To find out more about Gill Buchanan go to her author website: www.gillbuchanan.co.uk

Find Gill on Facebook: www.facebook.com/literallyforwomen

Also by Gill Buchanan

Birch & Beyond
The sequel to Forever Lucky

Unlikely Neighbours
Alex and his wine cellar arrive in Lodge Lane
sparking some unlikely outcomes

The Disenchanted Hero
Inspired by the true story of
Molly and Guy

'Perhaps I should end it for their sakes.'

'Katie!' Julia sat upright and turned to her dearest friend. 'After all you've been through! Let's not forget that David had gambled away all your savings and left you with very little. I know you've forgiven him and I think that's the right thing to do.' She relaxed back into the cushions again. 'But you've had to claw your way out of financial ruin. You've set yourself up as a virtual assistant and worked jolly hard to build up a client base.'

'I have, haven't I?' Katie suddenly felt proud of what she'd achieved. 'Harry's been a great help of course.'

'And Birch has been really supportive; he's the light in your life, you've said as much.'

'He is. He makes me very happy.' Katie smiled as she thought of how her life had turned around when he came into it.

'Ending this relationship, what's that going to achieve apart from heartache?'

'But if Celia wants him back...'

'That's her problem. The sooner their house is sold and the divorce is all sorted, the better. Hopefully she'll move away. A long way away from Highgate Village.'

'That all seems like a pipe dream right now. She called me a money grabbing bitch.' Katie said sighing.

'I'd call her the devil incarnate,' Julia joked and they both laughed and felt better for it.

'Before this evening I'd have said that was a bit harsh.' Katie took a gulp from her brandy deciding she quite liked it.

'But now, it's her new name.' Julia clunked Katie's glass.

***

Celia continued her tirade of insults and demands at the front door. Birch was red with embarrassment. 'I'm so sorry about all this. My estranged wife is giving me enough ammunition to divorce her on the grounds of unreasonable behaviour ten times over,' he explained, imploring his onlookers to have sympathy with him.

There was a squeal from outside followed by a concerning silence. Birch closed his eyes in despair, 'she's already fallen over once,' he informed the others.

Andrew put a hand on Birch's arm. 'Look mate, do you think maybe you and I should walk her home?'

Birch bit his lip and looked to Katie to approve the idea before he answered.

'That sounds like the best solution,' Katie said putting on a brave face.

'Right,' Birch braced himself, 'we'll be as quick as we can. It's only a few streets. You two go back in the lounge and, Andrew, let's get out of the front door as quickly as possible. I can't bear the thought of her barging in here.'

With the two men gone, Julia opened a bottle of brandy and poured generously into two tumblers.

'I don't like brandy,' Katie said with a smile but behind her eyes you could see pain.

'Nor do I, but it's good for a shock.' Julia sat next to her on the sofa in front of the fire and they both stared into the cinders as they tried to make sense of what had just happened. Julia got up and added more logs, stoking the embers to get some much needed warmth from it.

'Yes, shocking is the right word,' Katie said eventually. 'I'm wondering if my relationship with Birch was doomed from the start. I mean Bethan hates him with a vengeance and Alice only tolerates him...'

'They lost their father last summer,' Julia interrupted, 'they were bound to react to any man coming in to your life.'

Printed in Dunstable, United Kingdom